MAGNETIC SHIFT

LUCY D. BRIAND

Library of Congress Cataloging-in-Publication Data
available upon request

Published in the United States by Spencer Hill Press
www.SpencerHillPress.com

Distributed by Midpoint Trade Books
www.midpointtrade.com

This edition ISBN:
9781633920668 paperback
9781633920675 eBook

Printed in the United States of America

Design by Lorin Taylor
Cover by Jenny Perinovic

magnetic shift

Lucy D. Briand

SPENCER
HILL
PRESS

chapter one

I jumped down from the truck, gawked up at the fence arching over Daytona International Speedway's tri-oval track, and groaned as my gut twisted in the worst way. This death pit of metal, iron, and steel was going to be the end of me, I just knew it.

Okay, so technically this wasn't any worse than the mounds of scrap metal and car parts at the salvage yard back home. And the fact that I was sent here against my will really sucked—like bash-me-over-the-head kind of sucked—but that wasn't why my stomach was doing flips, either. Being thrown smack-dab in the middle of a media-crazed sport while trying to keep a lid on my magnetic influences, on the other hand …

Bye-bye, frying pan. Hello, fire.

I pulled a roll of cherry-flavored Tums out of my pocket, peeled the wrapper, and was about to drop my fifth one of the day on my tongue when a heavy twitch in my senses shifted my focus toward the track. A bright green-and-blue stock car had entered my awareness and roared past me through the banked turn ahead. A normal person would have thought that to be exhilarating, but me … every fiber of my body had actually felt the thirty-four hundred pounds of steel rolling at one hundred and eighty plus miles per hour around that bend.

Ah, hell. Who was I kidding? There was no way I'd be able to keep my emotions under control in this place. I was already more bitter than a key lime and my curse was teetering over the barriers I'd taught myself to keep up.

The car caused a gust of wind to whip by, barely stirring air that had turned thick and humid thanks to the series of freak torrential downpours we'd had all week. I closed my eyes, curled a few stray strands of hair around my ear, and gave my right temple a quick rub.

Throbbing temple. Never a good sign.

The dark-haired man, who'd introduced himself as Jimmy when he'd picked me up, set my suitcase down next to me. "This way, Lexi. Dean's waiting."

Ah, yes. Dean. The owner of the Cup series race team and the creep who'd accepted my douchebag stepdad's offer and taken me as payment for one whole year's worth of sponsorship ads for his salvage yard.

God forbid we make him wait.

Jimmy turned his back to me and started toward the garage area at the center of the track's infield without pausing for an answer or to make sure I was following. And why would he? In his eyes, I was nothing more than some glorified slave.

Huffing, I blew the long bangs out of my eyes. I never should've gotten off that bus—or better yet, never boarded it to begin with—but it wasn't like I'd had a choice. I'd been sold. All deals were final.

Blood boiling, I shot my hand out over my suitcase, and the metallic handle popped up and slapped into my palm.

Crap. I glanced around. It didn't look like anyone had seen what I'd done, but I'd have to be more careful from now on.

I glued my gaze to Jimmy's heels as I hurried after him. The wheels of my suitcase grumbled loudly over the pitted pavement and, though I refused to look up, when we reached the long stretch of half white, half yellow multi-car garages I felt eyes watching me as we passed the open doors.

"Ah, shit." Jimmy came to a halt, making me almost face-plant into his back. "I left the invoices in the truck. I gotta go back."

He swung around me and jogged off the way we'd come, calling over his shoulder, "Go on ahead to Colton's stall and ask for Dean, will ya?"

"Wait, what …?" Was he just going to leave me here? My gut tightened something fierce. "How am I supposed to know which one it is?"

He glanced back without stopping. "Look for the angel 129."

Angel 129? Was he kidding me? What did that even mean? He disappeared around the corner, and the weight of my backpack grew heavier on my shoulders.

Crap. Crap. Crap. This wasn't happening.

Techs and team personnel stared at me from the garage stall where Jimmy had left me stranded. The crew must've been wondering why a seventeen-year-old girl was hauling a suitcase and overstuffed backpack through the infield of the site best known for hosting auto racing's equivalent to the Super Bowl. The car sitting inside had the words "SunCorp Petrol" plastered all over it and the number 220 on its door. The stall belonged to two-time Cup Champion, Mitch Benson. The team owned by the great Carl Stacy.

Great, my ass.

My stepdad, Roy, idolized the man. Saw him as a role model of sorts. I didn't follow the sport much, but I'd caught enough highlights on the shop's radio and seen enough of his team's promotional posters plastered around the workbench to know who the ass was. Even the part-timers at the shop wouldn't shut up about him. If you asked me, the guy was a snobby old fart.

After passing a few more open doors, I looked up ahead, squinting through the glare of the mid-afternoon sun, hoping to figure out where the hell I was supposed to go. It was safe to assume the "129" part of Jimmy's instructions meant I needed to find team 129's stall, but how was I supposed to do that? The round yellow number signs sticking out above the doors only numbered the stalls, with no indication of which team was where. No way was I asking around for help. I was already a freak and I looked pathetic enough dragging around all my worldly possessions; I didn't need *newb* tattooed on my forehead, too. My only option was to wander around and hope I stumbled on it.

My plain, black t-shirt—the only one I owned that wasn't covered in oil or grease stains—clung to my skin. *Argh!* If I didn't find this Dean guy soon, I was going to melt into a pile of goop right here on the pavement. I cupped a hand over my eyes and found the clue I was looking for three doors down. A crew member wearing a dark mechanic's shirt with a white angel printed on the back strolled out, grabbed two Goodyear radial slicks from the stack outside the door, hollered a few words to one of the few scattered fans leaning over the railing of the roof's viewing area, and ducked back inside.

Bingo.

Now all I had to do was keep my fingers crossed that I would find the 129 car inside that stall.

I tugged my suitcase over the threshold and wrinkled my nose at my first whiff of motor oil and high-octane racing fuel. This stuff was way more potent than the gunked-up crap I spent day in and day out draining from the old cars back home.

My gaze landed on the shiny vinyl-wrapped black, yellow, and dark green stock car perched on the ramps inside. A white angel logo—large unfolded wings, a yellow halo, and dark green Guardian Auto Insurance lettering—gleamed and sparkled on its hood under the ceiling's florescent lights. The car also had a small, white 129 decal stuck to its bumper.

Found it.

But wasn't it supposed to be Roy's ad sprawled on that hood?

I leaned to the side a bit to get a better look at the roll call of different associate sponsor decals along the side of the car.

Great.

There it was. The four-by-twelve-inch silver-and-gold lettered logo of Roy's East Coast Salvage Yard.

Are you freakin' kidding me?

He'd shipped me out here so he could get that stupid little sticker put on the car? How were fans supposed to see that from the grandstands? I could barely see it from here.

"Are ya lost, little girl?" A deep, young voice spoke behind me.

I sucked in a sharp breath and my hand flew to my chest. I'd been so busy cursing that damn ad I hadn't noticed anyone approaching.

I spun around, ready to ask him who he was calling "little girl," and came face-to-chest with a guy who looked barely older than nineteen. My mouth turned to cotton at the sight of him staring down at me. I took a wobbly step back. "I, uh …"

The sleeves of his black, green, and yellow one-piece fire suit were tied low at his waist, showing off the white short-sleeved cotton t-shirt printed with the large winged Guardian Auto Insurance logo stretched tightly across his chest. I swallowed as I flicked my gaze up to his face. Sandy blond hair peeked out the back of the matching black ball cap pulled low over his eyes.

Oh, good God almighty.

I'd never swooned before—hell, I hardly knew what the word meant—but this guy's grin made me light-headed and woozy, and my heart raced at two hundred miles per hour. I picked up my jaw, cleared my embarrassing reaction from my throat, and, hoping it wasn't too late, tried not to look stupid.

He stepped closer and jutted out his chin. I met his eyes, and my breath hitched. His left eye was a deep sapphire color while the other was emerald. He had mismatched eyes. My temples pulsed. I'd never seen such odd, gorgeous eyes before. My awareness of every metal object in the vicinity grew stronger.

"It's called odd-eye."

I blinked hard. "Excuse me?" I'd been staring and not paying attention … to his words, anyway.

"It's called odd-eye. Heterochromia, if you want to get technical." He pointed to his eyes. "People stare all the time. You get used to it."

Used to it? I didn't want to get used to it. This was a guy who knew what it was like to get stared at, to feel out of place, to be different. I liked not being the only abnormal person here.

Okay, having different colored eyes was totally different from my ability to move metal objects with the flick of my wrist, but the small similarity gave me a sense of comfort.

"Sorry," I mumbled. My cheeks flamed. Nice. My face probably looked like a pair of lit-up brake lights right about now.

"Hey, no worries." His grin grew wider, raising the cute, tiny dark freckle on his left cheek closer to the corner of his green eye. A strange yet pleasant sensation tingled through me and scattered into tiny flutters inside my chest.

Something rattled behind me near my suitcase. I snapped out of it and shifted my awareness to the pulse throbbing in my temples.

No, no, no. Ah, crap. Not now!

I closed my eyes and pulled myself together. After years of control, I couldn't let myself lose it now. Not out in the open like this. Not in front of this guy. This gorgeous guy.

Within a split-second, the rattling had stopped. With a sigh of relief, I released my death-grip on the shoulder straps of my backpack.

Crisis averted. For now.

When I opened my eyes again, the guy had lost his grin. He glanced down at something behind me, but dismissed it and looked back at me. "So, you never answered my question."

I blinked hard, trying my darndest to keep my nerves from exploding. "Which was?"

"Are you lost?" He crossed his arms over his chest, eyed my backpack and suitcase, and narrowed his eyes at me. "Something tells me you're not here 'cause you're a fan."

"I'm not lost. At least, I don't think ..." His new posture intimidated me. I couldn't focus. "I'm looking for Dean ...?

Dean Grant?"

He shot his hand up, fingers pointing as if he were about to shoot me. I flinched. "Right, you must be Lexi, the girl who can drop a transmission in, like, fifteen minutes flat." He scanned me over from my thrift store steel-toed boots to my delicate, silver eyebrow piercing—a gift Mama had gotten me not long before she died—then twitched the corner of his lips into a faint smile. "You're not at all what I'd pictured."

I resisted the urge to give him the evil eye. "Yeah, well. Sorry to disappoint." What had he expected from a girl grease monkey, anyway? That I'd show up in a dress?

He fist-tapped the side of my shoulder and chuckled. "I'm not at all disappointed … I mean … I didn't mean it like that." He cleared his throat. "Anywho, Dean's in his office."

I glanced around the garage. The structure had no interior walls. I could see straight into the neighboring stalls on either side. Where did this guy see an "office?"

"It's in the hauler. Come on, I'll show ya." He started toward the long row of car carriers parked outside.

"You're not going to tell me who you are?"

He turned. "You're kidding, right?"

"Why? Should I know you?"

His expression fell but perked up again. "My bad. I just assumed …" He held out his hand. "I'm Colton Tayler, driver of this here 129 Angel."

"Driver? Snap, I'm so sorry. I don't follow motorsports much." I slipped my hand into his. My heart swan-dived into the pit of my stomach. The heat of his touch seeped through my skin and wrapped me in a warm fuzzy feeling. A fog clouded my mind and the world spun around me. The last time I'd felt like this was on the night of my grade school graduation when my friends and I raided Roy's liquor cabinet. That was back when I still had somewhat of a normal life and boy, had I gotten in shit that time. Was my body trying to tell me something?

While keeping my breath steady and my expression neutral as best as I could, I tried to mentally shake away the weird sensation. I failed. Worse, I lost my focus—only for a second, but that's all it took. I turned just in time to see an old, rusty tomato juice can tip over and scatter a handful of wheel nuts all over the garage floor, some rolling under the car to where one of Colton's teammates was busy working. I jerked my now-shaking hand back, bit down around the one-inch scar on my bottom lip, and tensed.

Had I done that?

Please God no ...

Colton had lunged forward as if he'd thought he could catch the can, but he'd been a fraction too late. Instead, he surveyed the mess.

"It's my fault," I blurted, on the verge of panic. "I ... I knocked it over with my suitcase." My gaze shifted around the stall, making sure no one was close enough to have seen otherwise.

"No worries. Somebody trips over that thing at least once a day." He waved his hand up high in the air and let out a loud whistle. "Hey, Joe. Can you look after this spill? I need to get Lexi here to the hauler."

A curly-haired man wearing a two-piece black and white fire suit with the angel logo printed across the front popped his head out from behind the car. "Sure thing, Colt."

Colton's gaze dipped back to me. "Come on, newb." He

winked the green eye. "Dean's expecting you." He turned on the heels of his weird, dainty-looking running shoes and headed toward the haulers.

I snatched my suitcase's handle and hurried to keep up. "Hey, it's not like I'm totally oblivious. I've watched races on TV before. I just don't follow every race … I mean, you're new and—"

"It's no biggie." He chuckled, slowed down, and glanced back. "I can't expect everyone to be a fan. I get it."

"It's not that I'm not a fan, it's that I …" Colton looked back, eyebrow raised. "I … oh, never mind." Swallowing my words, I motioned for him to keep going. I followed the rest of the way in silence. Making friends with this guy—or anyone else, really—wasn't the goal here. The goal was to pay off Roy's debt. That was it. Getting close to anyone was a bad idea.

Colton led me between the haulers, up the side of the DSG Racing and Guardian Auto Insurance's black, forty-seven-foot-long rolling billboard, and held the side door open for me. I slid the propped luggage handle down and reached for the side handle, but Colton beat me to it. "I got it."

"Thanks." I gave him a faint smile.

"Head on up and to your left."

I stepped inside and peeked through the thick strands of dark brown, chin-length hair falling over my face, catching a glimpse of myself in the stainless steel surface of the bar fridge. I looked so out of place with my grease-stained, ripped jeans and large gold hoop earrings. No wonder people had stared. This was an entirely different world, a shiny one compared to working at the salvage yard. These teams all had matching uniforms that were, no doubt, professionally cleaned on a weekly basis. My wardrobe and accessories were going to need some serious rethinking.

Colton climbed up behind me, swinging my suitcase in before him. "Son of a … This thing's heavy. Whatcha got in here?"

"My whole life." I resisted the urge to look over my shoulder at him, not wanting him to see the scowl on my face. It wasn't his fault I'd been sent here against my will.

Colton brushed my arm with his hand and I jumped, darting a look in his direction. "Hey, now. Whoa. You have nothing to be scared of. Dean's a good guy, I promise."

I looked away. "Yeah. Says you."

"Dean," Colton shouted, "Your golden child has arrived."

I rolled my eyes. I couldn't help it. I *so* knew where he was going with this. This guy was as cheesy as the college frat boys Roy hired to help out around the shop part-time. Cute—in this case, gorgeous—but didn't have much going on upstairs, other than lousy jokes and ideas for stupid pranks.

A chair scraped on the hollow floor in the next room. "Now, Colton, I wouldn't exactly call you my—"

"Lexi's here," Colton corrected him before he could finish his sentence.

Dean appeared around the corner. He looked the same as he had the day he'd strolled into Roy's office: thirty-something, medium build, wavy brown hair. "Oh." His expression softened. "Hello, Lexi." He pulled his hand out of his dark jean pocket and held it out to me. "We haven't been formally introduced. I'm Dean Grant."

No, we hadn't. Roy hadn't had the decency to introduce me to the man who was going to rip me out of the only home I'd known for the past eight years and whisk me away for an entire NASCAR racing season, all because I knew how to turn a stupid wrench.

I looked down at his waiting hand, and then up at his face. "I know who you are." *Jerk.*

Don't get me wrong. It wasn't like I had the perfect life with Roy in that hellhole I called home. Dean had seen the fresh handprint-shaped bruise on my arm the day he'd toured the shop—now a faded yellow, unrecognizable mark hidden under my sleeve—but still. I'd managed fine on my own. I knew how to deal with Roy's temper, and I only had to put up with it until November. In her will, Mama had left me the old cottage by the lake—the one we'd lived in before she'd married that scumbag—and it would finally be mine on my eighteenth birthday. All I had to do was prove that I intended on graduating high school, which I did.

Colton dropped my luggage in the middle of the aisle and grazed my arm on his way to the bar fridge. The contact made my temples throb again, this time causing a tool to rattle on the workbench behind Dean.

Oh, come on. Not again. Lex, get a grip.

I clenched my fists and worked at regaining control while trying to keep my face expressionless.

Dean took back his hand, rocked onto his heels, and looked past me at Colton, oblivious to my struggles. "Move her bag over there, will ya?" He nodded to a corner between the workbench and the door. "I'll come see you before Link's practice."

Colton swallowed as he tightened the cap of a water bottle he'd taken from the fridge. "Sure thing, boss." He moved the suitcase, flashed me another grin, and then left the way we'd come.

Dean put his hand on my shoulder and pointed toward the next room. "Let's go chat in my office, shall we?" I flinched and gave him a sharp stare. I didn't like being touched, not without good reason. He pulled his hand away awkwardly, clearing his throat as he did so, and gestured for me to go in before him.

I slipped my backpack off my shoulders, dropped it on the floor, and sat in one of the two upholstered office chairs facing his desk. The room was gray and dull; not one picture or poster hung on the walls. The only dab of color came from the large green and yellow sponsor calendar that lay on his desk. Talk about boring.

Dean rounded the desk and pulled back the chair on the other side. "I hope you had a pleasant trip."

He meant the cramped, two-hour bus ride from Kissimmee to the Daytona International Credentials Office a few blocks from here, where he hadn't even had the decency to pick me up himself.

"Fine."

"Good." He smoothed out his yellow satin tie and sat.

I lowered my gaze, fiddling with the credentials badge hanging from my neck as I fought to keep my emotions in check. I didn't want to "accidentally" launch every metallic object in this room at his head, although knowing I could if I wanted to helped me relax. I forced myself not to smile at the idea of whacking him in the face with a stapler.

"Now, I know being here may seem somewhat odd to you. It's not exactly an ethical way of negotiating a sponsorship deal with your stepfather's business. But, after seeing you work from his office window, I couldn't refuse his offer."

Yeah, I'm sure he hadn't missed the part where Roy had

stormed down from his second story office to yell his brains out at me when the transmission I'd been removing fell and almost smashed my face in. I'd managed to deflect it to the floor with my ability, but Roy hadn't noticed that, and neither had Dean. He'd been too busy watching Roy scream at me for almost ruining the part his customer was picking up later that afternoon.

Dean stared at my not-so-pleased expression and sighed. "Look, Lexi, I realize you probably don't think much of me now, and I'm not going to force you to stay—"

"Like I have a choice," I mumbled, slouching deeper into my chair.

"Yes, you do."

I glanced up. "I do?" Hope began to stir, but then fear reared its ugly head. How could I go home now? Roy would beat the crap out of me for screwing up his deal. And, to be honest, did I seriously want to go back there?

Running away wasn't an option if I wanted to graduate or inherit the cottage, so that didn't leave me with many choices.

Dean narrowed his eyes, as if trying to figure out what was going on in my head. "Give me three days. Give me until Sunday's race to prove you'll fit in here, to show you what this new life has to offer, and then you can give me an answer on whether you want to stay or go. If you decide this isn't for you, I'll drive you home myself."

"What about your contract with Roy?"

He threaded his fingers together and leaned his forearms on the desk. "I'll honor my commitment to him for the remainder of the season."

Was this guy for real? Would he seriously let Roy's East

Coast Salvage's name stay on as a sponsor if I walked away? He was nuts. Sponsorship ads weren't cheap. That much I knew.

"Do we have a deal?" Dean stretched his open hand across his desk.

His eyes held a sincere promise, but this whole thing still seemed fishy to me. Something told me there was another reason I was here and it had nothing to do with my mechanical skills. But what did I have to lose? Worst case, I'd be back home in three days.

I firmly planted my hand in his and nodded.

"Deal."

chapter
two

I followed Dean through the infield down to the drivers' lot where I'd be staying for the weekend. People circled and stared like vultures nearing a fresh kill. Some even whispered as we passed by. I didn't belong here, and they all knew it. I gripped my backpack tighter and hoped that once Dean showed me to my room, I could have some alone time to calm my agitated nerves and my cursed senses. If I was going to function, I needed to get a grip on my emotions before I completely lost it.

Dean ushered me through the side door of a large, dark gray motor coach with green decorative swirls along its side. My eyes widened and wandered around the luxurious space, looking at the hardwood crown moldings and matching cabinet doors, the speckled granite countertops, and the black, polished floors that sparkled at my feet. Dean took the lead again and moved toward the back of the bus, passing two beige leather sofas before entering another room where he swung my suitcase onto the queen-sized bed centered against the back wall. "So … what do you think?"

I followed him in, taking slow and steady steps toward the bed. I needed time to digest the elegance that surrounded me. I mean … this was a bus. A freakin' bus. From the outside, I'd never expected it to look so spacious and rich.

"It's huge." The words slipped out of my mouth before I could stop them.

Dean chuckled. "Yes, well. This is the master bedroom. I thought you'd appreciate having your own space when at the tracks. You even have your own bathroom right through that door." He pointed to a narrow sliding door behind him.

I blinked rapidly to keep my eyes from bulging out of my head. "I get my own bathroom?" I slid my backpack off my shoulders and dropped it on the bed.

Dean nodded. "Colton and I are set up on the bunk beds at the other end. We share another bathroom up there."

I stared in awe at the room: the dark brown, built-in nightstands, the long dresser, the tipped out wardrobe that sat empty, begging me to fill it. I opened the bathroom door and gasped at its sheer size with crisp, white walls, a floor-to-ceiling mirror, and a stand-up shower in the corner. This was too much. My musty corner loft room above the garage back home would only have filled half this space, if that.

The shock wore off, and Dean's words sunk in. "Wait, Colton sleeps here too?" A static spark ignited in my head.

"He sure does. I gotta pamper my drivers." He tilted his head slightly. "That, and his parents preferred that he stay with me until he turns twenty-one. It's a condition they set when I took him on last year, but you didn't hear it from me. Colton doesn't like to advertise it."

"Huh." So not only would I be working with Colton, I'd be

sharing a living space with him for the whole weekend. The low hum of pulsating currents in my head didn't seem to like that idea much.

"I left you a few t-shirts and ball caps in the first drawer over in that dresser with our team logos on them. I recommend you wear them on race day, but I'll leave that up to you. And if you follow me into the kitchen, I have a few more things I want to give you."

More things? He *did* realize I worked for him, not the other way around, right?

Dean pulled out a large bag from a compartment under the seat of the eating area and motioned for me to sit.

"From what I gather, you've been doing your schooling through online independent studies. Correct?"

I nodded and shifted awkwardly. "It's a long story, I—"

He waved his hand. "No need to explain. It's actually a relief that I didn't have to pull you out of school." I bit my lip. He proceeded to pull out a black Toshiba laptop from a zipped protective casing and set it down in front of me. "I just want to make sure you don't neglect your school work while you're with us." I stared at it. A squeal lodged itself in my throat—this gift was too good to be true. "It's not new, but I had it reformatted and made sure you'd have all the software you need."

Who cared if it wasn't new? Anything was better than the old piece of shit computer I had at home that would greet me with the blue screen of death the second I attempted to surf the web and run MS Word at the same time.

My lip twitched, wanting to smile, but I suppressed it. I couldn't accept this gift, not when I had every intention of leaving Sunday.

"Sir, I appreciate what you're doing, but—"

"It's Dean. And consider the laptop a loan if it makes you feel more comfortable." Before I could respond, he pulled out a small wallet-sized case. "This is so we can reach you when we need to. Colton tells me it's the phone to have. He set it up for you. Added music and apps he thought you might like." He opened the case and placed a brand new iPhone on the table next to the laptop.

I picked it up, my hand trembling. I'd never had a cell phone before, nor had I ever had the need for one, but I'd wanted one so bad. My eyes itched. I took a conscious breath and set the phone back on the table. "Dean, I—"

Dean's finger shot up and stopped me. "Oh, and I almost forgot …" he reached into his back pocket. "This should be enough to get you started." He held out a folded envelope. I shot him a glance and then looked down at his hand. He pushed the envelope toward me. I took it, opened it, and pulled out a stack of twenty-dollar bills. A web of emotions spun in my throat and fed the curse, now pulsating hard in my temples. I dropped the bills on the table as if they'd bitten me and balled my hands together in my lap.

Get a grip, Lex. You're stronger than this.

"Is something wrong?" Dean asked, looking puzzled.

"Why are you doing this?"

Dean slipped his hands in his pockets. "Did you actually think me cruel enough not to pay you?"

Okay. Now I really didn't understand. "That was the deal, wasn't it?"

"With Roy, yes. But with you, it doesn't have to be."

I looked down at the money.

"Unfortunately, I'll have to pay you in cash—under the table, so to speak. Two hundred per week sound good?"

"Two hundred per—" My throat stopped functioning and pressure built in the back of my eyes. I'd never been paid for working at the Salvage Yard, nor had I ever gotten an allowance. Roy would show up now and then with a hand-me-down bag of clothes he'd picked up from God knows where, and if my luck aligned with the planets just right, he'd bring home a movie rental as a treat, but that was the extent of his kindness and fulfillment of stepfatherly duties. The only time Roy ever put money in my hand was for me to run his errands at the supermarket next door.

The Blackberry clipped to Dean's belt chirped. In a quick one-handed sweep, he unclipped it, thumbed the keys, and read the screen. "Ah, hell." He rubbed the back of his neck, clipping the phone back at his waist. "I hate to do this to you, but I have to go. The CEO of Guardian Auto Insurance decided to swing by unannounced. I need to clear my schedule and go schmooze the man if we want to keep him on as our main sponsor for the full season. Are you okay here?"

I batted my lids to dry the moisture building along my lashes and nodded. I was on the verge of crumbling—which was totally unlike me—and I didn't like it one bit.

The side door burst open, and Colton ran inside. "Dean, Mr. Langdon's—"

"I know. Jimmy just texted me," Dean told him.

My stomach fluttered when Colton's eyes shifted to me and didn't look away. I tried my best to look sane and not disturbed by the forces churning inside my head. I thought I'd imagined it before, but now I knew for sure that Colton had a strong effect on me, one that warmed my insides but also kept me teetering on the edge of going magnetically insane. It didn't help that Dean's gift giving had thrown my emotions all out of whack. I didn't know if I could control it much longer.

Dean glanced at his watch. "Link's practice is in forty-five minutes. Lexi, if you want you can meet me at the hauler later to get a feel for what we do around here."

I broke eye contact with Colton and looked back at the items in front of me. My energy was draining fast, and the pressure kept building. I couldn't remember the last time my head pounded and throbbed this bad. "I'd like to stay here and unpack … if that's okay."

"Alright …" Concern crept across Dean's face, dueling with his obvious sense of obligation, but he concealed it with a smile. "I'll see you later, then." He hesitated, and then turned to Colton. "Come on, kid. We can't make the man wait."

Colton followed Dean out and threw me a smile and a wink before closing the door behind him.

That did it.

My head exploded with pain. I threw myself over the phone and laptop to prevent them from moving, but the coffee machine and a few other objects on the counter levitated and swirled up above my head. Cupboard doors began to open and slam shut thanks to their spring-loaded hinges.

My first day of high school flashed in front of my eyes. It was all happening again.

I covered my ears and ran to the bathroom, trying to escape the clanging metal and vibrating walls, but the chaos followed. Why me? Why did I have to suffer with this curse?

I knew why. It was thanks to the father I didn't remember

and the stupid unexplained condition he passed onto me at birth, the one that caused my iron levels to fluctuate with my emotions and allowed my body to store it all without symptoms.

But I could live with that—and I had, for fourteen years. No one but my mother knew I could sense every metal object around me the second I walked into a room, more so if my emotions were heightened. Essentially, I was a human metal detector. But what Mama failed to explain to me was why my father felt the need to take his own life only days after surviving a power line accident when I was two, or why she kept me locked inside the house during electrical storms.

I understood when I'd survived my own life-altering encounter with high voltage the night of her funeral. My emotions had been at their highest, my iron level through the roof, when lightning had struck. I found out that night what had driven my father to end his life. And now the curse was mine to bear.

For three years now, I'd been dealing with this new manifestation of my ability, this new control I had over metal objects as if they were an extension of my body. I thought I'd finally mastered it—but then again, who can say for sure when emotions play a role?

A tight-fisted knot ached behind my ribcage. Who was I kidding? I couldn't stay here. I had to leave on Sunday before someone figured out what I could do, before they shipped me off to some institute or research facility. But did I really want to go back to face Roy and his rage?

I leaned against the wall and faced the long mirror in front of me. My usual storm grey eyes stared back at me, blood red and panicked from the intensity of uncontrolled magnetic currents flowing through me like a triple shot of caffeine. My eyes burned and tingled like pins and needles. They'd done the same that first day of high school, and every other time I'd lost control after that until I'd learned to contain it.

I wasn't doing a good job of it now, though.

I squeezed my eyes shut and sank to the floor, rocking myself back and forth to calm my mind. Mama did that with me when I got upset as a kid. If only she were here now to take me into her arms, rock me, and tell me everything would be okay. But things weren't okay. Every metal-hinged door flung open and slammed shut, over and over. I kept my hands over my ears to muffle the noise and prayed the shower door didn't shatter. The walls around me shook as if a hurricane was blowing through the lot outside. My lungs burned and ached. I wanted to scream.

Oh, God, make it stop. Make it stop.

I hugged my legs tight to my chest, put my head down, and forced myself to concentrate on something, anything other than the chaos around me. Imagining my mother's face was the only thing that worked in the past. That calmed me when this new ability first manifested, but as time went on, the details of her features, her smile, even the feel of her skin faded from my memory. I relied on pictures that contained some—not all—of the details my memory had lost, but it wasn't the same. Besides, I hadn't needed to be calmed in over two years. Why was this happening now?

I rubbed my temples, trying to soothe them. I couldn't think straight. All I could do now was clear my mind and wait it out, one deep breath at a time.

It took several minutes for my rattling senses to calm, and for silence to return. What a sweet sound silence could be.

I looked up at my reflection. My eyes were their dull gray selves again. "Thank you," I whispered to no one, and then slumped back against the wall, eyes closed, concentrating on catching my breath as the expected wave of exhaustion hit me with a cold sweat.

The creaking door to the motor coach opened and broke through my sweet silence. My nerves tensed, and I pursed my lips shut to try to contain the occasional whimpers that insisted on slipping out.

"Lexi?"

Shit. What was Colton doing back here so soon?

"Lexi, are you in here? Dean asked me to come ..." His voice trailed off, and I knew he had heard me.

A knock at the bathroom door pushed me to square my shoulders and bite down on my lower lip to prevent any more noises from coming out.

"Lexi, are you alright in there? If you don't answer, I'm coming in."

Could he? I couldn't remember if I'd locked the door. I didn't think I did. Crap. I didn't have the energy to contain another meltdown. I opened my mouth to ask him to leave, but a sniff and a sob replaced my words. I clamped both hands over my mouth, hoping he hadn't heard.

The door slid open. His eyes landed on me, half collapsed on the floor against the wall. He shoved the door wide open and dropped to his knees next to me. "Lexi, damn it, what happened?"

"Nothing," I choked out.

"You're bleeding. You've been crying."

Bleeding? I snapped a glance back to the mirror in front

of me. A nosebleed. "Oh. That. It's nothing. I get these all the time." Over the years, I'd learned that using my ability lowered my iron levels, so using it from time to time kept me balanced. But losing control like I'd just done dipped them dangerously low, bringing on more extreme symptoms. This was just another common side effect of my uncontrolled magnetic freak-outs. It'd been so long since I'd had one that I'd almost forgotten.

I stood and tore off a few hand-twirls of toilet paper from the holder and held it to my nose to soak up the blood. Colton towered behind me, so close that all it would take was a slight lean to rest my head against his chest. My stomach did that fluttery thing again and sent pulses rushing to my head, but this time, I was too weak to fight for control. The curse dulled to a low hum in the back of my mind.

I stared at his reflection in the mirror—more specifically, his mismatched eyes. "Me being here has nothing to do with my mechanical skills, does it? I'm a charity case."

Colton's eyes narrowed. "No—"

"That's why he accepted that deal. That's why you and Dean are being so nice ..." A sob cut me short.

Colton slid his warm hand up my right arm. The flutters spread to my chest and into my lungs, making it harder to breathe. He lifted my sleeve and uncovered the yellowed marking left over from last week's bruise. The discoloration stuck out against my skin. Colton's entire hand glided gently over the mark, and then he looked up and met my eyes through the mirror. A shiver ran across my shoulders.

"Dean knows what it's like. He's been in your shoes."

I stepped out of his touch, ashamed that he knew about my bruise and what kind of stepdad Roy really was. I balled up the blood-soaked wad of toilet paper and whipped it at the wastebasket next to the toilet with whatever strength I could muster. Colton took one of my elbows and gently turned me around to face him. "Give Dean a chance, Lex. He's a good guy. Trust me. Don't go through this alone. Not when you don't have to."

This would've been so much easier if Roy's tight arm grips and slaps were the only things I had to worry about—if I didn't have to monitor my own thoughts and analyze my emotions every damn second to make sure I didn't expose myself in public and get locked up in some mental institution. But my life hadn't been easy for three and a half years now. I had to live with the fear and the guilt. Images of overturned desks and screaming classmates flashed in my mind. I shook my head, looked up at Colton's questioning gaze, and whispered, "No one can help me."

chapter three

I knuckled the sleep from my eyes to the sound of muffled voices coming from the kitchen just outside my door. Dim light filtered through the tinted window next to the dresser. Morning had snuck up on me. I pulled back the covers, sat up, and dangled my feet off the edge. It'd been years since I'd slept in such comfort, and every inch of me protested against getting out of bed. But I couldn't stay in here all day, even if I wanted to.

The voices grew louder. I couldn't quite make out what they were saying, but it was none of my business—living with Roy, I'd learned real quick that I should never stick my nose where it didn't belong. A black eye had taught me that lesson.

I shuffled to the bathroom like a zombie and prepared to splash water over my face to liven myself up when I heard Colton's angry voice.

"Ah, come on, Dean."

I straightened. I could hear them clearer in here. My interest piqued. They were arguing. Colton was trying to make Dean understand something, but I still couldn't make out some of the words. The hell with it. I wasn't at home anymore. I tiptoed through the open shower door and leaned my ear against the wall.

"She shouldn't be here," were Colton's next words. They shot through me like a snapped engine bolt on the fly. Were they arguing about me? "You should never have brought her here. She's too fragile."

Fragile? What the hell?

"Fragile?" Dean asked, as if reading my thoughts.

"Yesterday, I found her in the bathroom after you asked me to come back and see if she needed anything. She had some sort of full-blown panic attack. You should have seen all the stuff she trashed in here before she locked herself in there."

"Why didn't you tell me this yesterday?" Dean asked.

"When did I have the chance? You were busy schmoozing Guardian's CEO most of the afternoon and then spending the evening with Link and his family. I picked everything up before she came out, in case she didn't remember doing it or whatever. But Dean, there's something not right about that kid."

"Hey. That *kid* is less than two years younger than you, and—"

"Uh, Dean? Don't bother. It's broken."

"It's broken?"

"Yeah. It's one of the many things I found on the floor yesterday."

"Ah, man. Not the Keurig." Dean's voice dropped.

I'd heard enough. I didn't have to listen to any more. It was obvious that Colton wanted me gone. How could I have been so naïve as to think that maybe, just maybe ... Colton had been so nice to me yesterday. So much so that I'd even toyed with the idea of staying, thinking this could be a good opportunity for me. A chance at a normal life. But I'd been wrong. The other proverbial shoe was dangling by a shoelace, just about to drop.

My eyes burned. So what if I had a panic attack? Why did Colton hide the mess? I hadn't realized I'd broken anything. After cleaning myself up and changing, I'd been relieved to see that my episode had left little to no evidence of collateral damage, but now I knew it was only because of Colton. He wanted me gone, and I had every intention of giving him what he wanted. Come Sunday, I was outta here.

I changed out of my pajama bottoms and vintage Mickey Mouse tee and slipped on a pair of denim shorts and one of the many DSG Racing t-shirts Dean had left me before pulling a ball cap low on my forehead. I took a deep breath, and then stepped out of my room. Both Colton and Dean fell silent. I took one glance at them, turned, and made my way to the door.

Dean broke the ice. "Morning, Lexi. There's milk in the fridge and cereal in the cupboard. Or some toast and jam on the counter."

"No, thank you. I'll go find something at one of the concession stands," I said, grabbing my lanyard with my credentials attached, hanging by the door.

"There's no need for that. I'm sure we can find something for you here," Dean said.

Colton tapped me on the arm. "Are you okay? Is something wrong?"

I wasn't very good at hiding my emotions, and Colton read me like a timesheet. Turning to face him, I flexed my hands at my sides, forced a smile, and prayed that the anger building within me didn't pierce through the control I was trying so hard to maintain. I could feel my senses vibrating, assessing every object with metallic properties in close proximity.

"Oh, don't you worry, Colton. I'm not about to have a panic attack or anything." His face and jaw dropped.

"Lexi." Dean stood up from his seat.

I snapped my head in his direction. "Tell your superstar that I'll be gone by Sunday night. He won't have to worry about cleaning up my messes anymore."

"Lexi, he didn't mean—"

I stormed out of the motor coach, refusing to let him finish his no doubt pathetic and defensive excuse, and slammed the door shut behind me with a wave of my hand—a stupid move that I hadn't thought through. Luckily, there was no one around to notice I'd shut it without touching it.

Securing my credentials around my neck, I ventured out to find some food, returning only when I was sure I'd have the motor coach to myself. I thought about not coming back at all, losing myself in the crowds that were pouring in for today's events, but there was only so much mindless walking and hordes of people I could endure. I craved the solitude—if you could call it that—of the infield, and I was in dire need of some quiet time. So much had happened in the last twenty-four hours and I still hadn't fully accepted that all this had happened in the first place. I sat on the bed in my new room, surrounded by my new things, and felt the need to dive into the familiar. I fired up the laptop Dean gave me, pulled out my schoolbooks, and logged into my online courses. I plugged myself into my iTunes library—Colton had programmed a bunch of good tunes—and continued where I'd left off back when my life was normal. Well … normal to me, anyway.

A half hour into my English assignment on *Hamlet*, someone knocked at the door. I looked up, debating if I should pretend I wasn't here. "Lexi, I need to talk to you."

Damn it. Colton. I let out a loud sigh.

"I don't wanna talk to you," I yelled over the music playing in my ears.

"Please. Just let me explain."

"There's nothing to explain. I heard what you said, and I'll be out of your hair by Sunday night."

"Please. Talk to me. I'm not going to leave until you do."

Ugh. "You've got five minutes."

"Can I come in?"

I contemplated leaving him out there, but decided seeing his face would help me determine if he was being sincere. I saved my Word document, pulled out my ear buds, and got rid of the annoyed expression on my face. "As you wish." *This should be interesting.*

The door creaked open. I regretted letting him in the moment I saw him. He moved closer to the bed where I sat, legs crossed, laptop balanced on my knees. He eased himself down on the corner and looked me in the eyes. I forced myself to keep a straight face and a tab on my curse's emotional levels. Cute or not, he was still a giant ass. "Well? You've got four minutes left."

He glanced away. "I didn't mean what you heard this morning."

"Oh, really? So you just enjoy going around saying things you don't mean for kicks."

He noted my sarcasm and nodded. "What I meant was, maybe the NASCAR scene isn't the best place for someone like you."

"Someone like me?" I crossed my arms. "What the hell is that supposed to mean?"

"The reason Dean accepted that deal with your stepfather was to get you away from him. He saw your bruises, saw the way he yelled at you, and he had to get you out."

So I'd been right. I *was* a charity case. I looked down at the blinking cursor of my still-open laptop screen. "And you know this because ...?" Had Dean run around telling everyone what he saw?

Colton shook his head. "I was the first person he saw when he came back and he told his wife over the phone, but that's it, I swear."

"Well, for your information, I didn't need saving. I was out of there in less than a year anyway."

"That may be so, but Dean knows what it's like. He's been through it. He had a rough childhood, possibly worse than yours, and no one helped him get out. I'm amazed he got through what he did and still managed to become the good guy he is today. He has a family now and a little girl of his own, and something inside of him snapped when he saw your bruises and your stepdad's temper toward you. He had to get you out of there. He played on your stepdad's greed to strike a deal to take you. Made him think it was his idea. The free advertising he's getting in exchange for you is coming out of Dean's own personal income."

My heart ached for Dean and for what he'd been through, but what did that have to do with me? Just because he saw one bruise and one of Roy's tantrums, what right did that give him to yank me away? "That's all nice and dandy, but that doesn't explain why you said what you said."

"When I walked in and saw the mess in the kitchen and then found you crumpled on the bathroom floor, I panicked. You looked so fragile, like someone who needed more than just an out from an abusive situation."

I eyed him and huffed out a laugh. "You think I need professional help."

"I—"

I scowled and waved my hand to stop him from saying more. The look on his face told me all I needed to know. "You don't know me. You don't know what I've gone through or what I'm going through right now. There are things you will never know about me, things that have nothing to do with my life back home, or with Roy. Things I have to deal with that not even a professional can help me with. So, thanks for your concern, but stay out of it."

"But I can't just leave you …" A sigh slipped passed his beautiful heart-shaped lips—an observation I couldn't stop myself from making, no matter how mad I was at him. "Please give Dean a chance. The man's like a father to me. He gave me the one thing I've always wanted—a chance to live out my dream when I thought it wasn't possible. I just don't want to see him embark on a personal mission to help you, and then fail. And if you go home on Sunday, he fails. If you're wrong and you do need more help than he can offer you, he fails. I can't just stand by and let that happen. So please, if you think staying might give you a better shot at a good life, then stay. If not for yourself, then for Dean."

I squared my shoulders and opened my mouth to fight back, but something in his eyes calmed every tense nerve, every vulgar word on the tip of my tongue, every tingle that ached to levitate the picture frame from the wall behind him and send it crashing over his head. He cared. He really cared. Not for me, but for Dean. Something churned inside me. Mama gave me that look often before she died. I'd forgotten what having someone care about me and protect me felt like. Colton cared for Dean. But what Dean did for me—the risk he took to get me here, whether I liked it or not—meant that he cared about me, even though he didn't know me. I slouched my shoulders and bit my lower lip to alleviate the remainder of my boiling anger toward Colton. He had a point, and I had to make a decision. This was my chance. A huge risk, but a chance nonetheless. All I had to do was not allow myself to get too close to anyone, regain control of my magnetic impulses, and maybe, just maybe, I could have the life I'd wanted before Mama died. Before all this happened to me.

I closed the lid to my laptop, tossed my schoolbook aside with a little more force than I'd wanted to, and closed my eyes. "Fine." The word tasted bitter on my tongue, but I had to give this a shot. Mama would have wanted me to.

"But—"

I shot Colton a cold stare. "I said fine. I'll stay. Happy now?"

Colton just smiled.

"Don't tell Dean just yet. You may trust him, but I'd rather make him sweat."

He nodded. "The brooding, bitter approach. Got it."

I let out a light chuckle.

"So we're good?" Colton reached out and touched my arm,

causing unfamiliar sensations to trigger the pulse of magnetic energy in my head.

I stiffened under his touch and suppressed the curse from trying to invade my senses. "We're good." For now.

chapter
four

Colton received a text message from Dean asking him to report to the hauler for practice. I told him to hold on while I put away my laptop and books, and followed him out. The realization hit me that I'd said yes to staying without having a clue what Dean expected of me, or what kind of work he had in mind for me. I really needed to get out of my self-loathing bubble and find out what working with a NASCAR team entailed. I just hoped I hadn't given Colton my word too soon.

On our way, Colton explained that Daytona was usually a week-long event that kicked off the regular season, but because of the storms we'd had, NASCAR officials had been forced to cancel all the races and qualifying sessions that determined the big 500 race's starting order, as well as most of the activities earlier in the week. Practices like this one were being squeezed in at the last minute, and the standard qualifying laps had been added to tomorrow's new busy schedule.

When we reached the hauler, a short, stocky man barreled toward Colton as though on an urgent mission. "Colton, there you are. You're on the track in ten."

"Keep your checkered panties on. I got plenty of time." Colton waved him off and grabbed a hold of my sleeve. "Come on." He opened the back door to the hauler and ushered me inside.

"Who was that?" I asked.

"That?" He pointed over his shoulder. "That was Lenny. My crew chief."

I nodded, although I wasn't sure what that meant. "Uh-huh."

As if reading my thoughts, Colton continued. "He runs the show from the pits. Helps me make decisions about pit stops and what strategies to use."

"So he's one of the guys that talks to you during the race?"

"Yep. Him and my spotter."

I was about to ask him who his spotter was and what he did when Colton stopped in front of a section of shelves on the end of one of the workbenches and untucked his shirt. Was he about to …?

"Give me one minute to get ready, and then I'll find you a headset and show you how to get up top where Dean is."

I pursed my lips, gave a slow nod, and leaned back against the rack of spare coil springs behind me. Colton turned away, pulled off his ball cap, and tucked it between his knees. Blond hair trickled down the sides of his face. My body tensed, my eyes grew wide and refused to blink despite my trying to make them cooperate. I'd been so sure that he had a short, preppy style under that hat. My fingers twitched, curious as to whether his hair was as soft and silky as it looked. It suited him.

In one fluid motion, Colton reached over his shoulders, curled his fingers into the fabric on his back, and pulled his shirt up and over his head.

A gasp forced its way up and balled in my throat. Keeping it from escaping and clamping onto the curse now humming wildly inside my head wasn't easy. The smart thing to do would be to look away right about now, but I didn't want to be smart and the struggle was *so* worth the view.

He tossed his shirt aside, snagged a stretchy black shirt with white stitching from the shelf, threaded his arms through the short, tight sleeves, and then turned to face me.

I gulped and swallowed the gasp back down.

The tips of his long, straight hair swept his cheekbones as he lifted his arms to pull the tight-fitting shirt over his head, granting me a full, uncensored view of his chest and abs. Oh, he definitely worked out. Those were not natural. No lazy nineteen-year-old could look this perfect. I tried to tear my poor virgin eyes away, but instead they centered on his ribcage, sprinted a lap and a half around his belly button and crossed the finish line at the belt that kept his fire suit from falling off at his hips. My temples ached as if they were being stabbed repeatedly with a pocketknife. What was wrong with me? It's not like I'd never seen a guy shirtless before. Many guys walked around the yard shirtless back home, some way more drool-worthy than the view I'd just seen, so why was I losing my marbles?

I closed my eyes, strained against the building pressure, and pushed up every wall I could to contain the magnetic currents, but it wasn't enough. A pair of bolt cutters next to me wobbled off the wall and fell off the workbench, followed by the hook they'd been hanging from. I hadn't seen them fall, but I'd felt them. Colton bent to pick up the fallen tool and inspected the jagged-edged hook. "Huh. Guess this anchor was a dud."

My face grew hot, probably turning the same shade of red as the coil springs behind me. The tension in my head eased, but still tried to fight me. I dipped my eyes to the floor and released the canine grip from my bottom lip. I had to say something, anything. I couldn't just stand here like an idiot. "You must be really hot with all those layers on."

Seriously? Out of all the things I could have said, that was what came out of my mouth? This moment desperately merited a face-palm. I was such an idiot.

His lips twitched and then formed a smile as he tucked the hem of his shirt into his suit. "It does get extremely hot in that car, but this type of fabric actually helps keep me cool. It's not mandatory, though. One guy I know likes to go commando under his suit." Colton winked.

My face boiled. I didn't want to look at him, didn't want him to see how his words and actions were affecting me, although the pink-to-red-to-purple trick my cheeks had surely done had more than likely given me away.

He reached for his cap, raked his hair back with his free hand, and slid the cap into place, setting the brim low on his forehead, shading his eyes and giving them an added air of mystery.

"So, now that *I'm* ready …" He rested his hands on his hips and glanced at the wall of aluminum cupboard doors lining half of the aisle. "Where are we going to find you a spare …?" He rushed to one of the doors, swung it open, shut it, and then opened the neighboring one with his other hand. "There we go."

He pulled out a set of large, red, retro-looking headphones. "This should do. Remind me to have Dean order you a set."

He moved toward me. An amazing scent filled my nostrils. He had a familiar smell—tangy and sweet, like men's cologne only better. It took me a few inhales to trigger my memory. Phoenix Axe body spray. That was it. Chris, a guy who sometimes helped out at the salvage yard on weekends, skunked himself with the stuff before leaving at the end of every day. I pitied his poor girlfriend for having to put up with it. On Chris, the scent was overwhelming, poisonous even, but on Colton, his natural sweet smell mixed in well. Even with the added hint of burnt rubber and racing fuel, it still managed to turn my knees into processed string cheese.

Colton hooked the headset around my neck, rested his hands on my shoulders and slouched down to my level, eye-to-eye. "You ready?"

I forced a smile despite the odd, uncomfortable tightening in my chest. And let's not forget my constant struggle to control the static sparks from flaring inside my head—about ready to burst and send objects flying—that seemed to intensify each time Colton got too close. "I guess."

"Good. Follow me."

Colton lifted his fire suit from his waist, slipped his arms through the sleeves, and led me out the back door to the aluminum ladder resting against the awning-like tailgate raised between the back door and the upper compartment where the cars were stored during transport.

"Dean should be up there already. He'll set you up."

"Thanks."

"Don't mention it." He winked, then turned to leave. "I'll see you after practice."

When I reached the top of the second ladder, Dean offered his hand to help me up the last few steps. "I was beginning to think you weren't going to show."

I looked past him at the track and the massive, colorful grandstands that stretched out both sides and murmured under my breath, "So was I."

Dean stood next to a tall man dressed in dark jeans, a white shirt, and a purple tie, similar to Dean's own attire. In front of them, a girl about my age wearing a pink headset that matched her tank top and denim shorts was leaning over the aluminum safety railing as far as she could, aiming her sights at pit road.

"There he is, Daddy," she said.

"Lexi, meet Mr. Langdon, the CEO of Guardian Auto Insurance, and his lovely daughter, Gwen."

"It's a pleasure to meet you." Mr. Langdon said, extending his hand my way.

Gwen turned and pulled back her left earphone. "Who's she?" Her eyes narrowed in my direction.

"Gwendolyn. Your manners!" Mr. Langdon glared at his daughter.

Dean placed a hand on my shoulder, "Lexi, here, might be helping us out at the shop this season. She's got some pretty impressive mechanical skills."

"Does she," Mr. Landon said, more as a statement than a question. He released his firm grip from my hand and smiled.

Gwen looked me over like I was nothing more than a goop of gum stuck to the bottom of her wedge shoe, then repositioned her headset and turned back to face the track. "He's starting her up, Daddy, look." She pointed again toward pit road.

Mr. Langdon ignored his daughter and tilted his head back. "Glad the weather finally cleared up. I was afraid we wouldn't see the Angel car fly her first race."

Dean followed the man's gaze while securing a scanner to his waist like it was second nature. "Schedule changes have been brutal, but everything looks good for Sunday's 500."

The big block V8 engines below roared to life. Dean motioned for me to put my headset on, clipped a scanner to my waistband, and then showed me how to tune it to the right channel. The instant he plugged me in, Colton's voice blared into my ears: "Let's go do this thing." I jumped and reached for the scanner's volume button.

Colton took to the track with the others, the sun glaring off his hood as he tilted up onto the sloped surface of the track and gradually inclined into the steep banked turns.

"Take a few laps to warm her up and then let her rip," the voice in my headset instructed him. That had to be Lenny.

"Roger that," Colton replied.

Colton brought the car up to speed, testing his lines. I'd at least retained that tidbit of knowledge from when Mama used to drag me to the dirt tracks as a kid to watch Roy race his small block modified. That was before they married and before his salvage yard business expanded into a hised enterprise. Before his temper got worse. He didn't have time to take out his stress and frustrations out on the dirt tracks on the weekends anymore, and with Mama gone and unable to keep him in check, he'd become the bruise-making bastard he was today.

"How's she feelin'?" Lenny said, snapping me out of memory lane.

Colton rounded out of turn four. "She's loose. Ass end's all over the place."

"Noted. We'll tighten her up."

"Not too much," Colton warned. "You know how I hate it when she's too tight."

"Ten-four," Lenny replied with a chuckle.

Gwen lowered her headset and turned to Dean. "Do I get to meet him after he's done practicing? I want to invite him to my eighteenth birthday party next month."

Mr. Langdon's expression fell. "Now, Gwendolyn, honey, remember what I told you."

She threw her hands up in the air. "Aww, come on, Daddy. He'll be in town that weekend anyway, and he'd be stupid to miss it. I throw the best parties." With that last comment, her eyes flicked toward me. I rolled mine and turned away.

Bratty and spoiled. Check.

After a few more laps, Colton ducked back into the pits, and Gwen made a beeline for the ladder.

Dean leaned in my direction and lowered his voice. "And so it begins."

I pulled off my headset and rubbed my ear where the foam piece had suctioned to my skin. "What begins?"

"Colton is the youngest driver in the Cup series. Teen girls are going to flock to him like seagulls on french fries."

I scrunched my face. "And what do I look like to you? I'm a teen girl. You don't see me flocking."

Dean laughed and glanced over at Mr. Langdon, who was chasing after his daughter, trying to talk some sense into her.

"You're different. You appreciate the mechanical side of the sport. I'm talking about girls who fawn over boy bands and *Teen Beat* magazine cover models."

I grimaced.

"Yeah, exactly. Colton has the look girls like and our PR rep Nancy thinks it'll get him tons of exposure. NASCAR's newest teenage heartthrob, she calls him."

"Didn't he race in the ProNation Series last year?"

"There are many young guns who come and go in the ProNation. It's like the minor league circuit of NASCAR. Racing the Cup series means you're in it for the long haul. At least we hope. And—"

"And girly-girls tend to get attached to their celebrity crushes," I finished for him.

Dean tapped my shoulder and laughed. "You catch on quick."

We made our way to Colton's garage, where Gwen was already in the midst of introducing herself to him, flipping her long blond hair and showing off her long, tanned legs by stretching one out in a runway model-type pose.

Unbelievable. The way she flirted with the guy, you'd swear it was a sport. But who could blame her? Colton Tayler was smokin' hot.

"I'll see what I can do," he told her in response to her party invitation.

I leaned close to Dean. "Is he for real? Would he actually go?"

Dean shrugged. "She is his major sponsor's daughter. He has to play nice. Guardian only signed on for seven races. The Board of Directors votes on sponsoring for the rest of the season after Texas in three months."

"Looks like she's milking it for all it's worth."

"You bet she is."

Gwen twirled a finger around a piece of her hair. "I'm going to be at all of your races. Daddy said I could use the corporate jet," she said to him, then curled her lips into a seductive smile.

Great. I hadn't seen the last of Little Miss Flirty Pants.

"Dean?" I caught up to Dean, who was wandering toward Colton. "Hey. Um. Would you mind if I headed back to the motor coach? It's been a long day." That and this chicky was making me nauseous.

Dean flashed me an understanding look. "Sure thing. I'll meet you back there for supper in about an hour."

I gave him a pinched-lip nod, took one last glance at Colton—who appeared to be enjoying every flirtatious advance Gwen threw his way—and took off in the opposite direction.

chapter five

A knock at the door snapped me out of my academic trance. I tugged at the cords of my ear buds and popped them out. "Come in," I said.

The door swung open, and Dean leaned in past the doorframe. Having ditched his shirt and tie combo for a pair of shorts and a t-shirt, Dean looked younger, less businesslike, and much less intimidating. "You hungry? We're heading over to Lenny's RV for some grilled burgers."

"Yeah, sure. I'll be right there."

"Ten-four. We'll be outside."

I nodded and watched the door close behind him. I'd only been here two days, and already Dean talked and acted as if he'd known me for years.

I saved my history assignment, logged off, and met up with Dean and Colton outside. My first breath of fresh air filled my nostrils with the sweet, smoky aroma of meat grilling nearby. Many of the drivers and their families were congregated outside their RVs, campers, and motor coaches while their kids ran around shouting and playing games. Some even had their dogs with them, playing fetch and getting belly rubs.

Colton had also changed into casual attire—green and blue knee-length board shorts, another Guardian Auto Insurance t-shirt, and a matching ball cap. His mirrored shades gave me a twitch of disappointment, though. A part of me had looked forward to seeing his fascinating eyes again.

He fell in step next to me without saying a word. We walked in silence. I looked around the infield, up at the tall palm trees, and caught a glimpse of the large body of water ran the length of the backstretch. I wondered if they blocked access to it during events like this, and made a note to check it out tomorrow.

The gentle graze of Colton's hand against mine pulled me out of my distracted thoughts. An instant chill traveled up my arm. I looked down at his hand, then up at him. His face had no expression and remained focused ahead. I looked away.

"I didn't see you after practice," he said finally, after I was forced to sidestep into him to avoid the two screaming kids chasing each other around the lot.

I looked up at him. "You were busy. I didn't want to bother you."

He slid his shades down to the tip of his nose, revealing eyes that matched the deep green and blue tones of his board shorts.

"That was nothing. Just you wait 'till race day. I'm going to have to fend the girls off with a tire iron."

I raised an eyebrow. "Is that supposed to impress me or something?"

"No. I was just stating a fact." With a tap of his index finger, he returned his shades to the bridge of his nose.

I rolled my eyes and shooed away the images of screaming

girly fans swirling inside my head. Did he know how arrogant he sounded?

Dean called out and waved to a group of people under a gray and teal striped awning at the end of the row. Lenny stood at the grill wearing a greasy white apron with the words "Flip This" across the front, flipping hamburger patties while the other crew members lounged in lawn chairs in the shade, sipping beers and drinks on the rocks. I recognized two of the guys from when I'd arrived at the track yesterday, but the others I couldn't place.

"Dean." Lenny raised his spatula in greeting. "You're just in time. Food's about ready."

"I timed it that way." Dean flashed him a grin and turned to me. "Lexi, these are the guys. Lenny here"—Dean patted him on the back—"is our crew chief, but he's also a seasoned cook. And, of course, you've met Jimmy, our spotter." I nodded at the man who had picked me up from the credentials office. "This is Dylan, our car chief, and Alan here is one of our jacks of all trades."

Colton leaned toward me. "That's Dean-talk for technician."

Dylan and Alan waved and I nodded and smiled at each of them.

"The other guys prefer to stay at the hotel," Dean added.

Dylan laughed and reached in front of him toward the cooler. "They're wussies. Real men shouldn't need silk sheets to get a good night's sleep."

"Ah, let 'em. Just means there's more food for the rest of us," Alan said.

Lenny pointed his spatula at me. "I hope you like burgers, sweetheart, cause you won't find any rabbit food on my grill.

You better not be one of those veggie whatchamacallits."

I folded my arms across my chest and smirked. "I was raised in a salvage yard and tore cars apart on a daily basis, *sunshine*. Do I look like a rabbit food-eating kind of gal to you? I'll eat a thick, juicy steak over a salad any day."

Lenny shot his brows up and snapped his head back to where Dean was. "I like this one. She's got spunk."

"Easy, Lenny. She ain't legal yet," Dylan cracked.

Lenny propped his fists at his round waist. "You callin' me a perv, Dyl?"

"If it quacks like a duck," Alan answered, bringing his beer bottle to his lips to take another swig.

Lenny's jaw dropped. "Don't listen to those twerps. I'm a happily married man. They're just joshin' ya." He flipped another patty on the grill and handed me a plate with an open burger bun on it. "Just for that," he said, raising his voice for all to hear, "Lexi gets the first one."

"Aw, come on, man! We've been waiting here longer than she has," Jimmy whined.

Lenny scooped up a patty and slid it onto the bun. "Welcome to the crew, sweetheart."

"Thanks."

Colton pointed me to the condiments table. I prepped my food, found a seat in the shade, and observed the crew. Their banter reminded me of the days when Roy went out of town, of how the mood lifted in the shop during his absence. Here, it seemed to be the norm. This whole day hadn't turned out the way I'd planned, and it just felt too good to be true, but I decided to enjoy it for the time being.

Colton reached into one of the coolers and handed me a

bottled water before sitting across from me. A loud roar pierced the chatter.

"Is it seven-thirty already?" Dean glanced at his watch.

"Yep," Lenny said. "Trucks are out." He meant the truck series scheduled to race tonight. "Music to my ears," he added, flipping another burger on the grill.

As the night wore on, Dean, Jimmy, Dylan, and Lenny reminisced about last year's ProNation season. Alan was new to the team this season. Some of the crew from last year had opted to stay on the ProNation team and Alan had been hired to fill one of the vacant positions—at least, that's what I'd managed to understand between all the jokes and nonstop laughter. Poor Alan was simply trying to keep up. At least I wasn't the only one.

Their stories consisted mostly of "remember when?" they'd played on each other in the shop and funny moments that had occurred at some of the races. Colton just sat there quietly, elbows resting on his chair's armrests, fingers laced together over his abdomen.

An odd breeze of awareness blew through me. He was staring at me. I couldn't see his eyes behind those mirrored shades of his, but I was sure of it. He was watching my every move. The unease made me fidget and shift around in my seat. I tried to immerse myself in the conversation and even got up to get another drink, hoping to shake the feeling—or his stare—but nothing worked. Had I done or said something wrong? Or was he still assessing the need to send me to a psychiatrist or to a loony bin? My insecurity pushed me toward the latter.

Blood simmering and temples aching, I sat back in my chair, arms crossed, and stared back at him. Two could play at this game. Within seconds, his leg began to fidget. I shot him a knowing smirk.

Busted.

But instead of looking away and pretending this staring game wasn't happening, he stood and removed his shades. "Well, guys, I'm off to bed. Another big day tomorrow."

The guys took their turns wishing him goodnight with pats and handshakes, and then dived back into another one of their stories. Colton looked down at me as he pulled the brim of his cap lower over his eyes and hooked the arm of his sunglasses into the neck of his shirt. With pursed lips, he gave me an expressionless nod and strolled off.

I got up and started after him. I had to know what his problem was, why he'd been making me feel like some kind of zoo attraction since we'd sat down to eat.

"Hey, Lex, while you're up, can you grab me another beer?" A tipsy Dylan asked me. I wanted to tell him to get it himself, but I couldn't. I was going to have to work with these people for nine months; I couldn't let them get the idea that I was some stuck-up teenage bitch. I reached into the cooler near the chair Colton had been sitting in and tossed Dylan another bottle of Budweiser. I gave up my mission and wilted back into my chair. If I left now, I'd have to explain why to the crew and draw attention to myself, which I loathed.

My questions were going to have to wait until tomorrow.

■■■

I sprinted through the infield, my uncombed hair tucked under a ball cap. Thanks to the state Colton's stare-down had left me in last night, it had taken me so long to fall asleep that I'd tuned out my alarm and overslept. Lucky for me, I'd found a text from Dean waiting on my phone that said Colton would be last to qualify. There was still a chance I could make it on time to see him run.

Dean stood alone on top of the hauler, holding a spare scanner and headset, and sporting a quirky grin. He'd seen me coming, running through security like a flailing idiot. I plopped my butt down on the drink cooler and heaved forward to catch my breath. "Am I too late?"

Dean shook his head. "You're just in time. He's going up next."

"Oh, thank God," I huffed.

Dean handed me the same scanner I'd used yesterday and went back to watching and timing the speed of the car currently out on the track. While waiting for my breathing to slow, I clipped the scanner to my waistband and slid the headset over my ears. Colton was already in his car, waiting for his turn to hit the track. The team with the fastest lap took the pole position in tomorrow's race, the first of forty-three cars in the field, and I knew without a doubt that Colton desperately wanted that spot.

When my chest stopped heaving, I joined Dean at the railing. "Who's the one to beat?"

"Take a wild guess," he said. I sensed bitterness in his tone. Bad history with the team to beat, perhaps? I took a peek at the clipboard in his hand. Dean had two-time Cup series champion Mitch Benson's name penned at the top of the page with a lap time of 194.087 mph. I guessed that meant Benson was this year's biggest contender.

"Okay, Colt, it's time to go," Lenny said through the scanner.

"It's time to show 'em whatcha got."

"Let's go do this thing," Colton voiced back.

I curled my fingers around the railing in front of me as Colton took to the track.

"Yee-haw!" Colton cried, and then laughed.

"How's she feelin'?" Lenny asked.

Colton cued his mic. The high-pitched growl of his car's engine filled my earphones before he spoke. "She's still a bit loose on that first turn, but it's nothing I can't handle."

"That's good. You have one more lap to go. Focus," Lenny told him.

"Bah, it's in the bag," Colton shot back.

Dean stood there, unfazed by the banter, with his clipboard and his stopwatch, clocking Colton's time. Race officials had computers that tallied up lap times and speed, but I got the feeling Dean had been around the sport for a long time and preferred the old methods of keeping track. My insides fluttered as Colton flew through turns one and two, ducking low, keeping to his lines. The car ran steady and perfect. He leveled out through the backstretch and then dipped thirty-one degrees as he went high, then ducked low again through turns three and four.

"Let's git 'er done!" Colton yelled in his mic as he came out of the last turn, heading toward the tri-oval and the start/finish line. Colton had definitely found his calling. He was good. Real good.

Dean held up his stopwatch just as Colton crossed the checkered line. "Yes. Yes. Lord, yeah!" A more prominent southern drawl found its way into his speech through his excitement. He cued his mic. "Colton, I think you've got yourself the pole in your first ever Daytona 500."

Colton screamed so loud I had to reach for my scanner's volume control knob.

"It's official, 194.738 miles per hour. Way to go, Colt, you did it!" Lenny said.

"No," Colton replied. "We did it."

"Bring 'er on home, kid."

Dean and I met up with Colton in the garage afterward to congratulate him. He grinned at me over Dean's shoulder as Dean raved on about how good he'd done. A wave of warmth ran up my arms. I looked away before I lost all of my senses and took a second to reorganize my thoughts.

"Hey, Lex."

Crap.

Colton approached, slapping the tips of his driving gloves against the palm of his other hand. This was the perfect time to ask him about last night. I took a deep breath, lifted my chin, and returned his slight smile. "Congratulations."

"Thanks. I'm glad you came to watch."

"Wouldn't have missed it."

An awkward silence fell. *Now. Ask him now.* I ignored the crampy knot in my stomach and seized the moment. "Umm … do you have a sec? There's something I wanted to—"

"Colton!" I cringed at the familiar brat-tastic squeal of Gwen's voice coming up behind me.

You have got to be kidding me.

She pushed past me—pretty hard, I might add—and practically jumped into his arms. "There you are, Colton Tayler!" Her high-pitched voice screeched inside my head like one of her manicured nails sliding down a sheet of scrap metal.

The way she said Colton's full name in a 1-800 number voice made me want to stick my fingers down my throat. "Daddy wants you to join us in the Superstretch Suite for the ProNation race." She let go of his neck and tugged at his waist.

Colton smiled and pulled back. "Sure, hold on a sec." He turned himself toward me. "Was there something you wanted to talk about?"

Gwen's beady little eyes burned through me. "Spit it out already. I don't want to miss Link's start."

Eighteen-year-old Link Bowers was another one of Dean's drivers. Dean had scouted him as Colton's replacement on his ProNation team when he moved Colton up to the new Cup team.

Dean had a good eye for talent … and hotness, apparently. Just saying.

I waved them off and backed away. "That's okay, we can talk later."

Colton stepped toward me and away from Gwen's reach. "Are you sure?" he asked in a lower tone. "If you need to talk, I can skip—"

"Oh, no. No worries. You go ahead." I pinched my lips together, then looked down at the ground. "It's not that important. I'll … I'll catch you later." I wrapped my arms around my midsection and walked away without looking back.

■ ■ ■

The race day crowd was overwhelming. I'd never seen so many people in one place. It was worse than Disney World during peak season. I pushed through the sea of fans, passed through the amped-up security, and made it to the hauler in one piece and on time to witness the crew pushing the car out onto pit road.

I hadn't seen Colton again last night or this morning and my urge to question him had faded. Maybe I'd imagined it. Maybe he hadn't been staring.

Dean greeted me when I reached the top of the hauler, handed me my headset and my scanner, and pointed over to the cooler. "Help yourself to something if you get thirsty."

I nodded. "Will do."

Mr. Langdon glanced back and nodded a greeting.

"You remember Mr. Langdon and his daughter Gwen?" Dean asked.

I shifted my weight from one foot to the other, uncomfortable in the presence of these rich people. "Yes, of course. You must be pleased to see the Angel Car starting first today."

"More than pleased. Proves we chose the right team to sponsor. He's going to give us a good name on and off the track, I think. We just need to convince the board of the same." He lifted his headset into place.

Gwen glared my way, her heavy-on-the-ruby-red-lipstick lips set in a frown. She mumbled something and then turned back to the railing, letting her pink pleated miniskirt twirl with her. Talk about inappropriate attire for a race. Even her tiny white halter top accentuated way too many body parts. She might as well have joined the models down on pit road taking pictures with some of the crews for publicity. I leaned closer to Dean. "What's her problem?"

Dean coughed out a laugh. "She's pissed."

"About what?"

"All the attention Colton's getting. You should have seen the herd of girls here earlier, asking for autographs. She complained about how insulted she was that Colt didn't pay any special attention to her." A suppressed laugh screeched in my throat. "She's been pouting ever since."

"Aww … muffin."

Dean whispered a laugh. "Shh, we mustn't piss off the sponsors." But the amusement on his face told me he couldn't help it, either.

I began to fasten my gear to my waistband and noticed the mic on my headset. "Hey, Dean, you got me the wrong headset."

"No, I wanted you to try this one on for size." He turned and helped me place it. "This is where you cue the mic." He placed my hand over one of my earphones and guided my finger to the button on the top. "And this is how you move it around." He swiveled the mic up and down.

I wasn't sure why I'd need a mic, but I went along with it. "Got it, thanks."

Within minutes, the anthem blared from every speaker and all the drivers and crew members stood on pit road next to their cars. The jets flew overhead, growling loud enough to rattle the inside of my chest. Adrenaline rushed through my veins as we all waited. This was it.

Drivers jumped into their cars, secured their steering wheels, and patiently waited along with the rest of us for the most famous four words in automotive racing.

Dean glanced back at me just as Colton cued his mic. "Let's go do this thing, boys." His excitement rang through in his voice. "Whooee!"

The sound system blared on, the crowd quieted, and the

celebrity guest gave her speech.

"Here it comes," Lenny said.

And sure enough, the Grand Marshal of the race went silent then called out, "Drivers. Start. Your. Engines!"

"Fire in the hole," Lenny said over the airwaves to relay the message to Colton that it was time to start her up.

All forty-three cars roared to life. Goosebumps rose on my arms. The hauler trembled under my feet, and the rumble of the idling cars vibrated through me like nothing I'd ever felt before. My temples pulsed in warning, but I locked it tight before anything noticeable happened. I didn't have many memorable moments growing up, but I was definitely going to add this one to my small collection.

One by one, the cars took to the track. Colton picked the inside spot behind the pace car, and Mitch Benson moved up next to him. The others fell in line behind them.

"We're green in five," Lenny said.

"Roger that," Colton acknowledged.

The cars lapped around the track, weaving side to side, warming up their tires and testing their suspensions. The strong, tangy smell of racing fuel filled the air.

"One lap to go, Colt," Lenny said. "Get 'er ready."

Colton kept himself low in turns three and four, maintaining the inside position while the cars behind him tightened up into a perfect side-by-side formation heading toward the start/finish line as the pace car ducked down. "Green, green, green!" Jimmy's cries came through loud and clear. The cars' rumbles grew louder as they charged the green flag and officially began the five-hundred-mile, two-hundred-lap race.

After a few laps, the four of us settled into our lawn chairs for the long haul as the cars circled the track. Colton lost the lead, but hovered in the fifth position on and off, keeping a decent pace. The radios went quiet except for the occasional repetitious "inside" or "outside" from the spotter telling Colton where the cars were around him. My nerves, on the other hand, weren't taking a break. They were as tight as when the race had first begun. I could almost swear I was the one sitting in the driver's seat out on that track.

The afternoon hours breezed by with no major accidents. The pits re-opened during a minor caution with fifty laps left to go. Air ratchets whined, large red canisters came out to top off fuel tanks, and tires were changed. Some teams opted to forgo the stop and risk it in a final attempt at making the front of the line.

Colton pitted, then took off again within seconds. "Great job, guys," he said.

"Forty-nine to go," his spotter called out.

When the green came out again, Colton pushed himself from seventh position to right behind the leader, Mitch Benson, and by the hundredth and sixtieth lap, it had turned into a full-blown battle for first.

Colton stayed glued to his ass, blocking some of the airflow to his radiator.

"Careful, Colt. Don't let her overheat," Lenny said.

"No worries, I'm keeping an eye on the temp gauge."

"Ten-four."

I stood and gripped the railing in front of me. With ten laps to go, my heart raced as fast as the car flying down through the turns. Colton dipped low going into turn one, trying to pass Mitch.

Mitch's back bumper clipped Colton's front end. I hissed. The car wobbled, but he recovered nicely.

"Ease off, rookie. He's not going to let you pass," Lenny said.

"Doesn't mean I can't try."

Colton pushed him in the backstretch then rounded high in turn three, but Mitch blocked him again.

"Four laps to go," Jimmy announced.

My palms clammed, and my knuckles ached from my death grip. Luckily, this particular railing was made of aluminum, or I would have magnetized the whole thing.

"Two laps," said Jimmy. "Up high."

Another car was attempting to bump Colton into third.

"Oh, no, you don't," Colton said, swerving his car up in front of him as he rounded turn four.

"White flag's out. One lap to go."

My mouth went dry. The hauler shook under my feet. I gasped. Had that been my doing? No! Gwen was jumping up and down, cheering as the checkered came out.

"This is it, kid," Lenny said.

Colton crawled up beside Mitch in turn three and rounded out of turn four, neck and neck with Mitch as they charged the finish line. So close, so close. The flagman waved the flag over the line.

"Good try, Colt. Second place in your first Cup race is a good place to be. And a great start to the season."

My body relaxed as the excitement evaporated, but Lenny was right. For a rookie, a second place finish in the Daytona 500 was nothing to frown upon.

"Good job, everyone," Colton said. "Oh, and Lexi ..."

My heart stopped. Was he actually talking to me? Dean gestured to the button on top of my left earphone, reminding me how to cue my mic. "Um ... yeah?"

Gwen whirled around, her mouth wide open.

"Time's up, little girl. Don't keep Dean in suspense."

Dean's lips curled into a slight smile, waiting for my answer. It was D-day, even though I'd already made up my mind days ago. My heart still pumped from the adrenaline of watching the race and the fact that Colton was talking to me when he should be celebrating his almost victory. This was my chance to experience what a normal life could be like.

This could *be* my life.

"Well?" Colton asked, impatient.

I swallowed hard and cued my mic. "Remind me later to kill you for putting me on the spot like this, Colt." I looked Dean square in the face and took a deep breath. *Here goes.* "I've decided to stay."

Dean's slight smile grew into a full grin as he draped an arm around my shoulders. "Welcome aboard, kid. I promise to make you never want to leave."

Gwen stomped off toward the ladder. Mr. Langdon tried to grab her arm but missed. "Where are you going?"

"I'm going to see Colt."

Mr. Langdon sighed, gave Dean an apologetic look, and chased after his daughter.

"Come on," Dean said, giving me a backhanded tap on the arm. "Let's go congratulate the kid before the camera crews attack him."

I paused and gulped. Camera crews? That meant reporters

and journalists. My gut clenched. *Oh, God.* I'd almost forgotten that they'd be part of my new life now.

Despite what Colton and Dean thought, deciding to stay might not prove to be in my best interest.

chapter six

Dean, Colton, and I headed to the airport where the company jet was fueled and ready to take us to Atlanta, the home of DSG Racing and forty-five minutes from where Dean and his family lived. Dean's home was going to be my home, and although my stomach turned into a ball of nerves every time I let myself think about it, I looked forward to settling in to my new life.

When we boarded, Colton sat next to me on the leather seat backed against the side hull of the plane. His complexion paled as the tips of his fingers clawed into the armrest and the front edge of the seat.

"Hey, are you okay?"

With a snap of his head, he glared at me, keeping his lips pursed in a thin line.

Dean chuckled. "Give him a few minutes." He bent to grab some papers from his briefcase. "I'm sure he'll explain once we're in the air."

Colton faced straight ahead and shut his eyes. Dean shook

his head and buried himself in his papers.

"Is he going to be sick or something? 'Cause if he is, I don't want to be sitting here when he barfs."

"Not helping," Colton said through clenched teeth.

"He's not going to be sick." Dean didn't seem to be worried, but the purple color settling on Colton's cheeks wouldn't let me take my eyes off him. The plane took off down the runway and pulled up off the tarmac. Colton gripped the seat tighter, his knuckles turning from tan to pink to white. He looked like he was either going to explode or pass out.

"Quit staring or I *will* punch you," he growled.

"I'm sorry." I glanced at Dean, who still sported half a grin. What was so funny?

The seatbelt light turned off, sounding a loud ding through the cabin. Colton ripped his seatbelt off, and hurried to the back of the aisle. He sat on a floor cushion with his back against the wall and his forearms resting on his propped-up knees. His heated blush faded, and the rise and fall of his chest steadied.

Dean pointed at Colton with the back of his pen. "Go talk to him. It'll distract him."

Still confused, I unbuckled my seatbelt and approached him, not sure what to expect. His creased eyes met mine. "Well, don't just stand there and stare. Sit down or go back to your seat."

I sank down next to him and crossed my legs. "You going to tell me what that was all about?"

His fingers braided and unbraided in front of him, and the blank stare returned to his face. He was really starting to creep me out. "You better not laugh."

"Why would I laugh?"

He cocked an eyebrow and glanced at me from the corner of his eye.

"Okay, fine. I promise I won't laugh."

Colton's hands stilled and his chest filled with air. "Heights and I don't get along very well. Never have."

Wait, what? Was he serious? "Are you saying you're afraid of heights?"

He hung his head.

He wasn't kidding. I didn't know what to say. I certainly wouldn't have guessed it on my own. An involuntary smile tugged at the corner of my lips.

"So much for promising," Colton mumbled.

"I'm not laughing, I swear," I said, before clamping my mouth shut to prevent the laugh bubbling in my chest from spewing out.

He shoulder-nudged me, curled his lip up slightly, and went on. "That's why I sit here. If I can't see out the windows, I can convince myself that I'm on a bus or in a car."

"Huh." I swallowed the laugh and forced my cheek muscles to push back the grin trying to spread across my face.

"It's not funny."

Apparently, I'd been unsuccessful.

"I'm not laughing." But I wanted to so bad. Come on. He drove a stock car for a living, going a hundred and ninety miles per hour on a weekly basis, yet the guy would shrivel at the sight of a bungee cord.

Colton rolled his eyes. "Fine. Laugh. Ha ha, I'm a freak."

"Whoa." Freak? … wow. If being afraid of heights made you a freak in his weird polka-dotted world, what in the hell did that make me? "I don't think you're a freak. Not one bit. Lots of people are afraid of heights. It just proves that none of us are perfect."

He peeked at me from under his lashes and revealed a set of dimples I hadn't noticed before. "You thought I was perfect?"

I blushed furiously, but before I could come up with a clever retort, heavy turbulence suddenly shook the jet. Colton's eyes widened before shutting tight. He dropped his head between his knees. I touched his rigid arm, wanting to ease him, but the feel of his skin under my fingers sent pins and needle like jolts through my body. I pulled back, embarrassed by my impulsive move and worried about the pulse beginning to pound in my temples. Losing control in a gazillion-ton jet made of sheet metal and steel was not my idea of a fun time.

Colton grabbed my hand, jerked it toward him, and squeezed. My lungs stopped functioning. What was he doing? Emotions swirled in and out of me, and I didn't quite know how to handle it. Neither did my curse.

The turbulence stopped. Colton opened his eyes and stared down at our hands, looking almost as surprised as I'd been when he'd taken it. He loosened his grip without letting go and grazed his thumb over the back of my hand. I breathed in sharply, quickening the magnetic pulse in my head.

"Colton, did you call your parents?" Dean's voice broke though the moment.

Startled, Colton jerked his hand away, slowing the currents in my head to a more manageable speed. "Shoot, no. I forgot. I'll call them when we land."

I held my hand in my lap, trying to rub away the strange feeling his touch had left behind. "Won't you see them when we get back?"

Colton leaned back against the wall. "No, they live in Rocky Mount, North Carolina."

"You have your own place?" I envied him if he did. I longed for November, when I could finally take possession of the secluded cottage my mother had left me. Only then would I be able to live the rest of my life in peace—and alone, just like I wanted.

"Dean." Colton sat up straight. "Did you not tell this girl anything?"

Dean's head shot up. "I only found out she'd be coming home with us a few hours ago. When did I have the time?"

I shifted my gaze between the two of them. "I don't understand. Home with *us* ...?"

"I live with Dean during the race season."

I blinked confusedly. "You mean ... we'll be living together?"

"Sort of. I stay in the apartment above the detached garage. I suck at cooking, so I usually eat with Dean and his family and hang out with them most of the time. Oh, and I babysit their two-year-old, Annabelle, on Monday nights. That's Dean's date night with Lorna, his wife."

I tried picturing Colton handling a two-year-old. "Babysit, huh?" But I couldn't see it.

"What? I'm great with kids."

"He is," Dean interjected. "Annabelle just loves him."

"So, why do you live there?" I asked. "I mean, why can't you live with your parents?"

"When I was an only child, Pop took me anywhere I needed to go to pursue my dream of racing professionally, but it got harder when my little brother, Robbi, was born three years ago."

"He's a handful?"

"There's that, but there were complications during his birth and Mom ended up paralyzed from the waist down. She manages fine now, but there are a lot of things she needs Pop around for. So when Dean came and offered me a ride in the ProNation circuit last year, he offered me room and board as well. If it weren't for Dean, I probably never would've been able to drive for NASCAR."

"You would have, just maybe not right away," Dean said.

"We both know that's not true. My parents would never have let me do it on my own, and I would've had to give up racing entirely."

Dean shrugged.

Ding. The seatbelt light turned on. Colton's face drained of all color.

Dean tucked his files away in his briefcase. "Come on, Colt, back to your seat."

Colton climbed to his feet. "I know, I know."

Back in our seats, Colton buckled his seat belt and gripped the armrest to his left. I buckled myself in, rested my palm on the seat between us, and leaned toward him. "Is there anything I can do to help you feel more relaxed?"

He squeezed his eyes shut, placed his palm next to mine, and hooked his pinky finger with mine. My body froze. I flashed a glance at our linked fingers, at Dean sitting at an angle across from us, looking out the window and then back at Colton. My cheeks burned.

Activate your cooling fans, Lex. He's just trying to cope. He's not making a pass at you.

No way would a guy like Colton Tayler ever be interested in a girl like me. Besides, I couldn't fall for anyone, ever. Even him.

...

We arrived in front of Dean's brown, two-story house at around half-past eleven at night. The curved driveway stopped in front of a detached three-door garage, with only a cast iron gate separating the two structures. Colton grabbed his bags from under the cover in the back of the truck, said his goodnights, and headed up the steep wooden staircase built along the sidewall of the garage, gripping the iron railing for dear life.

"Aww, that's just cruel."

Dean followed my gaze and laughed. "Hey, I offered him a room in the house, but he chose the apartment. That's his own fault."

Dean helped me carry my luggage inside, where a tall redheaded woman sat at a computer desk in the family room.

"Hey, hon. I saw the race. Colton killed it." She stood and gave her husband a kiss.

I let out a slight cough.

"Lexi. I'm so sorry. Where are my manners?" He stepped aside. "This is my wife, Lorna."

She smiled and reached out to shake my hand. "Lexi, Dean's told me all about you. I'm so glad you're here."

"I'm happy to be here."

My curse vibrated inside me, detecting the new concentration of metallic properties in the room. *Breathe and smile. Breathe and smile.*

Dean moved toward the stairs. "Can you show Lexi to her new room? I want to go kiss Annabelle good night."

"Not a problem, but don't you dare wake her. It took me

two hours to put her down." Lorna turned to me. "She's in her terrible twos, and this weekend of all weekends, she's decided that she doesn't like going to bed anymore."

I forced myself to smile wider.

Dean gave his wife a glance of sympathy. "I'll be sure not to, then."

Lorna picked up my suitcase and motioned for me to follow her up the stairs after Dean. "Come on, your room's up here."

On the second story, Dean disappeared into one of the rooms at the end of the hall. I assumed that one of the other three closed doors would be mine, but Lorna stopped abruptly in front of a linen closet-looking pocket door at the top of the stairs. She slid the door open, revealing behind it a narrow wooden staircase that led up to the attic.

Great. From dirty, rundown, second-story garage storage loft to dingy, old attic. I was literally moving up in the world.

She glanced over her shoulder. "Don't worry. It's not what it looks like." Oh, so I wasn't going to be sleeping in the attic?

She hoisted my suitcase ahead of her, headed up the stairs, and turned to me once she reached the top as if to say, "What are you waiting for?" I readjusted my backpack on my shoulder and made my way up.

At the top, I took in the sight of what would be my bedroom for the next nine months. The room ran the length of the entire house, spacious, open concept with tastefully covered beams. A lemon scent wrapped around me, and wall-to-wall, cream-colored shag carpet tickled my toes as I advanced into the room. A desk sat in one corner, and a golden brown sofa against one of the walls faced a large flat screen TV. A dark wood bedroom set occupied the far end of the room and a large picture of Colton's ProNation car—now driven by Link—hung over the headboard of the queen-sized bed.

"Not what you were expecting, is it?"

"Are you kidding me?" My words cracked due to my constricted throat. What I loved most was that, apart from the TV, some hinges, and a few other minor items, the space was proving to be a safe haven for the magnetically inclined.

"I'm glad you like it."

I met her elated gaze. "What's not to like?"

She dropped my suitcase at the foot of the bed. "We'll just leave your stuff here for the time being. Dean and I would like to talk to you downstairs about what's expected of you, now that you've decided to take us up on our offer. You'll have plenty of time to make this space your own later."

I slipped my backpack off my shoulders, dropped it on the floor, and followed Lorna down to their country-style kitchen, where Dean was already seated at the old, refinished wood table. I sat across from him, and Lorna took the seat on my right. I kept my hands in my lap, fiddling with the ring I wore on my middle finger—the one I'd stolen from Mama's jewelry box before Roy sold all her belongings. "First off," Lorna started, "Dean told me you wore those drab and boring sponsor shirts he left for you all weekend."

"Yeah, about that ... I've—"

"No excuses. I'm the one who suggested he leave you those clothes, but I'm sure you don't want to be wearing them all the time." She snapped a pre-paid MasterCard onto the table in front of me. "This is my gift to you. From one girl to another." She winked. "Colton's going to take you to town tomorrow. I want you to buy yourself some new clothes."

I slid my hand over the table, picked up the card, and stared at it. I opened my mouth to protest, but all the words I tried to form melted together into one big lump in my throat. My eyes fought to keep the wave of tears from falling. *Control, Lex. Don't you dare have a panic attack now.*

I extended the card back toward her, shook my head, and forced my teeth to unclamp from my bottom lip. "I can't accept this. Your husband has given me more than I could've expected. It's more than enough—"

"That money is for your daily expenses, lunches, entertainment, savings," Dean said.

Lorna placed a soft, gentle hand on mine and pushed the card back toward me. "If it makes you more comfortable, don't think of it as a gift. You now represent DSG Racing and the crew of the Guardian Auto Insurance team. We need you to look presentable."

"It's not like I'm actually part of the team. I'm not even a licensed mechanic."

Dean squared his shoulders proudly. "No matter. You'll be helping out in the shop, which means you're part of the team. We leave no one behind."

"Now." Lorna leaned back. "I want this wardrobe to include at least three fancy dresses. There will be banquets and events to attend. Also, keep in mind that you'll need some work clothes for the shop. Colton can help you with that, and don't forget some shorts and tops for your days off and to wear at the track. Sponsor tees and caps are supplied, so no worries there."

I nodded, not knowing what to say.

"So, as Lorna mentioned, tomorrow Colton has been tasked with taking you shopping and to show you around the nearby town of Bellfrost. Monday night, as Colton mentioned to you on the plane, is the night Lorna and I go out, just the two of us. We consider it essential to keeping our marriage sane in this crazy business." He took Lorna's hand. "We'd like you to help Colton out a little with the babysitting. Annabelle is becoming quite the handful."

"Does that sound reasonable to you?" Lorna asked.

Reasonable? Were they kidding? Too overwhelmed and speechless to speak, I nodded.

"Any questions?" Dean asked.

I swallowed, hiding my shaking hands under the table, flipping the MasterCard between my fingers.

"When will I start working?"

"Tuesday. You'll keep working at the shop until we fly out to the next track on Thursday. This is the regular routine unless the race is on a Saturday, in which case we'll fly out on Wednesday. Monday is your day off."

"Oh, I don't need a day off."

"Nonsense, everyone needs at least a day off," Lorna said.

A tear escaped and ran down my cheek. "How will I ever repay you?"

"You will in time, Lexi. We just want you to feel at home here," Dean said. "I'm sure you've heard by now that I, like you, didn't have an easy life. It's no secret. And no one deserves what we've gone through."

Lorna reached over and squeezed my shoulder. "It's been a long day. I'm sure all of this has been pretty overwhelming for you. You should go get some rest, and we'll see you in the morning."

I thanked them both and headed back to my new room in the attic. As I lay on the bed, finally letting the tears fall, I couldn't help but wonder how long I'd get to enjoy this new life before the evil inside me destroyed it all.

chapter seven

The house smelled of bacon, eggs, and fresh strawberry jam. My stomach growled.

"Good morning, Lexi." Lorna stood at the sink, a little redheaded girl in pigtails latched to her leg.

"This must be Annabelle," I said.

"This is her, the holy terror in the flesh."

I waved at her. She grimaced and hid her face behind her mother's leg.

"She's shy now, but just you wait till she warms up to you."

Annabelle giggled, but firmly kept a grip on her mother.

"I set a plate for you on the table. I hope you like bacon and eggs. Colton should be in soon."

"I do, thanks." I couldn't remember the last time someone had cooked me breakfast. Not since Mama died, I guessed.

The kitchen's side door swung open, and Colton walked in. I almost choked on my first mouthful at the sight of him dressed in board shorts, a white t-shirt with a Reebok logo printed across his chest, and an Atlanta Braves ball cap.

"Well, well. Look who decided to show up on time for once." Lorna turned and raised a brow. "You'd swear a boy whose life purpose is to cross the finish line first would be on time for breakfast more often."

Colton smiled, his hidden dimples making a rare appearance. He gave Lorna a peck on the cheek. "Good morning to you, too, Lorna. Did you lose weight?"

"Yeah, yeah. Flattery will get you nowhere. I left your plate in the microwave to keep it warm, but you might have to zap it a little."

He slipped by her, patted Annabelle on the head, and retrieved his plate. "I'm sure it's fine the way it is."

"Cotton," the girl said with an elated grin, clapping her hands.

"Hi, Anna-banana," Colton said to her. She giggled and wobbled off into the family room, her pigtails swaying with every bouncing step.

"She calls you Cotton?"

"Yeah, she has a hard time saying Colton, so I've become Cotton." He shook his head and sat next to me.

"That's so cute."

"Hat." Lorna said, without turning around.

Colton pulled off his ball cap and hung it on the back of his chair, letting his damp hair fall around his eyes. I brought my attention back to the plate of food in front of me. Lorna dug through her purse hanging by the door and pulled out a set of keys. "She'll get your name right eventually." She threw the keys on the table in front of Colton. "Now, you take care of my SUV. One scratch and it's coming out of your paycheck." Colton bit into a slice of toast and nodded. "And Lexi, we're going to need your driver's license info to add you to our vehicles' insurance coverage."

"No need," I said, picking up my last strip of bacon. "I don't have one."

Lorna's eyes widened and Colton hurried to swallow his mouthful of food. "You don't know how to drive?"

I flashed him an annoyed look. "I know how to drive—I grew up in a salvage yard, remember? Roy just never let me get my driver's license."

"You're kidding," Lorna said with disgust. "We'll have to rectify that. I'll make an appointment for you to get your learner's permit next week. We'll have to establish your residency here first, but that shouldn't be too hard."

"Good luck getting Roy to sign off on that," I said.

"You don't have to worry about that. Dean made sure Roy signed over temporary guardianship of you as part of the deal. So, legally, he has no say in the matter."

I sat up straight. "Really? You mean I can finally—"

"Yep." Lorna took away my empty plate and reached for Colton's as he scooped up the last bite. "You two better hurry. You've got a lot of shopping to do. I want you two back here in time for dinner to watch Annabelle."

"Oh, we will, Lorna. Don't you worry." Colton raked his hair back, slipped his ball cap in place, and grabbed the keys off the table. He looked at me. "You coming?"

I stood from the table, still in shock about being able to get my learner's permit. "Thanks for the breakfast. It was delicious."

"You're welcome. Now go have fun."

Once outside, Colton gave me a once-over.

"What?"

"I don't suppose you have another t-shirt that you could wear?" he asked.

I pulled at the hem of my 129 Colton Tayler swag wear. "Not exactly. Why?"

"Although most people in town already know who I am, it's probably not a good idea for me to be seen with my very own walking billboard."

I bit my bottom lip and dipped my eyes to the large Guardian Auto Insurance car printed across my chest.

"Come on." He tugged at my wrist. "I'll lend you one of mine."

"Oh, no, I couldn't." I couldn't fathom the thought of wearing his clothes.

"You can and you will. Come on." He cautiously led me up the staircase with the same death grip on the railing I'd seen him use the night before, and ushered me inside. The room opened into an open apartment, roughly the same size as my attic room, only with a kitchenette and a bathroom at the far end. The air smelled of soap and Axe body spray, no doubt from taking his shower before heading down for breakfast. As if I needed confirmation, my eyes fixated on a damp-looking towel draped over the dumbbell of his home gym set next to his bed.

"It's small, but I like it," he said, stepping past me toward his dresser. He rummaged through one of the drawers and tossed me a black T-shirt. "Here, this should fit you. It's a little snug on me."

I pointed at the bathroom, and he nodded in approval. I went inside and pulled off my shirt. As I slipped his on, the fruity smell of his fabric softener and fresh cotton invaded my nostrils. Once on, I couldn't resist pulling the neckline to my nose to give it another whiff. I caught my reflection in the mirror, dropped the neckline back in place, and watched my cheeks grow a candy shade of pink. Ugh. What was I doing? I blinked away the embarrassment and raked my fingers through my hair to shake the sides loose from behind my ears before walking out.

"That's better," he said. "Just leave your other shirt on the dresser. We'll come back for it later."

We headed out to the SUV and made our way to town.

"Don't you have your own car?" I asked.

"I have a '69 Mustang back home, but it would be too expensive to drive it out here."

"So, do you always have to drive Dean's truck or Lorna's SUV when you want to go out?"

"I have a Kawasaki Ninja in the garage, but it isn't really ideal for shopping trips." His lips curled at the corners.

"I guess not, but why a motorcycle? Why not just buy a car?"

"When you drive one for a living, it's kind of nice to have something different, you know?"

I rolled my eyes. "Boys and their toys."

"Don't mock the Ninja." He laughed. "I'll take you out for a ride sometime."

I winced at the thought. I'd never been on a motorcycle and I did not intend to change that fact.

Colton pulled into a large parking lot surrounded by a variety of shops and stores. "Lorna thought you should start at the dress shop."

"Where will you be?" I asked.

"Oh, you're stuck with me—I'm going with you. You need a man's opinion."

My face grew warm at the thought of parading in front of him in clothes I wasn't used to wearing, but I shook away my unease with a retort. "Then why isn't Dean here?"

"Ha, ha. You're funny."

Inside the store, tall racks lined the walls with a variety of different colored gowns and cocktail dresses.

"Holy ... Where do I start?"

Colton laughed.

"Can I help you with anything?"

I turned to the sales lady approaching, then looked back at Colton.

"Yes ma'am," he said. "She needs three new dresses. Fancy ones."

"Well, I can certainly help you with that." She looked me over. "Let's get you set up in one of our fitting rooms and we'll start by taking your measurements."

Measurements? Ugh ... What had I gotten myself into?

She showed Colton to the seating area near the mirrors and led me into a large room off to the side before whipping out a measuring tape from the pocket of her perfectly tailored pantsuit. She measured my hips, waist and bust, frowning at the latter. "You're not very well supported," she said. "Have you ever been properly fitted?" I looked at her as if a different language had tumbled off her tongue. "A bra, have you ever been properly fitted for one?"

I shook my head. As if Roy would have ever brought me out to shop for one. This cheap sports bra I'd found in one of my hand-me-down bags was the closest thing to a bra I'd ever owned.

"Well then, we should do that first. Remove your top, please."

Embarrassment twisted my insides, but I didn't bother arguing with her. My mother hadn't been around to teach me these things. Better late than never.

I did what she asked of me, feeling awkward as she prodded at my current sporty undergarment.

"I'll be right back," she said, leaving me alone and shirtless. She came back a few minutes later with a bra and a few dresses. "This one should fit you nicely, and I brought a few dresses for you to try on. I'll leave you to it."

"Thank you."

I held up the new garment, all lacy and dainty. Ah, geez, really? I'd sworn I'd never be caught dead in one of these Victoria's Secret looking things. I gave my temple a quick rub and surrendered my morals.

I finally walked out of the fitting room wearing a black, knee-length cocktail dress that hugged my waistline a little more tightly than I was comfortable with. It had laced frills at the bottom and a V-neck collar that dipped lower than anything I'd ever worn. The new bra didn't help matters much either, jacking my girls up to new heights, so to speak.

Colton stood, his expression hard to read. His eyes roamed high and low—mostly high.

"That bad?" I asked.

"It's perfect on you."

"You need to have your eyes checked."

"No, Lexi, I … I'm telling you, you look … wow, you look great."

"Whatever." I turned to look in the tall mirror behind me and found a stranger staring back at me, her reflection beautiful. It couldn't be me, no way. This girl had curves and legs and …

boobs! Where had those come from?

My eyes traveled from my toes up until they landed on Colton's reflection standing right behind me.

"What?"

"Nothing." His hands fell to my hips and turned me around. He stood close, his Axe body spray and natural sweet smell filling the air around us. His eyes were filled with a hint of something, but I didn't quite know what. My insides vibrated, and my curse pulsed in my temples again.

Focus, Lexi.

"I never thought I could look like this," I said, looking down at the dress, trying hard to suppress my impulses.

Colton placed a finger under my chin and raised my gaze back to his.

I swallowed. *Please, don't.* The tips of my fingers tingled. My control weakened. I tried to look away, to step away, but I couldn't. My body had frozen in place, my gaze glued to his mismatched eyes sparkling down at me. His finger swept up my jaw line and tucked my hair behind my ear before grazing my cheek. *Oh, God.*

I closed my eyes as the racks of clothing started to rattle. Fitting room doors shook on their hinges and picture frames crashed to the floor. Glass shattered everywhere. Colton stepped away, startled and confused.

"What's happening?" the sales lady screamed from behind the counter.

Free from Colton's grasp, I snapped out of my frozen state and did the only thing I could. I covered my ears, ran back into the fitting room, and cowered into the corner on the floor, rocking myself back and forth. What had I done? Had he seen my eyes before I shut them? Did he realize this was my doing?

Colton burst into the room. I squeezed my eyes shut again before he dropped down and wrapped his arms around me. "It's gonna be okay. Maybe it's just a small earthquake or something." He rocked with me, his lips near my ear, murmuring words of reassurance. His warm breath caressed my neck, not helping matters at all. I stopped fighting the uncontrollable force inside me. What was the point? With Colton so close, I'd never be able to control it.

Instantly the noise stopped, and silence fell around us. I didn't dare move or open my eyes until I was certain my senses had calmed completely.

"Look at me," Colton whispered.

I shook my head.

"Lexi, look at me. It's over." Again, he placed his finger to my chin and turned my head to face him. "Open your eyes."

I did. He smiled as our eyes met, but it faded as his lowered. Shit. Were my eyes still red? Something trickled down to my upper lip. Something wet.

"Lexi, you're bleeding."

I wiped a finger under my nose. Bright red blood stained the skin of my index finger.

The sales lady ran into the room. "Is everyone ... Oh, my God, you're bleeding. I'll go call an ambulance."

"No, really, I'm fine. Don't do that."

"But ... but you're—"

"It's just a nosebleed, I get them all the time. Nothing a few tissues won't fix."

"Sure, anything you need." She rushed back to her counter and fetched a box of Kleenex. Colton took it from her and handed me a few tissues.

"I am going to have to ask you to leave, though. This place is a mess, and I have to close the store immediately to clean up all this glass and these racks that have fallen over." She looked back over her shoulder. "I hope none of the dresses were damaged."

Colton eyed the dress I still wore. "But what about the—"

"I'll knock it down to half price along with those two other dresses if you leave the store so I can lock up." Colton nodded and grabbed the dresses, which had fallen to the floor in the fitting room, and then left to wait for me at the register while I changed back into my clothes.

When he was out of earshot, I called the sales lady over. "Can you add another one of these bras to the bill, and I'll just wear this one out?"

"Can do," she said with a knowing smile.

I changed, paid, and left the store with Colton.

On our way to the SUV, Colton glanced around at the different stores, looking puzzled. "That's funny. It doesn't look like any of the other stores were affected by the quake—or whatever that was."

"Maybe they just haven't locked their doors yet," I said, trying my best to deflect his curiosity. "Is there anywhere else we can go to finish our shopping?"

"There's a mall on the other side of town, but if that really was an earthquake—"

"Maybe it wasn't an earthquake—maybe something hit the building out back? A truck or something. Or a gas explosion."

Colton shrugged. "I guess we can go check out the mall and see."

My nerves relaxed once we got back on the road and away

from the store. The good news—I'd gotten three new dresses and two new bras at half-price thanks to my little episode. The bad news—being around Colton had caused the episode to happen in the first place. To survive the next nine months, I'd have to stay away from him. I couldn't let him get close to me like that again … ever.

chapter eight

I snapped the tag off the neck of my new black cotton work shirt, shimmied it over my head, and pulled the hem down over the waist of my cargo pants. I had to hurry, or I'd be late for my first day.

Boots, boots. Where did I put those boots?

I scrambled around my room, rummaging through the stuff I'd bought and still hadn't unpacked. I spotted the corner of a shoebox under a pile of clothes on the dresser.

"Ah, there they are." I flipped the lid too fast and sent all of my purchases to the floor. Shit. I didn't have time for this. Leaving the pile there, I snatched the brand new pair of steel-toed boots and ran down to meet Dean as I gnawed at the plastic tags attached to them.

"Lexi!" Lorna called from the kitchen.

"I know, I'm sorry. I'm late. Is Dean already outside?" I stopped at the door, shoved the tags in my pocket, and fumbled with the laces. Mornings and I didn't get along, and it totally pained me to think that I was going to have to reset my alarm clock for an earlier rise thanks to the long commute.

Lorna poked her head out into the hallway. "Dean's already gone."

My gut jumped into my throat, and I gave up my one-foot balancing act, trying to tie my other boot. "What?"

"Relax. Colton's waiting outside. He'll drive you there. Dean had an early meeting he forgot about. I swear that man would lose his own head if it weren't for me."

"Colton's going to drive me?" My gut crawled back down to the pit of my stomach and landed with a horrible splat. Please, please let it not be on his motorcycle. Please.

"He's waiting for you by the garage. Here. Take this." She handed me one of Annabelle's yogurt treats. "Can't have you leaving here on an empty stomach."

So much for sticking to my fantastic plan of avoiding Colton. "Thanks, Lorna."

"You're welcome, sweetie. Have a good first day."

First day. I hated first days. Ever since my first day of high school, the thought of experiencing something new made me nervous, sweaty, and feeling icky all over. The first time my new lightning-induced ability emerged was on that day. Some stupid bully made a crack about my mama being dead and my emotions had erupted. Desks and chairs came to life, rose up, and circled the room. Even the stall doors in the girls' restroom wouldn't stop banging and twisting when I tried to retreat into one of them to get away from all the screams. And let's not forget activating the sprinkler system. The principal had found me hours later, collapsed on the tile floor in one of the stalls with a nosebleed. Saying that my life was never the same after that would be an understatement. It's also why I never went back.

After I ripped open the yogurt tube and sucked it empty, I found Colton leaning against the doorframe of the open garage door, holding an extra helmet and a riding jacket. His shiny black Ninja 650 rested on its kickstand next to him.

I shoved the empty yogurt tube into my pocket and propped my hands on my hips. "You're nuts if you think I'm getting on that thing."

"Well, the way I see it, you don't have much of a choice."

He moved toward me.

"I hate you."

"Hate me all you want, but you're late, and I'm your only option, so let's get a move on." A sly grin spread across his face as he helped me with the protective gear and buckled the helmet strap under my chin. He sat on the bike and motioned for me to get on behind him while he fastened his own helmet then reached back, grabbed both of my arms, and wrapped them around his waist.

"Now, just relax and let yourself lean when I lean, okay?" I gave him a nervous nod. "Alright, let's go do this thing."

The engine wound to life and my chest filled with butterflies. What if I accidentally let go? What if I fell? God, what had I gotten myself into? Colton threw back the kickstand with the heel of his left boot, flicked his right wrist to rev the engine, and took off.

I squealed and closed my eyes, hoping that if I couldn't see anything, I could pretend it wasn't happening, but the high-pitched whine of the bike's engine, the pressure of the wind around me, and the feel of Colton's hard abs through his jacket kept bringing me back to reality. A slight throb tapped at my temples, but nothing threatening, thank God. I molded myself against his back and forced myself to open my eyes. This wasn't so bad. Not as scary as I thought it'd be. Actually, it was kind of fun. I decided to let myself relax and enjoy the experience.

We made it to the shop in record time, regaining the minutes I'd lost that morning. Most racing shops were out in Mooresville—Race City, Colton called it—but DSG Racing's glass and concrete complex was based out of Atlanta.

I followed Colton through the main entrance and into a huge high-ceilinged lobby. Colton approached the large reception desk near the back wall. "Hi, Becky, is Dean free?" Colton asked the dainty woman behind the desk.

"Good morning, Mr. Tayler. Yes, his meeting ended twenty minutes ago. He should be in his office now. I'll let him know you're on your way."

"Thanks. Oh, and Becky, this is Lexi. Do you have her building pass ready yet?"

"Ah, yes, the new recruit." She turned and pulled out a plastic key card attached to a retractable clip from a drawer behind her and placed it on the counter. "Glad to have you aboard, Miss Adams."

"Thanks." I took the pass and clipped it to my pant pocket as I followed Colton into the elevator.

We got off on the fifth floor. Colton walked me to Dean's office at the end of the hall. "Welcome to DSG Racing," Dean said with pride, greeting us at the door. "What do you think?"

He had a massive office with a large oak desk and a big picture window overlooking the park across the street behind it. Wall-to-wall shelving full of awards, trophies, and framed certificates lined the wall to my right. Behind me, framed pictures of the crews and cars at various tracks hung over the love seat. To my left a large window overlooked the shop below, where the crews, technicians, and specialists were busy building and testing the ProNation and Cup series race cars.

"Impressive," I said, gawking down at the shop.

"You ready to get started?"

"As ready as I'll ever be."

"Well, let's get at 'er, then." Dean showed me the way back down to the shop. Assembly lines ran along both sides of the arena-sized warehouse. Crews down the left side worked on Colton's 129 Angel cars—I do mean cars, plural—and on the right, the 396 Watson's Steel and Lumber ProNation car. Link's car. It was like looking into mirror after mirror after mirror. The cars lined both sides, all tweaked with the specifications for different tracks: restrictor plated, not restrictor plated, short tracks, long tracks. In front of them, the car Colton drove last weekend sat on blocks, hood open and motorless.

"Is something wrong with it?" I pointed.

"Oh, no, we always strip the motor out to test the engine after every weekend." Dean pointed to a room on the far end. "We test the engine's horsepower output to see how much it's lost throughout the race."

"Wow, I never realized how much work needed to be done post-race." I watched as swarms of workers analyzed data and tinkered with parts.

"Colton," a crew member called out to him.

"Stewart, hey!" Colton looked back. "I'll catch you two later."

Dean waved him off, and Colton headed to fist bump and

man-hug some of his crew members.

"What will I be doing?" I asked Dean, eager to get to work.

"Well, since dismantling things seemed to be your specialty, I thought I'd set you up over here."

I followed him to a back room that housed rows and rows of aluminum shelving full of car parts.

"What is all this? Looks like the stock rooms back home."

"Well, it's sort of the same thing, only these don't all work. These are salvaged parts from wrecked cars and malfunctioning ones that still have usable parts attached to them, but we never had the manpower to assign someone to dismantle them."

I gawked at each row of shelves as he led me to the front of the room. "So, it's like an auto parts graveyard?"

"Yeah." Dean chuckled. "Basically."

A large stainless steel counter stretched along the wall ahead. It had three sinks and racks of open-front bins fixed to the wall above them.

"So, your job will be to dismantle these completely, clean every part—nuts, bolts, everything—and put them in the proper bins. The large parts can go on these shelves over here"—he pointed to some empty shelves off to the side—"to be analyzed by the techs to see what's good and what will get tossed. You up for it?"

My lips crept into a smile. "Hell, yeah!"

I longed for the peaceful distraction that came with working with my hands, the release of pent-up emotions and pressure from the iron levels in my system in small controlled doses when no one was watching. It's how I'd been able to stay in control back home. There were far too many witnesses on the other side of that wall, but I was confident that the work would keep me calm and give me back some balance.

"Good. All the solvents you need are behind the cabinet doors under the counter, and everything else is in the large toolbox at the other end there. I'll leave you to it."

"Thanks."

Dean turned back toward the doorway. "If you need anything, I'll be in my office for most of the day. Don't be shy."

"I won't," I called back as he disappeared around the corner. Alone at last.

I took a deep breath and eagerly raided the toolbox for tools I needed but wouldn't use, laying them on the counter next to where I'd be working. I filled four buckets and all the sinks with solvents, oil, and brake cleaner, and got to work.

This was where my ability didn't feel so much like a curse. When away from curious and prying eyes, it had its advantages. My fingers hovered and twirled over bolts and nuts, unscrewing them with ease, and levitated them into the solvents, oils, and bins with a flick of my hand. I had a one-girl disassembly line going, all while keeping my ears peeled in case someone came to check up on me. I couldn't let anyone see my mechanical version of the magic mop and water bucket scene from Disney's *Fantasia*.

I lost track of time and almost didn't hear the heavy footsteps coming in behind me. In a panic, I reeled back my magnetic hold and let the handful of bolts that were currently making their way to the bucket fall to the counter. I cringed at the loud noise, but ignored the mess and dove for the socket wrench. I pretended to struggle with a nut on the starter I had in front of me. I had just enough time to take a quick glance down at my reflection in the stainless steel countertop to make sure my eyes weren't bloodshot and red before the footsteps got too close. I never could figure out how much time or energy it took for my eyes to change.

"Looks like you've got a good rhythm going," Colton said, leaning against the rack closest to me. "Dean was right, you're good at this."

"Thanks." I put the socket wrench down and lifted my goggles over my head.

"You should probably wear gloves, though." He pointed at my grease-covered hands.

"I can never get the hang of working with gloves. Can't get a proper grip with them on."

"I know what you mean." He pushed off the rack and moved closer. "You ready to break for lunch?"

"Is it lunchtime already?"

He nodded. "Time flies when you're having fun."

"Yeah, I guess."

"Most of the guys are ordering in, but I thought we could go to the diner next door. What do you say?"

My mind screamed *no*, but my heart thumped *hell, yes*.

"Sure, why not?" My lips spoke before I could stop them. Traitors. I was going to have to watch out for that in the future.

"Wash up and meet me out front."

■ ■ ■

The Park Side Diner overflowed with various industrial park employees, but we found a booth near the back corner. It felt a little too intimate for my taste, but I didn't have much of a choice. The waitress took our orders and returned with our food not fifteen minutes later.

"So, you ever thought of going to school to be a licensed mechanic or technician?" Colton asked, taking the first bite of his club sandwich.

"Never really thought much about anything after high school. The plan was to wait until I turned eighteen, and then move the hell out of Roy's place and into the cottage Mama left for me. Besides, I could never afford it." I sliced into my fish and chips and shoveled the first forkful into my mouth.

"How about now, though? You could probably save up enough throughout the season for one semester and get a loan for the rest. Dean told me you were fast-tracking your studies. You could probably get into college by next fall."

"Fast-tracking only gets me graduated one semester ahead of time, meaning I'll be done in January. I doubt I'd be able to get in then. Like I said, I never gave it much thought."

"You could come back and work for Dean."

I cut up another piece of my fish. "Oh, I don't know about that."

A quick flash of disappointment shifted into a puzzled look. "Why not?"

I had to have imagined it—as if he cared whether I came back or disappeared after this season.

"Dean hired me out of pity. If I was certified, I'd want to be hired on skill alone."

Colton took another bite of his club and wiped his fingers with a napkin. "Dean didn't hire you out of pity."

"Yeah? What else would you call it? Don't think I'm not grateful, but I don't know if the racing world is all that safe for me."

"What makes it any less safe for you than it is for me?"

Shoot. Bad choice of words. I stabbed a few fries in the small cup of ketchup on the edge of my plate. "Never mind. Can we talk about something else?"

"Why, what's wrong?"

I tossed the fries onto my plate, unable to eat another bite. "I don't want to talk about it, okay?"

"Okay, fine. I just wanted to get to know you better, that's all."

I leaned back from the table, away from him, and folded my arms. "Don't you get it? There's nothing to get to know. I'm an abused little girl without much of a life or a future. I'm a statistic. Now, can we drop it?" I looked away, unable to stare at the hurt on his face while he ate the rest of his lunch in silence. I forced a few morsels down, paid for my meal, and returned to my job without as much as a "see you later."

■■■

To avoid another confrontation with Colton, I rode back to the house with Dean and immediately jumped in the shower. Afterwards, I returned to the kitchen and sat down for dinner with Dean, Lorna, and Annabelle, who fidgeted endlessly in her booster seat. Lorna placed a serving of roast beef, mashed potatoes, and salad in front of me. Everything smelled so yummy, my taste buds couldn't wait to savor the flavors of a home-cooked meal. It had been so long. I looked over at the empty place setting next to me. "Where's Colton?"

"Cotton," Annabelle gleefully shrieked.

I giggled, still finding it adorable that she couldn't pronounce his name right.

Lorna reached for the butter at the center of the table. "Friends of his from town picked him up a half hour ago while you were in the shower."

"Oh." It's not like I planned to apologize. I still thought I should leave things the way they were, but his absence rankled. It wasn't his fault I'd been born a magnetic freak. I wasn't being fair by taking out my frustrations on him. Ah, crap. Maybe I did owe him an apology.

Later that night, I sat outside at the bottom of his stairs and waited for him. By then, my urge to fix the situation was all I could think about. Colton had been nothing but nice to me, and I'd shit all over it. I'd even brought him a peace offering—a piece of leftover cheesecake Lorna had made for dessert. Time passed, and darkness fell. I looked up at the stars in the clear night's sky. They shined brighter then I'd ever seen them. Mama used to love looking up at the stars on warm summer nights. I always thought it so boring to spend hours just looking up at the sky, but now I cherished the memory of those moments I had with her.

Bright headlights pulled into the driveway and interrupted my thoughts. Music blared from the yellow Scion's open windows. The driver stepped out and stood behind his open door, laughing at something. A tall brunette climbed out of the passenger seat and folded the seat forward. Colton stepped out from the back seat of the two-door coupe.

"It was a blast hanging out with you again. We should do it more often," the driver said to him.

"Yeah, man, but it's the busy season, you know that."

"It's good to have you back in town."

"It's good to be back."

The girl wrapped her arms around Colton's neck and pecked him on the cheek. "We should all go to the movies next week." She looked at him as if by all, she meant just the two of them. But then she added, "Maybe we could finally meet this Lexi chick."

I stiffened at the sound of my name, realizing they couldn't see me sitting in the shadows.

"Nah, don't count on it." Colton slid his hands into his back pockets and hunched his shoulders. "She … kinda doesn't like to talk much. I don't really think she's the type that would enjoy hanging with us, if you catch my drift?"

My jaw swung open. What? I clamped my mouth shut, analyzed my surroundings, and flung a discarded decking screw I sensed on the ground near the front veranda at the back of his leg.

"Ouch, what the hell was that?"

"What?" the girl asked, backing away from him.

Colton reached down, picked up the screw, and rubbed the long scratch down his calf.

"This"—he held out the screw to show her—"freakin' thing scratched me."

"Aww, poor baby," she said, giving him another kiss on the cheek.

I looked away for a second to control myself from sending anything else flying—this time at her head. Was I jealous? No. Couldn't be. I was too mad at Colton to be jealous … right?

"Anyway," the driver said, "give us a call if you're free next week."

"Will do."

The guy got back in his car. The girl gave him the seductive "call me" gesture while mouthing the words, then got back in the car and shut the door. Colton waved as they drove off, and then walked toward the stairs. He froze when he saw me, his face dropping as if fifteen daggers were pointed directly at him. A tear rolled down my cheek. I hadn't realized my eyes had welled with them. I stood and stepped toward him.

"Lexi! What are you …?" He bit his lip, likely realizing what I'd overheard, and knew he needed to come up with some lame excuse.

"Here." I held out the Saran-wrapped plate and fork.

He glanced at it, but made no attempt to take it from me. "What's this?"

"I saved you a piece of cake to apologize for earlier today, but for some odd reason, I don't feel very apologetic at the moment. You know … because I 'don't like to talk much.'" I mimicked his faint drawl. "Or maybe it's because I just learned that you don't think I'm good enough to meet your friends."

"Lexi, that's not what I … I can explain."

"Please do. I'd really like to see you squirm your way out of this one." I kept my expression stern, but I couldn't get my face to stop throbbing.

He just stared at me, his lips twitching as if trying to form words.

"That's what I thought." I stormed past him, shoving the plate in his hands as I did so, and headed back to the house.

"Lexi, wait!"

I closed the door behind me and didn't look back.

chapter nine

Today we were flying out to Phoenix. I'd managed to avoid Colton like the plague all day yesterday and most of the morning, but he wasn't making it easy. He even had the nerve to try to corner me at breakfast, but I'd successfully snaked passed him and locked myself in my room.

When it came time to leave, I climbed into the back of Dean's crew cab pickup truck, giving Colton the front seat. No way was I going to let him stare at the back of my head for the entire ride.

"Okay, you two." Dean hoisted himself into the driver's seat in front of me and pulled his door shut. "What's up with the silent treatment?"

I leaned my head against the window. "It's nothing, Dean. I promise. Nothing you need to worry about."

Colton looked back at me. Our eyes met. His gaze tugged at my emotions, but the hurtful words he'd said about me still lingered in the back of my mind. Not once had he tried to apologize. All he kept trying to do was explain why he'd said them. Explain what, exactly? Clearly, he'd meant every word. Why had he been so nice if he didn't consider me the type of girl he could introduce to his friends? I mean, I may be a freak, but he didn't know that. What was it about me that was so not their type?

I looked away and stared out at the scenery passing by my window. Dean didn't pry or try to make small talk, and I was grateful.

When we boarded the jet, I sat in the same seat I'd sat in last week, thinking that Colton would have the nerve to sit next to me. He did. I debated changing seats, but then I'd have to explain to Dean why. I buckled myself in and kept my hands in my lap, remembering what had happened last time. Dean took his paperwork out and kept himself busy, leaving me to stare out the window.

The jet turned and headed down the runway. The air to my left tensed. Colton looked so scared and fragile—the urge to comfort him pounded against my chest, but I resisted. I couldn't let him get to me again. The jet lifted off the ground. Colton sucked in a breath, reached over and yanked my hand from my lap, threading his fingers between mine.

I scowled at him, but his eyes were shut tight and his body jittered with anxiety. My insides melted. I couldn't take away his only comfort, as much as I hated him right now. I knew what it was like to feel scared and vulnerable about something out of my control. I stared down at our hands, wondering what it would be like to hold his hand for real. To feel the warmth of his skin seep through mine while knowing that it was because he wanted to feel the same thing, not because he was latching on to help himself cope with his fear.

Stop. Stop it. You're anti-social and not his type, remember?

The seatbelt light turned off. Colton released my hand, unbuckled his seatbelt and hurried to his cushion at the back of the aisle. Once seated, he leaned back and glanced up at me. He mouthed the words "I'm sorry," then hid his eyes under the brim of his ball cap.

Sorry about what? For what he'd said, or for using my hand as a coping mechanism? It didn't matter. Either way, staying mad at him now was going to be a challenge.

When it came time to land, Colton returned to his seat and gave me the saddest look I'd ever seen. The one a puppy would give his master when in trouble for peeing on the carpet. I let out a soft sigh and slapped my hand onto the seat between us. Even though I knew it was coming, my body flinched the second I felt his fingers lace with mine. I was still angry, only now it was with myself. I had let my emotions be affected by him again. I was growing weak, and I didn't like it.

The wheels of the jet hit solid ground and rolled to a stop. Without looking back, I tore my hand out of Colton's grasp and got as far from him as I could.

■■■

Dean kept busy all afternoon and the better part of the morning with Link and his crew, preparing and qualifying his car for the next day. He also stuck around to watch Colton's practice runs. I, on the other hand, wasn't needed, and took the opportunity to do some sightseeing and to catch up on some of my online course assignments. I didn't want to fall behind, and it was an excellent excuse to keep some distance between

Colton and myself.

He'd tried to corner me a few times, but each time his PR rep, Nancy, came and whisked him away for interviews and sponsor promo shoots. My plan of staying in the motor coach until race day was working out nicely until my phone chimed with a text message from Dean, asking me to meet him atop the hauler for Colton's qualifying runs. With a sigh and a figurative kick in the butt, I left the motor coach and headed out to meet with him.

I still didn't understand why I needed to follow Colton and his team to every race, but Dean assured me that my dismantling skills would someday come in handy. Unfortunately, that meant many more weekends and handholding jet rides with Colton.

Dean stood at the railing timing Mitch Benson, the returning champ and, according to the sportscasters, the lead contender for this year's championship. But they also said Colton might be his biggest competitor for the top spot in The Chase—the top ten drivers in season points that advance to contend for the cup championship. Dean motioned for me to wait. He turned back, raised his stopwatch, and clocked Mitch as he crossed the start/finish line. "Shoot. He's going to be hard to beat." Dean removed his headset. "It's nice to see you out and about."

"Did I have a choice?"

Dean frowned. "Listen, I don't know what Colton did to get you so upset, but you can't let it keep you locked up in your room every weekend."

"I know. I'm sorry."

Dean stepped toward the cooler. "I have a gift for you and I wanted you to test it out before tomorrow's race." He picked up a turquoise-blue headset and a scanner, turned them over, and passed his thumb over the black lettering printed on the side. "Got them personalized." He grinned and handed them over. "You like?"

They were new and shiny without a scratch or a scuff. My full name, Lexi Adams, stood out against the light turquoise color on the left ear piece. "Are you kidding? I love them. Thank you so much."

"The dial is tuned to our channel. Go ahead and take them for a test run—Colton's about to take the track."

I clipped the scanner to my waist and placed the headset over my ears.

"You're next," I heard Lenny say to Colton.

"You think I don't know that?" Colton replied, disdain in his voice.

I pulled one earphone off and nudged Dean. "Who pissed in his corn flakes this morning?"

"He's been like this since Wednesday. No one's been able to calm him down."

I replaced my earphone and stood off to the side. He couldn't seriously be like this because of me, could he?

Colton took the track next and hammered up to full throttle, zipping around the track.

"She still feels pretty loose," Colton grumbled.

"We made the changes you wanted. We don't know what else it could be."

Dean cued his mic. "Colton, just calm down and give us your best lap."

"Yes, boss," he replied, his tone harsh and mean.

Colton finished his laps. "How was that, boss?"

"Fourth," Dean said. "Possibly fifth. There's one last team

still to qualify."

"Damn it," Colton yelled, so loud that my headset screeched.

"Now, Colton, that's a good start."

"Not good enough."

"Colton!" Dean's face hardened. "Okay. That's enough. Get your ride back to the garage and see me in my office ASAP."

Silence fell over the airwaves. Dean yanked his headset off and stormed down the ladder. I paced a few laps along the railing before making my way down. I didn't want to bump into Colton on his way to the hauler. The crew huddled outside the side door, trying to listen in.

"Guys, I don't think—"

Jimmy shushed me and leaned in close to the door. Not that he needed to—I could hear Dean and Colton yelling from where I stood.

"I don't care if you have personal issues and I don't care to know what they are, but when you're out on that track, you're going to be respectful to me and to your team. We aren't the only ones on this frequency, Colt. Fans out there and at home are listening in, as well as officials and any of our sponsor reps who might be in attendance. Man up and stop taking your foul mood out on everyone around you. Apologize and move on."

"But she won't even talk to me."

"Not my problem. You put yourself in this mess, you get yourself out of it. Is that clear?"

"Crystal."

My head swayed back, and the crew's eyes all landed on me.

"Don't look at me," I said. "He's the jerk." Lenny shook his head and walked away.

Colton burst out, letting the side door slam against the

hauler, and narrowed his eyes at his crew. "Don't you guys have shit you should be doing?" The men scattered back toward the pit.

Colton grabbed the hanging sleeves of his fire suit and began tying them around his waist as he turned. He froze when he saw me standing there, and our eyes locked.

My heart pounded. The urge to crumble into his arms came out of nowhere. Where had that thought come from? His stern expression faded. We stood there for what seemed like minutes. Finally, he sidestepped around me and left me there alone to catch my breath.

■ ■ ■

Saturday evening I opted to eat with the boys at Lenny's RV, knowing that Dean and Colton would be at the hauler watching the ProNation race. As I finished my plate, a tall, creepy, salt-and-pepper-haired man in a two-toned navy suit and Stetson hat approached.

"Lenny. Long time no see."

"I'm at the same place you are every weekend," Lenny answered him.

"Can we talk?" The man eyed us all. "In private?"

Lenny put down his grilling utensils and took his apron off. "Sure, lets walk." They hobbled off together.

I nudged Jimmy, who'd been sitting beside me. "Who was that?"

"That, my dear, is Carl Stacy. Team owner of the SunCorp 220 car."

I pointed over my shoulder. "That was Carl Stacy?" I knew

who he was thanks to Roy, but I'd never seen the man's face. He didn't look at all how I'd pictured. "What's he want with Lenny?"

Dylan cleared his throat and leaned forward on the edge of his seat. "Rumor has it he's going broke, so he's putting another team together next season, hoping to supplement his income. Looks like he's trying to recruit."

"Can he do that?"

"He can," Jimmy said. "Question is, would Lenny jump ship?"

"Depends on what Carl offers him." Dylan leaned back in his folding chair and chuckled. "Man, Dean's not going to like this."

I glanced to where Lenny and Carl were deep into conversation. "I guess not."

"Oh, darlin', you don't know the half of it. Carl is Dean's stepdad's cousin."

I snapped my glance back at Dylan. "His stepdad?"

"Yeah. The guy who beat him to a pulp every time he came home from a race. Dean's stepdad drove for Carl until he died in a racing accident shortly after Dean went to the police with his allegations. Carl blames him for his cousin's death." He leaned back in his chair. "I tell ya, Carl practically blew a gasket when he heard Dean was starting up his own team last year and even more so now that he's got himself a Cup series team."

"Shut it, Dyl. Dean's coming," Jimmy said in a loud, throaty whisper.

Colton and Dean sauntered over and joined us.

Jimmy cleared his throat. "Hey. Didn't expect you guys here so soon. Race ain't over yet."

Dean pulled up a folding chair and took a seat. "Link's done. Got caught in a pile-up in turn four. Car's totaled."

Dylan sighed. "Shit."

My hand flew to the front of my chest. "Is he okay?"

"Oh, yeah. Medics cleared him twenty minutes ago. He's with his family now." Dean glanced around. "Where's Lenny?"

Everyone looked away, pretending to be preoccupied with other things.

"He's with Carl Stacy over there." I nodded to where they stood in the distance. Jimmy elbowed me. "What?" I glared at him. "He is."

Colton hooked his thumbs into the front pockets of his cargo shorts and stepped back. He had his shades on and his ball cap set low. It was too dark to see his full face, but something told me this was going to end badly.

Just then, Carl and Lenny returned. Lenny averted his eyes when Dean tried to meet them.

"Carl." Dean stood and extended his hand out. "To what do we owe the displeasure?"

Carl took his hand, ignoring the jab. "Came to talk to my friend Lenny here." He patted Lenny on the back with his free hand. "But he didn't sound too interested in what I had to say."

Dean let go of Carl's hand and gave Lenny a side-glance. "I'm happy to hear that. No offense."

"None taken. I heard you had a hard time controlling that rookie of yours during qualifying today." Carl nodded in Colton's direction.

Colton's head dipped as his remaining exposed fingers curled up into his palms.

"Nah. Just a small misunderstandin', ain't that right, Colt?"

Colton lifted his gaze. "Right, boss."

"Well, you better keep your kid, Rocket here, from trading any more paint with my 220 or there will be hell to pay."

"What are you complaining about? Mitch won Daytona last week," Dean said.

"Your rookie damaged my car real good. Repairs don't come cheap, you know."

"Rubbin's racin', Carl. It's all part of the game. And since when do you worry about money?"

"That may be true, but if he as much as grazes my car tomorrow, we're taking him out. I can't afford to throw money around because of this kid's inexperienced, immature nonsense."

Dean's face hardened. Carl laughed and tipped his oversized cowboy hat to the rest of the group. "Have a good night, boys. Oh, and Dean, one more thing."

Dean squared his shoulders and folded his arms across his chest. "What's that?"

Carl jutted his chin up at Colton. "Your pops would've liked this one."

Dean lunged toward him. Colton, Dylan, and Jimmy rushed to hold him back. "You son of a bitch. Stay away from my driver and crew, do you hear me?"

Carl strolled off, laughing. Dean pulled himself out of his team members' holds, but Dylan kept a hand on his shoulder while Dean snarled at Carl's back. "He's not worth it, Dean. Let him go."

Dean cursed under his breath and stormed off toward his motor coach. No one dared to follow him. My gut churned, knowing what he must be going through. As much as I liked to think that I had bigger things to worry about than Roy's abusive behavior back home, I still cringed at the memory of his hand coming down on me more times than I could count. So many times I'd thought of using my ability to end him, or just threaten him, but I knew it would've made things a lot worse. Dean and I shared that. He'd found the courage to report his stepfather, but was still paying the price thanks to Carl. In situations like ours, you were damned if you did, and damned if you didn't.

chapter ten

"I still say you should report him," I heard Colton telling Dean in the kitchen. I reached for my cell phone on the nightstand to check the time. It was almost noon.

"It's his word against ours, Colt. NASCAR's not going to do anything about it. Not until he actually does something."

"Yeah, after the damage is done and he costs me the race."

"He's just trying to get under your skin, Colt. Don't let him. You do, and he wins regardless. Now get your butt in gear. The team needs you out in the garage."

I buried my face in my pillow for a few seconds then grumbled as I pulled myself out of bed and shambled over to the door. I reached for the door knob.

"Is *she* coming?" Colt asked in a softer tone.

I hesitated. Was he talking about me?

"She'll be there."

I picked that moment to step out of my room. Both Dean and Colton glanced my way.

Colton slipped his shades on, his face hardening. "I'll see

you later, Dean." He spun and ducked out the door.

Dean set his elbow on the table and pinched the bridge of his nose. "You two are going to have to talk sooner or later."

Ignoring his comment, I shuffled past him to the cupboard and pulled down a box of Frosted Flakes, then snatched the milk from the fridge, closing the door with a hip check. Not the best choice of food this late in the day, but I didn't think I could stomach anything else.

"Lexi?"

"Dean, all I want is an apology. Until then …"

Dean sighed. "Okay, well, I'll see you out there." I nodded. Dean shook his head and left me to eat alone.

■ ■ ■

With an hour left before the race I began making my way to the hauler when my phone chirped in my back pocket. I reached for it and swiped my thumb over the screen. Dean had sent me a text.

911. Where are you?

911? What could have possibly happened for him to summon me via 911? I picked up speed and turned the phone sideways to make the screen keys bigger. I wasn't used to this texting thing yet.

On my way to the hauler. What's up?

Within seconds, my phone chirped again.

Get your butt here now! How fast can you Re & Re an engine?

Remove & Reinstall? Shit! I didn't bother replying, I ran past fans, golf carts, security gates, and rounded into our garage stall. White smoke wafted through the air and lingered at the ceiling. Blown head gasket. It had to be. But how and why? I glanced back at the hauler. Crew members were hauling a new engine down from the top compartment.

"Son of a bitch. Son of a fu—"

"Colton!" Dean yelled from in front of the toolbox.

"Dean. I'm here. What the hell happened?"

"Lexi, oh, thank God. No time to explain." He handed me some safety glasses and a few tools. "Get under that hood and start dismantling. We need all hands on deck. I want that engine removed yesterday."

A stabbing pain shot out from my core. "You want *me* to dismantle the engine?" My eyes flicked to the engine bay of the car. "Here?"

Dean wanted my speed, but I couldn't use my ability now. Not in such a public setting.

"This one's finished and the backup car will never be ready in time. This is your moment, kid, now get to work." Dean patted me on the back and rushed off to help the others.

Shit.

I bit my lip and glanced around to pinpoint everyone's distance. Fans were being redirected to the neighboring stalls to give the crews space to work, and the crews were so busy that no one besides Dean seemed to know I was even there. Could I pull this off? I plunged my hands down into the engine bay and mimicked the normal removal process with my wrench while loosening every one with the twitch of my wrist. No one hovered, and the noise from the neighboring team's air guns and impact wrenches masked my lack of tool use. The task took longer than if I'd been alone, but was fast enough to put a smile on Dean's face when I told him to bring the engine crane over.

I ducked under the car, unbolted the engine and transmission from their mounts, and gave them the go-ahead to lift her on out.

I stood off to the side, wiping my hands with a shop rag, antsy as I watched the techs take the transmission and exhaust from the damaged engine and install them onto the spare one, preparing it to be dropped into the car. I fought the urge to push everyone aside and yell out "let me do it," knowing that, in a perfect setting, I could have done it all in half the time it was taking them. Instead, I just stood there, biting the inside of my cheek into hamburger meat. Colton stood opposite of me, watching his crew hurrying to reconnect the cooling and ignition systems. I wanted to help so bad, but with all the techs now elbow-deep in the engine bay, there was no room for me.

When Dylan finally leaned into the driver side window and fired her up, she growled and purred like a charm, and everyone cheered.

Dean motioned Dylan to shut her off and got everyone's attention. "Good work, guys. Do a final check for coolant and vacuum leaks, and let's get her to the inspection booth."

The boys rolled the car out, leaving Colton and me alone in the garage.

"Son of a bitch," I heard him mutter from where he stood near the door, arms crossed over his chest.

"What's with you?" I asked. "It's fixed." It hadn't been my intention to sound so harsh. I actually wanted the tension between us gone, but Colton took it the way it sounded.

"It's fixed, but now I'm forced to drop from a fourth starting position to the rear of the field for doing a last-minute engine swap."

"Oh … I didn't realize—"

"Yeah, well." he dropped his arms. "That's just another reason why NASCAR's not the place for you." He took off before I could react.

My gut burned with not-so-nice words that begged me to chase after him so I could throw them in his face. He had some nerve getting mad at me.

I washed up, retrieved my new headset, and climbed up to the top of the hauler. Dean arrived a while later with Mr. Langdon in tow, but no Gwen. Thank God—I didn't think I could put up with her twirly miniskirts and her whiny daddy's princess voice, but then Mr. Langdon said the only thing that had the potential to make me feel worse than I already did.

"Wasn't it nice of Colton to ask Gwen to walk him to his car?"

Dean stared at me and tilted his head slightly as if waiting for Mr. Langdon's words to sink in. They had. Big time. I looked over the edge of the railing. Colton stared up at me and slid his arm around Gwen's tiny waist. She looked up at him admiringly, but his eyes were fixed on me until the jets flew overhead and Lenny nudged him to get in his car.

Once Colton hit the track, Gwen came running up the ladder and proceeded to tell her father every detail of her experience. My stomach churned. *Oh, my God, shoot me. Or better yet, shoot her.*

"I'm heading to the ladies' room," I told Dean, annoyance crawling down my spine at Gwen's non-stop verbal diarrhea. How did her father put up with it? She was almost eighteen, for crying out loud. Grow up. At Dean's nodded approval, I scaled down the ladder. I thought of removing my headset, but decided to keep it on in case the team needed me while I ventured around the infield.

I hadn't planned to return, but with fifteen laps left and Jimmy's announcement that Colton was closing in on the leader, I had to see how it would end. Dean smiled when I reached the top of the hauler. I smiled and stood next to him, gripping the railing.

"Eight to go," Lenny said.

"Clear low," his spotter added.

Colton dipped low, then tried to pass his opponent in turn three. Mitch ducked and blocked him.

"We've got company," Jimmy said.

"Who is it?" Colton asked.

"Danny Morris, 160."

"Crap!"

Colton dipped again, got up next to Mitch, and stayed with him while blocking 160's attempts to get by.

"Two to go, Colt."

Colton and Mitch came out of the last turn side by side, almost touching. The 160 lost control and clipped Mitch's rear bumper. Mitch's ass end shot up into the wall and his nose-dived straight down into Colton's car, sending him sideways onto the shoulder. All three straightened out, but the 160 took the lead, crossing the finish line first, with Colton second and Mitch Benson third.

"That little punk," Colton screamed over the airways.

Dean cued his mic. "Nice recovery, Colt. Could've been a lot worse."

We all headed down to the garage where camera crews and news reporters buzzed around Colton while the crew worked at packing things up.

"What a remarkable recovery by Colton Tayler to get him the second-place finish here at the Phoenix International Raceway. Tell me, Colton, did you think you'd make it back up to the front after having to make a last-minute engine change?" asked a perky blonde.

I stood off to the side, watching Colton get microphones shoved in his face.

"We have a great team and a dedicated crew this year. There was no doubt in my mind that we could recover," Colton answered. He seemed calm, but I knew better. He was fuming behind that façade.

"What happened to your previous engine, any thoughts?" the slim dark-haired reporter asked before shoving his microphone back in Colton's face.

"Not sure at the moment, but the team is eager to get it home to the shop to have a look. Now, if you'll excuse me, I need to get back to my team. Thank you."

Colton turned away and took off toward the hauler.

"Well, there you have it, folks ..."

"Colton!" Gwen yelled as she ran to catch up to him, her long blonde ponytail bouncing behind her. Colton turned just as she launched herself into his arms. I stared as her hand reached up behind his neck. A twitch of anger went through me. Wow, this girl had no shame. Colton caught me watching them. He wrapped an arm around Gwen's waist and brought her into the hauler with him. *Ugh!* Why did I even care?

Once the cameras and media personnel left the garage area, Dylan called Dean over to where the old engine sat. I followed, curious.

"Take a look at these head gaskets," he said, leaning over the engine.

"Okay, what am I looking for? They look fine to me."

"Exactly. Nothing's wrong with them—the water pump's fine too. The pistons and cylinders, on the other hand, are scorched to shit and the oil is garbage, but no hoses are leaking. The only way coolant could have gotten into this engine is if someone put it there. Someone had to have poured it down into the throttle body earlier this morning or sometime last night and let it sit in the intake manifold."

"Are you saying the engine was sabotaged?"

"Looks like it, boss."

Dean ran his hand over his face, then rubbed the back of his neck.

"Lexi."

"Yeah, Dean?"

"Go get Colt. I want him here when the officials arrive."

"Sure thing." I sprinted to the hauler, threw open the side door, and let myself in. I put the brakes on at the sound of voices coming from Dean's office.

"Yes, I'll be there. I already told you I would. But not as your date, Gwen."

"Why not? Don't tell me you have a thing for that Lexi chick?" Gwen whined.

"I … God, no. Lexi's—"

I'd heard enough.

I cleared my throat before he could say anything to make me hate him even more. Colton poked his head out. "Lexi, what are you—"

"Dean sent me to get you. He's calling the NASCAR officials over."

His head snapped back, sending his flattened hair sweeping back. "What ...? Why?"

"Your first engine was sabotaged."

"Sabotaged? Are you sure?"

"Dylan seems to be sure."

"Son of a bitch." Colton reached around me for his ball cap and stormed out.

I turned to follow him when Gwen came walking out of the office. "Where'd Colt go?"

"Back to the garage. Racing business."

"Huh. Well, can you tell him I'll see him next weekend? And remind him that I'm going to save him all the slow dances." She licked her lips, wiggled past me, and hopped off the hauler step. "Oh, and honey, I know you have the hots for him. I can see it in your eyes."

"I do not." My head throbbed. She had some nerve.

"Oh, please. Not like it matters anyway ..." She stink-eyed me from ball cap down to steel-toed shoes. "The boy's mine."

My fingernails dug into my palms, and my teeth clenched so tight that my jaw threatened to seize. I wanted to pounce on her and claw out her eyes. Instead, I smirked. "No worries, Sunshine. He's all yours."

With her next step, the tall heel of her glossy pink shoe snapped.

"What the ..." She caught her balance and picked up her shoe. The heel hung from the inlay of the sole.

I hid in the shadows and smiled to myself.

Darn those metal shoe pins.

chapter
eleven

I sat and dangled my feet over the ledge of the open hayloft door of the old blue barn, staring at the piece of paper in my hand. I had a learner's permit. Me. It didn't matter that it wasn't a full license and that I could only drive with a licensed adult of twenty-one or older. I had a permit. An identity. I'd be damned if I ever let Roy take this one away from me.

I'd wandered off when Lorna and I had returned from town, wanting to be alone. To take in what this all meant for me. By this time next year, I would have my full license and could go wherever I wanted. Now all I needed was the deed to Mama's cottage and I could disappear.

A creaking floorboard startled me. Colton approached behind me, looking pale.

"What are you doing here?" I snapped, looking out at the field that stretched out to the tree line of the neighboring property. Way to kill a girl's good mood.

"Lorna told me you got your permit this morning."

"Yeah, so? It's not like I can drive alone or anything."

"Must still feel good. I remember how I felt when—"

"You're *so* not in a position to compare. You've been driving around dirt tracks since you were a kid and probably got your learner's at fifteen like everyone else."

After a few minutes of silence, the floorboards creaked again. "Lexi, can we talk?"

"We're talking right now, aren't we?"

"No, I mean talk about what happened last week and this weekend."

"You going to tell me I don't belong here again?"

"No."

I hoisted one leg up from the ledge and turned to look at him. He was rigid and tense, hands in his pockets. "Come sit next to me. It'll be easier to talk." I smirked to myself, knowing that his fear of heights would never let him make the extra steps.

"That's not fair."

"Neither are you."

I leaned back against the frame and gazed back out over the field. The floorboards creaked once more, but instead of moving away like I thought, Colton moved closer. My eyes followed him as he eased himself down on the ledge. He leaned and looked down, his face turning a light shade of green.

"Ugh." He grazed the bare part of my thigh below the hem of my denim shorts as he swung his arms out behind him and leaned back. The touch seared my skin.

I waited for him to say something, but he stayed silent. The only sound around us came from the breeze blowing though the nearby trees, rustling the leaves. He kept his head aimed at the sky and his eyes closed as if repeating something in his head to control his fear. Didn't seem to be working, though—

the color in his cheeks had yet to return.

"You okay?"

His lip twitched, but he said nothing.

"Colton?"

Again, no words. I tapped him on the knee. He jolted, his eyes wide, and grabbed my hand.

"Oh, God, don't do that."

I laughed. "You're too funny."

"I'm not *that* funny."

He fell silent again, looking down at my hand. I debated pulling my hand away. My mind conjured up a hundred warnings, but I defied them all and did what felt right. My skin warmed, but still I shivered. He stroked his thumb over my knuckles. My knees weakened. I really hoped I wouldn't need to get up soon.

"I don't know why," he said, his head still dipped low, "but I'm not as scared when I hold your hand."

A shallow breath caught in my throat and my whole body stiffened. I ached to look at his face, but the beak of his ball cap hid it from me.

"Lexi?"

"Yeah?"

"I'm sorry about what I said to Adam and Dezzi. I didn't mean it the way it came out."

Adam and Dezzi? The friends who dropped him off the other night, I guessed.

"I was mad about what had happened at lunch that day," he continued. "You shut me out and all I wanted to do is get to know you better. I don't quite understand why I felt the need to or why it made me angry when you … And then I was mad at myself for prying and mad that my stupid need was the reason you were avoiding me. I just ..." His mouth shut for a second. "Wow. I'm not making any sense right now, am I?" He sat up straight and looked up at the sky, not seeming to care that he was teetering on the edge of a second-story hayloft, his legs dangling over the edge. I wanted to say something, tell him I understood, even though I really didn't. I mean, why did he want to know me? Why did he even care? "I get it now, though. After everything you've been through," he added.

He'd puzzled me. "Everything I've been through?"

"I mean, it can't be easy to live in that kind of environment. Roy—"

"Roy wasn't all that bad. Yeah, he lost his temper and was rough with me sometimes, but it wasn't all bad."

"Stop saying that. What he did was wrong, Lex. No one deserves to be hit like that."

"I never said that. It was just the cards I was dealt after Mama died. I knew what buttons not to push."

Colton's eye narrowed. His free hand reached up and traced his finger along the two-inch scar that angled toward my ear, causing me to shiver and inhale a deep breath I had no intention of releasing. His eyes fell to my lips. I swallowed hard. His finger left my temple and landed on the half-inch scar on my lower lip. I flinched and pulled my head back. His touch still lingered on my lip. My senses vibrated and blood pounded in my skull. Every metal or metal-coated object in close proximity tickled the edge of my sanity. I squeezed my eyes shut, breathing short, shallow breaths, struggling to focus on keeping my control.

"Did Roy give you those scars?"

"No. Those were an accident." I hadn't lied. I should've told him that it had been Roy's fault to avoid further questioning, but giving him credit for something my curse had caused felt too much like praise.

"What happened?"

What really happened? I'd lost control after Roy yelled at me for not having dinner ready on time. I'd run away and gone out the back door, into the fenced-in scraps part of the yard. I had sent sheet metal flying toward the upstairs window where I knew Roy was at the time. When I tried to stop, one large piece swooped low and knocked me out cold. I'd woken up hours later with a gash across my temple and a split lip. In a screwed-up way, I guess it *had* been Roy's fault.

"A pile of scrap metal toppled over me in the yard a few years ago."

"I'm sorry. I didn't mean to—"

"Look." I tucked my hair behind my ear. "I'm not as fragile as you think I am. There are things I fear much more than Roy and his shitty-ass temper."

"What scares you, Lex? What makes you so afraid to open up?"

"I can't." My insides recoiled. "You wouldn't understand." I got up and started toward the old plank board stairs, but Colton jumped to his feet and reached for my arm.

"Lexi, please talk to me."

"I can't."

He kept his hold on my arm, but instead of pulling me toward him, he moved closer to me—*too* close. His eyes gazed into mine, the sapphire one hazed with sadness and the emerald one clear with wonder. He raised his hand to the side of my face, combed my hair to the back of my head, and then cradled the base of my skull. My mouth went dry. My body froze. His face inched closer. His gaze lowered and focused on my lips. Fog rolled through my pounding, aching head and my survival instincts faded. My heart beat fast, too fast—or was that his heartbeats chasing mine? My lids fell as his body came closer to mine. *Oh. My. God. He's going to kiss me.*

A scream came from downstairs, followed by a loud crash.

"Lorna?" Colton bolted for the stairs, leaving me breathless and weak. It took me some time to register what had just happened.

Oh, crap! No. No, no, no.

I flung my eyes open and ran, but then stopped and took a step back. My eyes, were they red?

If Lorna was hurt, I didn't want to scare her. I pulled out my phone and used the reverse camera as a mirror. Red shimmered in the corners of my eyes, but nothing anyone would notice at first glance.

"Lexi, I need your help."

I shut my screen off, slipped it into my back pocket, and hurried down the steps. Lorna sat on the ground crying, surrounded by scattered old chains and tree-cutting tools, some sharp enough to have hacked her into pieces. I slapped my hand over my mouth to contain my horror. I'd done this. I'd lost control in an intimate moment. Tears rose to my eyes.

"Lexi." Colton turned to me. "Help me get her to the house."

Focus. I needed to focus. I ran to Lorna's side and hooked my arm under hers. Colton did the same on his side, and together we pulled her up and brought her into the kitchen.

"I'll get her some water," I said.

Colton nodded and sat Lorna down in a chair from the

kitchen table. Her eyes were glazed over and her hands shook uncontrollably.

"They were floating in mid-air," she murmured.

Colton pulled out a chair and sat across from her, taking both her hands in his. "Lorna, what was floating?"

"The tools," she said, her eyes finally focusing on Colton as if she'd just noticed he was there. "The knives and saws."

I handed her a glass of water. She sipped from it, still shaking. Water spilled over the edge onto her lap.

My heart skipped a beat. "Annabelle? Where's Annabelle?"

Lorna glanced up at me. "She's sleeping. I put her down late for her nap. I'd just gone out for a second to ask you two what you wanted for dinner, since Dean and I won't be here, and then …"

"And then what, Lorna?"

"I walked into the barn and things just rose." She raised her hands. "Like this, and just floated there. And when I screamed, everything fell."

I backed myself up against the counter. How could I have been so stupid? I had, against my better judgment, allowed myself to maybe experience what it felt like to kiss someone. Someone whom I'd wanted to kiss so desperately, and what had that gotten me? I almost got Lorna killed. I couldn't let that happen. I couldn't.

Lorna's eyes teared up again. Colton wrapped his arms around her and soothed her back with a rubbing hand.

"Take her to the family room," I told him. "I'll go wake Annabelle up."

Just then, Dean pulled into the driveway. I rushed upstairs to avoid hearing Lorna recount her horrid experience, knowing full well it had been my fault she'd been traumatized.

Annabelle slept quietly in her Tinkerbell bed, oblivious to the commotion happening downstairs.

I sat on the floor against the far wall, watching her peaceful sleeping face, and cried. I needed to keep my distance from Colton. But how? My heart was drawn to him. I'd had crushes. I used to gawk over the guys who worked at the yard over the summers. There was this one guy who'd come back two years in a row, and we'd gotten pretty close, but I didn't feel nearly as pulled to him as I seemed to be to Colton. He hadn't triggered my curse the way Colton did. Not that it mattered how I felt. I could never let myself go there with him. I could never let my feelings screw all this up for me.

My only choice here was to find a way to co-exist in this family without losing control.

chapter twelve

Colton retreated to his safe spot and I stared out the window at the clouds. Work had become my number-one focus these past few days. It'd given me something constant, controlled, and similar to what I used to do for Roy. I felt like myself again. The lack of supervision allowed me to test my ability more fully, something I never got to do under Roy's watchful eye. Things like the levels of energy needed for long-range reach, weight tolerance, and manipulation for easier control with attracting and pushing away objects. It gave me a better perspective of what I could control, and it also distracted me from thinking too much about what I'd done to Lorna. Thankfully, she wasn't the skeptical type and believed the barn to be haunted. She never even suspected my involvement, but had forbidden any of us to go anywhere near it. Colton tried explaining to her that the shelf couldn't handle the weight of those tools and that it was just a coincidence that she'd been there when it gave way, but she would hear none of it. "I know what I saw," she kept saying. That meant I'd lost my favorite spot to hide out in other than my room. If only Lorna knew that she had an even bigger threat than some silly ghost living in her attic—a dangerous freak.

I indulged in a private chuckle. *Pfft.* The freak in the attic. Sounded like a good premise for a horror flick or a suspense novel.

Unfortunately, I hadn't been able to erase the almost kiss with Colton from my mind, which caused a few mishaps when the thought popped into my head during my ability experiments. I was lucky no one questioned the racket going on at my workstation.

The jet was due to land in Vegas in about five minutes and Colton's cheeks were still drained of all color. He'd be asking for my hand again soon, a comfort I hadn't had the heart to take away from him. What would he do next season without me? Suffer in silence, I guessed. Like he did before I came along.

Ding. The overhead seatbelt light came on and Colton came back to sit next to me. I offered him my hand as I'd done when we'd boarded. He took it, his eyes wide. Things were awkward between us now. I avoided any talk about me or the kiss that might have been. I became determined to keep Colton at arm's length.

Nancy waited for us outside when we landed and whisked Colton away for more media appearances. If my memory served me correctly, he had a radio gig this afternoon.

Dean and I headed off to the track.

The garage area was crawling with security. Last week's sabotage had hit the news and NASCAR was taking every precaution to make sure it didn't happen again. I spent my time catching up on my online classes, doing some sightseeing, and helping out at the garage—the old-school way, of course. It'd be hard to blame ghosts here.

Friday morning, I woke up early. Colton had an early qualifying run scheduled and just because I wanted to avoid a close relationship with him didn't mean I couldn't cheer him on.

Sporting my black Guardian Auto Insurance shirt and green Fizzy Pop ball cap, another of Colton's sponsors, I headed out to the hauler. I hooked my headset around my neck, clipped the scanner to my waistband, and made the climb up to the top of the hauler. I had the roof to myself today. Dean watched from the pits, keeping a close eye on things down below. Last week's incident had him nervous and suspecting that someone had been out to ruin their season. In my opinion, the culprit was obvious, but the officials couldn't place the blame on Carl Stacy without proof.

"Everything workin'?" Lenny said over the scanner.

"Ten-four," Colton responded. "I hear you loud and clear."

"You're up next."

"Sweet. Let's go do this thing!" Colton hollered. I could almost see the grin on his face in the sound of his voice.

He took to the track, jerking the car side-to-side to warm up his tires, and then hammered it to full speed. He entered the turns high, then dipped down low, following his line in every turn.

"She's gripping good," Colton said.

"It shows," Dean answered. "You're lookin' good out there."

Colton sped through the turns with great ease, not one tug or wobble. Pride swelled inside me as I watched him. I was beginning to know what it felt like to be part of something, part of a team. I hadn't felt that since Mama had passed, and it felt good.

Colton ducked back into the pits.

Dean cued his mic. "Good job, Colt. You got the pole by a long shot so far, but there's still many more to go."

Colton was already inside the hauler when I went back to store away my headset. His black fire suit hugged his body in all the right places. I'd become more aware of Colton's appearance since we nearly kissed in the barn four days ago. Not that I hadn't noticed how gorgeous he was before—obviously—but now he looked somehow different. His appearance was now enhanced by his personality. He wasn't just the hot guy who called me a little girl on that first day, he was so much more. He was just so damn hot—inside and out. To make matters worse, when I snapped out of my thoughts, he took off his ball cap, raked both his hands through his flattened hair, slipped out of the top half of his suit, and hoisted the hem of his sweat repelling short-sleeved shirt over his head. This had to be what heaven looked like. I shook my head and cursed under my breath.

"Something wrong?" he asked, grabbing a t-shirt from the shelf.

"Huh? Uh, no, nothing's wrong."

He smiled, causing his eyes to glint as they creased. Damn him.

He flipped his t-shirt over and pulled it over his head. I tried to look away as his arms and abs flexed. Yeah, right. Who was I kidding? What girl could look away from that?

"Okay," I said awkwardly. "I'm going back to the motor coach."

I turned to leave, but Colton loosely wrapped his fingers around my wrist. "Wait."

I snapped my hand back, startled. A sharp pounding thundered in my temples.

"Sorry. I … I was about to head to one of the concession stands. You wanna come with?"

Was he serious? "Are you nuts? You're going to get mauled by fans."

"I can't keep avoiding them—they're the reason I get to do this every week."

I readied myself to say no, no way, not a chance, but my lips betrayed me. "Sure, why not?" *Why not? Because around you, I levitate steel objects and almost kill people, that's why not.*

He reached behind him and pulled another t-shirt from the shelf.

"Here, put this on while I go change. It'll help sort through the real fans from those just jumping for an autograph to sell on eBay."

I unfolded the shirt, which had Link's face printed on the front. I laughed. "Nice decoy."

"Yeah, it works too. And here …" He reached for the top shelf, pulled down two Watson's Steel and Lumber ball caps, and handed me one. "Matching fan gear. What do you say?" Before I could comment, he disappeared into a room down the aisle. Oh, good Lord, what was I doing?

I changed in Dean's office and emerged to find Colton already dressed. "You ready?"

I switched hats, leaving my Fizzy Pop one on the shelf. "Lead the way."

As much as we tried to blend in with the crowd of race fans, Colton got spotted a few times. But without an ounce of annoyance, he signed everything from t-shirts to program guides to toy car replicas and even one chick's cleavage with a smile and a thanks for rooting for him. Especially on that last one. The cutest were the kids, the little ones whose eyes would grow wide at the sight of him when they'd realize who he was.

We managed to order our food and find a spot in the shade to eat, away from the massive crowds.

"You're one popular guy," I said, dipping my French fry into the little container of ketchup.

"I try."

"You love it, don't you?" I bit into my fry.

"I do. It's all part of the gig." Colton raised his burger with both hands. "The fans are the best part."

"I don't think I could do it. I like being able to slip into the shadows, unnoticed."

He put his food down. "You would."

My lips curved into a slight smile. "What's that supposed to mean?"

"You need to live a little, Lex. You've been cooped up way too long. You don't even realize that you have so much to offer."

"Ha. Yeah, right. Like what?"

"For starters, your mad mechanic skills."

I leaned back. "Okay. I'll give you that one. I'm good at that."

"Secondly, you're great with kids."

"Not so sure about that one." I crossed my arms.

"Come on, Annabelle loves you. She talks about you all the time when you're not around."

"That kid says she loves anyone who's not the one trying to put her to bed."

"Point taken. But you also …" He paused.

"But I also what?"

He laughed, reached over, and wiped the corner of my mouth with his thumb. "Ketchup," he said, then transferred it onto a napkin.

The gesture caught me off guard. "Thanks." I grabbed my own napkin and wiped the corners of my mouth. "So, what else were you going to say?" I didn't care about the warning signs flashing in my mind. I ignored them. I wanted to know what else Colton thought I had to offer.

He stared, as if debating whether to tell me or not, then looked down to push a fry around his basket with his finger. "You have a great smile."

Heat crept up the back of my neck and up to my cheeks. I grabbed a leftover fry from my basket and threw it at him. "Whatever."

He jumped too late to dodge my fry attack and picked it off his lap, laughing. "No, really. I mean it." His eyes met mine and his smile faded, showing me his more serious side.

I glanced down at my watch as an excuse to look away. "We better get back if you don't want to miss the start of Link's practice."

Colton looked down at his now-empty food basket. "I'm not watching him practice."

"How come?"

He shifted in his seat. "I have a ... a thing."

"Oh."

"But you're right." He looked back up at me, a frown tugging at his lips. "We should get back. I need to shower and get ready."

We returned our baskets to the concession stand, trashed our wrappers, and headed back through the crowd. By the time we crossed through the heavy security at the gates to the infield, my head had calmed. I'd managed to not lose it, although I wasn't quite sure why that was.

Dean stepped out of the motor coach as Colton and I arrived. "Where have you two been?"

"Grabbing a late lunch," Colton said.

"Don't forget, you got that thing later. You better get a move on and get ready."

Colton looked uncomfortable. "I know."

"Why don't you take Lexi along with you? She might enjoy it."

Colton glanced at me then back at Dean. "I don't think that's a good idea."

Dean tapped him on the arm. "Oh, come on."

I shook my head. "No, that's okay. I'd just be in the way."

Dean grinned wide. "Nonsense. It's a party, after all."

"A party?" Confused, I glanced at Colton, who was now averting his eyes as he slipped his hands in his pockets.

"Yeah, Gwen's birthday party. You remember Gwen, right?" Dean added.

Gwen's birthday? He was actually going to that thing? Of course, how could anyone say no to Bimbo Barbie *Gwen*? I stepped back slightly. "Oh, I'm not sure she'd be very happy to see me there."

"Don't be ridiculous. She's a fan of the team and you, my dear—" he flicked the beak of my cap "—are part of the team."

I groaned internally.

"It's settled, then. Colt, show our girl here a good time. Maybe take a detour down the Vegas strip to see the lights on your way back." He winked. "Just don't be too late. You have practice early tomorrow."

Dean walked away, leaving me and Colton outside the motor coach.

I turned to face him, touching his arm to get his attention. "You don't have to take me. I understand."

"You don't get it." He kicked a pebble hidden in the grass at his feet. "I want to take you, it's just—"

"Don't worry about it." I reached for the door.

"No." Colton's head tipped up, revealing the sparkles in his eyes. "I want you to come."

chapter thirteen

I stepped out of my room and into the kitchen wearing the aquamarine cocktail dress I kept in my luggage in case an occasion ever called for such fancy attire. The double-layered hem puffed the skirt out from the sash that was cinched way too tight at my waist to breathe, but gave me an amazing hourglass shape. The built-in bra and the one-shoulder strap design left my right shoulder bare and a tad more naked than I was used to. The little make-up I wore felt unnatural and heavy on my lids, and the long earrings dangling from my ears were annoying the crap out of me. Bottom line, I felt ridiculous, overdressed, and stuffed like a sausage.

Colton emerged from his room at the far end, his suit jacket draped over his arm, adjusting his green silk tie. In that instant, my mission to find my shoes and any thoughts of my uncomfortable attire melted away.

Hot damn.

His black dress shirt, tucked into the waistband of his black dress pants, showed off his wide upper body. His hair, usually flattened by his ball cap or tousled by his helmet, was carefully groomed and hung down each side of his temples to his cheeks, making his mismatched eyes more noticeable and just totally gorgeous. Now I really couldn't breathe.

He looked up and froze, his hand still gripping the knot of his green silk tie. His lips parted as his gaze drifted over me. I gulped. My cheeks radiated with heat. "What?"

His eyes lingered a second longer, and then he looked away, pursing his lips. "Nothing. You ready?"

"I guess, yeah. I just need to find my shoes."

Realigning my focus, I struggled to get a grasp on my surroundings, as though I'd just gotten off a theme park ride. Not that I remembered what that felt like, since I hadn't gone to a theme park since Mama took me to Disney World when I was six, but I imagined this came pretty close. I looked in the small closet near the door, and then returned to my room, half shutting the door to peek behind it, still unsure where I'd put those damn heels I dreaded having to walk in.

I located them near the tip-out wardrobe, snagged them by their flimsy straps, and sat on the edge of the bed to fasten them. I got one done, but couldn't seem to contort my arms in the awkward angle needed to buckle the other. The tiny buckle kept slipping through my fingers, and I couldn't get the little hook in the loop of the strap. Why couldn't they make these things out of metal or stainless steel? It would make my life that much easier. The buckle slipped again and pinched my finger. "Shit."

A light knock at the door jumped my pulse. "You need help in there?"

I brought my finger to my mouth to ease the sting. "I'm fine.

It's just these friggin' shoes, sandals, whatever."

Colton inched the door open, spotted me, and moved closer. "Here, let me help."

I let out a frustrated breath, catching the tail end of it in the back of my throat as he knelt down on one knee in front of me. His hand reached down, cradled my foot and ankle, and lifted it to rest on his knee. His warm hands made my heart race. I watched as he maneuvered the buckle with ease and precision, and wondered what else those hands could handle, but I quickly shooed the thought away as awareness of my cursed senses heightened. My eyes pinched closed, and I forced myself to suppress the tingling magnetic vibration pulsating in my temples, just like I'd practiced at the shop. Only, the more I fought against them, the stronger they got.

"There," he said, bringing my foot down off his knee. I opened my eyes and blinked as he extended his hand to help me up. I met his gaze and instantly, my mind calmed and the pulses slowed. Not sure why, but I wasn't going to complain.

I accepted the gesture. He pulled me up and paused, his hand in mine. His eyes trailed from my toes up to my face. He cleared his throat and released me. "You clean up nice."

I smiled. "So do you." Oh boy, did he ever. This was bad. This was not the staying clear of Colton I had in mind, but I couldn't help it. He was just too … Aaargh!

"We better get going, if we don't want to be late."

I nodded, afraid to open my mouth and say something stupid like "you're hot," or "let's just stay here together, in my room." *Snap, Lex, get your mind out of the gutter.*

He raised an eyebrow, as if trying to read my thoughts. All I could do was swallow against the dryness in my throat and try not to flutter my lashes like the wings of a hummingbird in flight.

"Come on," he finally said, heading toward the door. I followed as close as I could, considering I wasn't used to walking around with spikes sticking out of my heels.

In the parking lot, Colton pulled out a set of keys and pointed the remote lock at a gorgeous yellow Camaro SS with black racing stripes like the one I once saw in a movie.

"That's the rental?"

"Yeah, what do you think?"

"Wow … I mean, just wow."

Colton opened my door like a gentleman, then came around and slipped into the driver's seat. He turned the key in the ignition, and the sound of the motor's deep, throaty roar sank me back against the leather seat.

At the salvage yard, I never appreciated the sound of an engine coming to life or the rumble of an idling one. Most of the cars that came through my shop were old and sick, or just plain garbage begging to be taken out of their misery. Since joining Dean and his team, though, I'd learned to appreciate the goosebumps and the internal rush flowing through my veins at the fierce sound.

We rode in silence most of the way there. My nerves grew stiff the closer we got to our destination. Gwen was *not* going to be happy to see me. That was a fact. I toyed with the idea of staying in the car, but something told me Colton probably wouldn't go for it. I didn't want to screw up his night—or his sponsorship, for that matter. The girl was Daddy's little spoiled brat, and Daddy was Colton's ticket to acquiring Guardian's sponsorship for the full season.

We pulled up in front of a large, iron-gated fence that seemed to hug the road for a quarter mile in both directions. Guards stood on each side as cars pulled in. Colton lowered his window when it came our turn. "Hi, I'm—"

"Colton Tayler. I know who you are," the husky guard said. "Go on in. Miss Gwen is expecting you."

"Thanks."

"Oh, and good luck on Sunday." The man leaned closer, winked, and flashed a toothless grin. "We're all big fans."

"I appreciate it … thank you." Colton raised his window and continued forward down the long tree-lined driveway, giving me a quick sideways glance. I chuckled. I wasn't sure if I could ever get used to people recognizing me all the time like that, but Colton seemed to embrace it as part of who he was and wanted to be. I admired him for that.

Within seconds, the tall trees opened up to a clearing, revealing a large, four-story red brick house with huge white circular columns framing the entrance. Manicured lawns and lavish flowerbeds stretched out around the property and tall, strategically placed palm trees added to the rich feel of the home. I was so way out of my element, it wasn't funny.

We climbed out of the car in front of the oversized front door, and Colton handed the valet his keys. No joke. They had a valet servicing an eighteen-year-old's birthday party. Unreal.

The doorman ushered us inside, and all eyes turned on us. Loud whispers rippled through the crowd over the booming music coming from the DJ's booth on a stage-like platform overlooking the ballroom-style dance floor.

Word of Colton's arrival must have spread like a tabloid scoop, because Gwen came out of nowhere through the crowd and threw herself into his arms. "I'm so glad you came! I was starting to think you wouldn't show."

"I promised I'd come, didn't I?"

Girls around the room, most of whom I'm sure Gwen didn't even know personally, stared at the two of them with envy. Hell, I did it too.

Gwen was perfect for Colton, as much as I hated to admit it. She was gorgeous, petite, and loved being in the public eye. They looked good together, which made me want to puke, but I knew I could never fill those shoes. Hell, I could barely walk in mine, and hers were two inches taller.

She let go of Colton and did a double take when her eyes landed on me. Her ear-to-ear grin faded. "What is she doing here?" She wasn't skilled at hiding her snarky attitude. "She wasn't invited."

"Come on, Gwen, the team thought it would be nice for Lexi to go out and have a good time. And what better place to do that than at one of Gwen Langdon's legendary parties?"

She smiled at his compliment. "Fine, she can stay. But remember, you're mine tonight."

Colton threw an apologetic look my way. "You know I can't stay long. I've got an early practice in the morning."

She flipped her hair back over her shoulder. "I know that, silly. I have your race schedule programmed on my phone."

Yeah. That wasn't creepy at all.

"Gwen," Mr. Langdon called her from the doorway to another room.

Gwen looked back, annoyed. "Make yourself at home. There's hors d'oeuvres over there." She pointed at the far end of the room along the wall. "I'll meet you back there in a snap."

With another flip of her hair, she took off.

Colton gestured for me to lead us toward the food. As we made our way through the crowd, he pressed his hand to the small of my back, sending chills up my spine. I glanced back. Colton's lips curled to one side.

The long table at the far wall offered an array of finger foods at the foot of a large ice sculpture in the center. I grimaced at the carved features of Gwen's perky nose and high cheekbones. Seriously? Overboard, much? That had to be the tackiest thing I'd ever seen. I wrinkled my nose at it, and caught Colton doing the same.

After taking a few nibbled bites of the goods, the music faded, and a slow song started. A sea of bodies scattered off the dance floor, leaving only couples wrapped in each other's arms, swaying in circles to the music.

Colton set his plate down on the edge of the table and extended his hand toward me.

"Oh, no, thanks. I've never danced with anyone before. I don't want to break your toes before your big race."

"Oh, come on," he said, taking my hand. "It's easy, I promise." He led me to an unoccupied spot on the dance floor next to a couple that was sucking face more than dancing, and pulled me close. I made it a point to keep track of my cursed senses. Being this close to Colton brought on some never-before-experienced emotions, and I didn't trust my iron levels to stay in check.

Colton wrapped my hands around his neck and let his fall to my waist, tugging me even closer. I swallowed hard as he lowered his lips to my ear. His hair brushed against my temple. "Relax and just follow my lead."

Relax. Yeah, right.

He leaned his head to the side, pressing it against mine, and moved in slow circular steps to the flow of the music. "That's it," he said. "You're a pro already." A girly giggle escaped from my lips. A giggle—really? I don't giggle. Never like that, anyway. My distracted thoughts threw off my momentum and I clipped the tip of his shoe with my heel.

"Shit." I pulled back. "I can't do this. I'm going to hurt you."

He drew me back to him. "No, you're not. You're doing great." His hands slid from my waist around to the small of my back, bringing me close. His eyes sparkled under the shimmering lights above us. My heart grew weightless and I lost myself in the moment. I leaned into his embrace, letting my head rest against his chest. He dipped his head lower into the slope of my neck. His breath warmed my bare shoulder. I couldn't remember ever feeling this nervous, happy, and content.

The song ended and another started. Colton's hands remained fixed, not allowing me to step away, which was fine by me. I was where I wanted to be.

A long-nailed finger poked me in the ribs.

"Thanks for keeping him warm for me, but scat." Gwen waved her bony fingers in front of my face. "I got this."

I stepped out of Colton's arms, which were trying to keep me from leaving. "I'm sorry." I turned to walk away.

"Wait!" Colton cried.

"No. It's okay. You're here for her. It's her birthday. Dance with her." I went back to the food table and watched as Gwen's fingers crawled up his biceps and grazed the back of his neck while she gazed up at him. One of his hands wrapped around her waist while the other stayed in his pants pocket. The impersonal gesture surprised me. I wished I could get a glimpse of his face, but his hair hid mostly everything. She was talking to him, though I couldn't hear what she was saying.

My heart wept. Who was I kidding? I could never get a guy like Colton Tayler. If he found out what I truly was—a freak of nature—he'd drop me like a rusted-out muffler. He'd hate me. I couldn't deny that, against my better judgment, I was falling for him. The glass of punch I'd swiped off the beverage table trembled between my fingers. This felt like more than a crush. I was falling … No! I couldn't even let myself think the words. It was just so wrong on so many levels. I couldn't be. I'd only known him for a short time.

The song reached its end. Colton spotted me over Gwen's shoulder and smiled. Gwen noticed and glanced back. An evil smirk crossed her face. She looked back up at Colton, reached for his collar, and pulled him into a full-on lip lock. The glass slipped from my hand and shattered on the floor. Or had that been my heart shattering into a million pieces?

I couldn't look away, even though I desperately wanted to— like a bad car wreck that just wouldn't end. Tears clung to my lashes and a lump formed in my throat. My curse vibrated and pulsed in my head.

The kiss ended and Colton looked up at me right away. My tears defied my orders and leaked down my cheeks. The thumping in my temples grew stronger. I needed to get out of here. I pushed through the crowd toward the front door, but it was too late. Everyone's gasps filled my ears. I knew it was my fault. I'd felt the stainless steel pitcher of water fly through the air. I turned in time to see it hit Gwen square in the chest. Water poured down the front of her cotton candy pink dress.

"Who threw that at me? Who?" she screamed, her eyes

filling with rage.

Colton looked down at his damp shirt, then back up in time to spot me. "Lexi, wait." He left Gwen's side and started making his way through the crowd, but I didn't wait. I didn't want him to see me like this. I wasn't sure if my eyes had turned red or not. I could never tell, but I didn't want to take any chances. I couldn't let him see what I was, what I could do, or how I honestly felt about him.

He could never know.

chapter
fourteen

Dark clouds hovered overhead, hiding the stars. I wished I could see them right now to calm my nerves. I'd lost control again. At least this time I hadn't almost killed someone.

Colton found me on the side of the house where I sat on the grass, in the shadows, wiping away my tears. I hid my face behind the curtain of hair that fell from behind my ear, too embarrassed to face him.

He knelt beside me. "Are you okay?"

"I'm fine." I wiped away another tear with my forearm.

He leaned in closer. "Why are you crying?"

"I'm not. It just got too stuffy in there all of a sudden. I had to get out." I looked at him. It was clear he wasn't buying it.

"Come on. Let's get out of here." He stood and extended his hand.

"What about Gwen?"

"What about her? I came here as a favor to her father. I owe her nothing." He smiled down at me. "Come on."

I took his hand, not expecting his firm grip to pull me up so fast. My heel dug into the grass and tripped me into his arms. He straightened me and stilled his hands on my hips. His eyes shone in the dim light as he brushed back a clump of hair that clung to my damp cheek.

Gwen appeared from around the corner, still drenched from the pitcher of water I'd flung at her. "There you are," she said with a grin the moment she spotted Colton.

Colton turned to face her, slipping one hand around my waist. "We're leaving."

The grin melted off her face. Her eyes traveled from him to me, then back to him. "But you just got here."

"Lexi's not feeling well." He stepped past her, taking me with him.

She spun around. "But, Colton, you can't just kiss me and then leave."

Colton released me and stepped toward her. "You ambushed me, Gwen. That wasn't a kiss. Thank your father for his hospitality. I'll see you at the track."

Gwen let out a sharp grunt and stomped back toward the house.

Colton slipped his arm around me again and led me to the valet attendant out front.

"Wait here," he said, releasing me to go have the car brought around. I shivered at the sudden lack of warmth.

"Are you cold?" Colton asked, returning to my side.

"A little." There was a chill breeze blowing that wasn't helping. Colton loosened his tie, shirt collar, and sleeve cuffs while we waited. When the car pulled up, he reached into the back seat where he'd left his suit jacket and draped it over my shoulders before helping me into the car.

The jacket didn't help the chills much. I wasn't just cold, I was scared. Scared of my growing feelings for Colton and my need for him to feel the same. My head and heart were on opposing sides. And if he knew what I could do … I couldn't let him find out. I couldn't let anyone find out. Not now, not ever.

The ride back to the track was a quiet one. Neither of us dared break the silence. Colton took a detour down the Vegas strip. The blinking lights and show displays were hypnotic and larger than life. Tourists and gamblers alike flooded both sides of the street. Fliers and papers littered the sidewalks. I'd never seen anything like it. The strip was alive, unlike me. My insides mourned the life I wanted. The life I would've had if I'd just been born … normal.

I thought back to the night of my mother's funeral, after everyone had left the cemetery. Roy had taken off, leaving me there alone so he could go have a few beers with his friends. He hadn't cared that she was gone, only that he'd inherited the burden of having to raise me.

I'd sat at the foot of the fresh mound of dirt over her casket, staring at the cheap tombstone Roy picked out without consulting me—a small, thin oval top rock, like those Styrofoam ones you see on people's lawns on Halloween. Only her name, her date of birth, and the date she left me were on its surface.

It stormed that night, hard. The rain fell like pebbles against my umbrella until the wind ripped it from my hands. It didn't bother me. I'd been too numb to care.

The shock of having lost her overwhelmed me. I couldn't leave her alone there in the ground. In the cold. Thunder rumbled and lightning lit up the sky, but still I stayed, staring at my mother's name, dark against the grey stone. I shouldn't have been out there. I knew that. Mama told me time and time again, even made me promise her before she died, to never go outside during a storm. I never quite knew why, only that it had something to do with what had happened to my father and that the same thing could happen to me.

My father.

Was she with him now? Had he greeted her when she opened her eyes in the afterlife?

That's when it happened—the instant flash of bright light jolted through my body, making me seize up with pain so hard I blacked out. Hours went by before I woke again. Weak, stunned, and tingling all over, I managed to walk the three miles back to the salvage yard on my own. I never told Roy what happened—or anyone else, for that matter. Who would have believed me?

Mama never told Roy that I could detect and sense metal as easily as a normal person could sense a cold breeze on their skin. Roy didn't know what kind of impact lightning could have on me. I hadn't known either, until Roy forced me to attend my first day of high school the next day. I found out then why my father thought himself too dangerous. That was what had happened to him. Now it was happening to me.

●●●

Sunday morning I woke up early. With last week's sabotage hanging over the team's head, Dean wanted me there at all times, in case he needed my speedy skills. That meant hanging around the garage … and Colton. I hadn't seen him much yesterday. He'd been tugged away to different promotional things, and I'd skipped going to his practice. The moments we did run into each other were awkward and uncomfortable.

"Hey, Lexi." Dean waved at me from the other side of the car when I got to the garage. Colton hadn't returned from his driver's meeting yet. "I have a favor to ask."

"You need something dismantled again?"

"No. I need you to watch the race from the pits today."

Confused, I cocked an eyebrow. "Why's that?"

"Mr. Langdon and his daughter are here, and Miss Teen Beat requested that you not be anywhere near her." Dean rubbed the back of his neck, looking disturbed by his own request. "Of course, Mr. Langdon thinks she's being unfair, but has requested that you stay down here, just this week, so he can have a chance to talk to her later."

I'd known that her royal highness disliked me, but hadn't realized she held the power to exile me from the hauler's roof.

"Just this week, Lex, I promise."

I wiped the hurt from my expression and forced a smile. "No worries, I've never seen a race from the pits before." I shrugged. "Could be fun."

"You could sit next to Lenny in the pit box. I'm sure Dylan would let you have his spot."

I amped up the smile and enthusiasm in hopes of taking some stress off Dean's shoulders. He had enough to worry about. He didn't need the added worries of Gwen's tantrums.

"It's okay, Dean. I don't mind."

Colton came back in time to help the crew push the car out to the inspection booth. We exchanged glances and nods, but nothing more. Things were awkward once again.

He knew.

He knew how I felt. He'd be stupid not to. He saw me storm out like an idiot after Gwen planted one on him.

I took my time going to the hauler to retrieve my headset and met the crew out at the pit stall once all the inspections were done.

The cars lined pit road in starting order, ready to go. Colton ran off for his driver introduction, where they paraded all the drivers in the backs of pickup trucks around the track for the fans. Meanwhile, I stood to the side, trying my best to stay out of the crew's way.

Gwen glared down at me from the hauler, as if trying to zap me with laser beams. That girl had a serious problem, and it wasn't that her colored nails didn't match her purse.

"Walk with me." Colton's whisper came from behind, startling me.

I spun around and smiled. I couldn't help it. His sheer presence brought one on every time. "Walk with you where?"

He stood before me, gloves in one hand, helmet in the other, and a sexy half-smile on his face. "To my car." He winked and tapped me on the arm. "Come on."

The remainder of the crew followed behind us as we walked by the other cars and drivers. Some stood around with their wives and kids, others with their girlfriends and parents, all anxious to start the race.

Colton placed his helmet on the roof of his car and threw his gloves inside on the dash. He stood by me, talking to the crew as my attention wandered to the massive grandstands ahead. Everything looked so much more majestic from down here. Camera crews and reporters threw themselves in front of any driver willing to talk. I prayed that none came toward us.

My nerves were tightly strung enough as it was, I didn't need a microphone shoved in my face.

Speakers blared, and the crowds in the pits and grandstands settled when the anthem started. Colton removed his ball cap, reminding me I'd forgotten to wear mine again. Maybe, with a little luck, my green Fizzy Pop one would still be in the hauler. Colton's hand rested on the small of my back. I bit my lip, skin tingling under my shirt. It took every ounce of my willpower not to look at him. I focused my eyes on the rows of cars and the crews lined up in their matching team uniforms, mentally gearing up for the long afternoon. Being part of a NASCAR team was like being part of a whole different kind of family. I laughed and covered my ears as the jets flew over our heads at the end of the anthem. Maybe I could get used to this life.

Lenny smacked me on the shoulder. "Put the boy in his car, sweetheart." He winked. "For good luck."

"Put him where … what?"

Colton laughed. "He means see me to my car."

"But we're at your car."

Colton leaned back against his front fender and pulled me toward him. He looked down at me, at my lips. A chill traveled down my arms and legs despite the scorching heat of the sun. *Please don't kiss me*, I prayed. I looked around. Too many people. Too many reporters.

Ah, who was I kidding? I wanted him to kiss me.

He tucked my hair behind my ear, leaned in, and pressed his cheek against mine, his lips practically touching my ear. My lids fell.

"Wish me luck," he whispered, then pulled back.

Resisting the urge to touch the tingling skin of my cheek, I lifted my lashes and met his smile. "Good luck."

Lenny pushed me aside and shoulder-shoved Colton. "Alright, now. In the car you go."

Colton climbed through the window, put on his gear, buckled himself in tight, and snapped his steering wheel into place. Lenny fastened his window net, tapped the hood, and walked away.

"I hear you," Colton said, his voice muffled by his helmet. Lenny or Jimmy was likely testing the mic.

"Be safe," I told him.

He winked and gave me a thumbs-up. Dylan tugged my arm. "Time to go."

As I walked back, something tapped me on the thigh. I looked down and found Colton's Guardian Auto Insurance ball cap hanging from my belt loop. Without me noticing, he'd attached the Velcro strap to the belt loop of my denim shorts. Sneaky little bugger. I removed it, put it on, and then raised my headset over it.

"Fire in the hole," Lenny shouted over the airwaves, just as the words. "drivers, start your engines!" rang out over the loudspeakers.

I shuddered when all forty-three 850-horsepower engines roared to life at once, angry and ready to attack the track. Everything sounded so much louder from down here. The cars rumbled around the track two-by-two behind the pace car, warming up their tires and easing in for the long haul.

"One lap till the green," Colton's spotter voiced.

"I'm ready. Let's go do this thing," Colton answered. The caterpillar of cars rumbled down the last turn toward the start/finish line. The fans in the grandstands stood, the flagman leaned forward, and then Jimmy yelled out, "Green, green, green," over the airwaves.

The race was on.

Colton had started sixth and hovered in that position for most of the race. I'd made sure to stay out of harm's way when Colton pitted, but close enough to catch a glimpse of him through his net.

With ten laps left to go, Colton began forcing his way to the front of the pack. One by one, he knocked the others back. He was behind Mitch now in the 220 car, the leader, with only five laps to go. He lingered, toying with him in the turns.

"What are you doing, Colt?" Lenny voiced.

"Just setting him up, chief."

"Two laps to go," Jimmy chimed in.

Colton went high in the next turn, and so did Mitch. Colton slingshotted low behind him and passed him on the inside.

"Yeah!" Lenny yelled beside me.

"Clear, clear, clear," his spotter said as he fell in line ahead of Mitch.

Colton pushed forward, gaining half a car length on the former leader.

"White's out," Jimmy cheered. Just one more lap to go.

"I can hold it. I can hold it," Colton said.

The crew and I lined the edge of pit road, watching. Lenny wiped his brow; we were all covered in sweat.

"Checkered's coming out," Jimmy said, then added, "220, up high."

Mitch was gaining on him, attempting to pass, but it was too late.

"Checkered's out."

"Whooo-hooo!" Colton hollered as he crossed the finish line. I jumped up and threw my fist in the air. "Yeah!"

The crew jumped over the barriers and ran toward victory lane while Colton performed his victory lap. "This one's ours, boys, this one's ours!"

My heart filled with pride.

After tearing up the infield grass and smoking his fans with burnouts, he eased her over to victory lane.

"Lexi, I better see you over there," he said. And the airwaves fell silent.

How did he know I planned to stay behind? He knew me too well already. I chased after the crew and joined them all on the stage. Colton was already being interviewed, and his PR rep kept switching his ball caps every few seconds so that each sponsor brand got media time. He spotted me standing behind Lenny, and I flinched. I just knew he intended on pulling me to him.

That's exactly what he did.

I squealed when he wrapped his arms around me and lifted me up over him. My hands gripped his solid shoulders tight, afraid to fall. Everyone cheered, hollered, and patted each other on the back. Containers behind us burst with confetti, sending it fluttering all around us—a shower of shiny, colorful paper. Colton lowered me to my feet, and before I could register what had just happened, his lips met mine in front of everyone—the crew, the sponsors, the media, and the fans gathered around the winner's circle. Heat rose from the center of my core and burned my face and neck. I lowered my lashes and let my surroundings fade. The cheers and crackling fireworks that lit up the sky disappeared.

Colton released me, his eyes scouring my face. Only he existed, no one else. The kiss had only been a peck, but a long one, more intimate and more shiver-inducing than any kiss I had ever experienced.

Jimmy wrapped his arm around Colton's shoulders from behind and pulled him back a few steps. I snapped out of my trance. The chaos of celebration returned and the moment we shared ended. I fought the urge to touch my lips. Everything had happened so fast, not even my curse had a chance to react. How? Why? Had it actually happened? Had I imagined it? The questions bounced inside my head and wreaked havoc on my pounding heart.

The excitement of winning his first Cup race had to have confused him. He hadn't meant to kiss me, had he?

Mistake or not, he *had* kissed me, and no kiss would ever compare to the emotional web Colton Tayler had tangled me into today. I was in big trouble.

chapter fifteen

I hadn't spoken to Colton since his very intimate, very public show of affection three days before, but he was due back some time today and my nerves were coiling into tight little balls. I couldn't take it anymore.

Dean and Colton were still in Vegas with Nancy, Colton's PR rep, to do some major Guardian Auto Insurance promos. With a win in his sponsor's hometown, Mr. Langdon had insisted they stay.

I, on the other hand, was too chickenshit to face Colton and the media frenzy surrounding him, so Dean made arrangements for me to fly back to Atlanta on a commercial flight and cab back to the house.

When I'd walked in the door, Lorna batted her eyelashes and flashed me a dish-it-girl grin. "I saw you two on TV. You were both so cute."

"No, we weren't," I'd scoffed before locking myself up in my room.

Dean gave me some extra days off work, not wanting to

bother Lorna and Annabelle's daily routine since he wasn't going to be there to drive me.

For the next two days, I'd snuck out to the barn to work on controlling my ability. Something odd had happened this past weekend, and I needed to understand what. My ability hadn't reacted to Colton's kiss. Obviously, my feelings for Colton had been the cause of my outbursts—yet I'd been closest to him during that kiss, and not one warning bell had gone off.

I opened myself up to the full range of emotions that surfaced when I thought of his touch, his lips, his scent, and—let's face it—his total hotness, in hopes of evoking a way to train myself to shut off my magnetic impulse at will. I hadn't had much luck as of yet.

The guys were due home any minute. Desperate, I opted to hide out in the barn and keep trying.

My current challenge was circling three items in midair while letting the memory of the dance Colton and I shared fill my mind. How his body had hugged mine, the feel of his arms around my waist, his breath hitting my neck. I even tried to conjure up the thoughts I had that night. My head pulsed, and whirlwinds of magnetic energy fogged my mind. One of the items, a large tire iron, strayed from the rest. With a firm image of Colton's vivid eyes looking down on me while surrounded by flickering DJ lights, I managed to sense the straying object through the emotions and focused it back into the circle.

"Yes!"

Then, just as quickly, the tire iron wobbled and then shot itself across the barn, heading for the one of the old hay stalls. I scrunched my face and squeezed my eyes shut. The tire iron broke through the wall with a loud, wood-splintering crash.

Oh, please God, tell me Lorna didn't hear that from the house.
"Lexi?"

My eyes shot wide open. My heart leaped into my throat.
Shit. Colton.

I launched the remaining two items into a pile of old hay
in the corner of another empty stall, then rushed to preoccupy
myself with gathering a large braided rope off the ground at the
far end of the barn.

"Lexi, are you in here?"

I took a deep breath tried to find my inner calm. "In here."

Colton appeared in the doorway with a half-smile on his
face. "I thought Lorna didn't want us in here?" He leaned his
forearm against the doorframe above his head.

I turned away and hung the rope on one of the hooks
protruding from the wooden beam above me. "She didn't—
doesn't. She doesn't know I'm here." My knees weakened. It was
like I'd forgotten what he looked like and I was seeing him again
for the first time. His arms bulged from his plain brown t-shirt,
tight at his chest and loose at his waist, leaving his abdominal
situation to the imagination, but what made me almost lose it
was the hint of a thin black necklace around his neck.

He nodded to the hole in the plywood ahead. "What
happened there?"

I picked up an old leather tool belt from the ground and
hung it on the hook next to the rope.

"Not sure. Maybe one of Lorna's ghosts did it."

Colton laughed, then moved closer. "Why didn't you answer
any of my texts?"

"I've been busy with school and stuff."

He reached for my hand. "Lexi."

I faced him, trembling and nervous. Noticing, he let go, frowned, and shoved his hand in his pocket. "Dean asked if we could watch Annabelle while he and Lorna go out tonight. He feels kinda bad for missing their date night on Monday."

"Sure. I'll go wash up." I dusted my hands together and stepped past him toward the house. I didn't look back, but his heavy footsteps followed me up the slope. Dean and Lorna were on their way out when we reached the front porch.

"Oh, good. We were just about to holler at y'all. Annabelle's playing in the family room."

Colton went straight for the door. "I got her. You guys go have fun."

An evening alone with Colton. The reality sunk in, and my stomach turned.

Lorna pursed her lip, and she leaned in close. "Are you okay? You don't look so good."

"I'm fine. Promise. Go on and have a good time."

"Okay. We won't be too late." I watched them get in the truck and pull out of the driveway, then headed inside where a tickle fight had already begun. Annabelle screamed and giggled.

Anxiety clutched my insides. I couldn't do this. I aimed my sight at the stairs. "I'm going to take a shower. You two eat. I'm not hungry." I hurried out of sight before Colton could respond. What was wrong with me? I couldn't think straight. I couldn't even look at him.

I took my sweet time, afraid to face the living, breathing temptation waiting for me downstairs, but after two hours, I didn't have much of a choice. As I neared the bottom of the stairs, my attention drew to Annabelle laughing and clapping as the big, strong Colton held her tiny toy phone in his massive looking hand and conversed with whoever Annabelle told him was on the other end. A muffled laugh escaped me, and Colton turned.

"What are you laughing at?"

My heart fluttered. "You."

He smiled and turned back to Annabelle. "I think it's bedtime."

"Nooo," she protested.

"Come on, Anna Banana, you promised after this last phone call that you would go to bed like a big girl."

"No." She stomped her foot and shook her pigtails. I bit my lip to stop from laughing. Her attitude reminded me of Gwen.

"Will you go if Lexi takes you?"

Annabelle looked at me and grimaced, then dropped her head in a sulk. "Okay."

I held out my hand, and she dragged her tiny feet, pouting. I picked her up, brought her up the stairs to her room, and tucked her into her Tinkerbell bed sheets. I swear this kid was obsessed with the green leaf-wearing fairy. Her room looked like Pixie Hollow had thrown up all over the walls. I stayed with her for a bit, avoiding having to face Colton downstairs, but I knew I couldn't stay here all night. I had to go back.

When I finally built up the nerve, I found Colton standing in front of the bay window. A nest of butterflies deep down in my gut opened and fluttered into my chest at the sight of him, his back to me, his hands in his jeans pockets.

I began picking up Annabelle's toys, dumping them one by one into the open toy box near the TV next to where Colton stood. I caught him glancing at me from the corner of his eye each time I came close.

Man, why was being alone with him so awkward now?

"You're good with her," I said finally, not daring to look at him.

"I wish it were that easy with you," he replied, still gazing out the window.

His words caught me off guard. I straightened, clutching a stuffed pink elephant in both my hands. What was that supposed to mean? I spun around to ask him that very question, but stubbed my toe on the toy phone on the floor. I winced, dropped the stuffed animal, and skipped forward with an ungraceful flail of my arms. Colton lunged to catch me. I latched onto him with more momentum than he expected and took him down with me instead. His back hit the floor, and I stumbled over the top of him, our arms and legs tangled and knotted together in a mess.

He looked up at me, eyes bulging. An uncontrolled laugh burst from my lungs. "Oh, my God, are you okay?"

His jaw relaxed, and a smile spread across his face. His body, stretched out under me, convulsed with laughter. "I'm okay." He reached up, grazed my cheek, and slid his hand to the back of my head. "I'm okay," he repeated, this time with a soft exhaled breath.

He lifted his head off the ground, closing the gap between our faces. My heart quickened, pounding in my chest faster than a piston at red line. My gaze was caught in the net of his stare. It was as if he were waiting for me to move, bolt, kick him in the nuts, something—all things I should have thought of doing. Instead, I froze, and all I could think about was his breath on my lips. I wanted to be free from his spell, from the way he made me feel, but I couldn't. I couldn't laugh away this moment. My mouth refused to let me. Colton tucked in his lower lip, slid it back out from the grasp of his teeth slowly, as if restraining himself. Then, without warning, he tilted his head and pressed his lips against mine.

Every nerve and muscle in my body melted together. His fingers trailed from the back of my head to my neck, then down to my waist where his other hand already rested, leaving behind a path of warm tingles and shivers. Was this really happening?

I moved my hand to his neck, his shoulder, then flattened my palm against his chest. The rush of his pulse intoxicated me, seared my skin with heat, and flooded my mind with a static haze.

Static. Haze. Thumping temples … Hell, no. Not now.

I pushed myself up off him. "I can't. Colton, please. I can't do this. I just can't." I backed away and squeezed my eyes shut.

"Lexi."

"Please, Colton, don't." I turned and held the tips of my fingers over my lips. I'd never been kissed before, not like this. Not like … My temples flared and pulsed worse than they ever had before. Not without losing control.

"Why?" Colton stood. "Have I done something wrong? Do I disgust you?"

I shook my head. "No. Oh, God, no."

"Then what is it?" He walked up close behind me and squeezed my shoulder. "You don't like me that way. Is that it? If it is, please tell me. Tell me I read you wrong when we danced the other night. Tell me you didn't feel what I—"

I raised my hand, palm out. "Stop. I can't tell you that. I can't tell you anything." Tears clung to my lower lashes, on the verge of spilling over. I wanted nothing more than to give in to what

I truly wanted, but I couldn't do that. He'd never understand.

"Talk to me, Lex. Trust me, confide in me. I'm here for you." He looked at me with the same look Annabelle used when pleading for her favorite afternoon snack.

"I can't. No one would ever understand. I don't want to hurt you."

"Hurt me? This *is* hurting me."

My heart plummeted. "No, it's worse than that. You don't—"

"I don't care." He wrapped his arms around me and raked his fingers through my hair, pulling it away from my face as he searched my eyes.

"Please," I pleaded, looking up at him. "Please, I don't want to hurt you or anyone else."

Colton's lips twitched. "I can't stay away from you."

"You have to try." I pushed him back. "You really have to try."

I headed for the stairs. I had to get away from him, away from all this, but he caught me by the waist, swung me around, and pulled me against him with a low, whispered plea. "Please don't deny me this."

His lips parted and pressed against mine once more, this time harder, needier, his tongue caressing mine with quick, soft touches as his arms enveloped me in tingling euphoric heat.

I tried to fight it, but lost.

My pulse quickened again, and so did the throbbing in my temples. What was odd was that I didn't feel the pain that usually accompanied the warning. Colton drew away. I opened my eyes and met his waiting gaze, and then scanned the room. Nothing had moved, levitated, or overturned. How could that be? All the signs were there but one—I felt no pain. Shit should have started hitting the fan by now, but for some reason, I had complete control. It was as if acting on my feelings for Colt caused my body to not fight back. My senses were embracing him the way *I* desperately wanted to. Could it be that simple? Could learning to embrace my emotions and stop fighting them be the answer?

Colton's arms loosened around me, and his whole face frowned. "I'm sorry. I shouldn't have—"

"No!" I smiled at him, still shocked, and pulled him back toward me. "I am. I'm the one who's sorry."

This time, I kissed him, not wanting to think of the consequences. This was where I wanted to be for the first time in my life. To hell with the rest.

Colton backed me against the wall, hips pressing against mine. I tugged at his shirt, wanting to touch his skin underneath, but then let go and clenched my hands. Was I moving too fast? I was new at this. I didn't know what to do.

He backed away, pulled his shirt over his head, and reached for the hem of my tank top. I raised my arms and let him pull it off me, revealing my black lace bra. I thought I would be embarrassed, shy, maybe even scared, but I wasn't. I'd never felt so comfortable. He slid my bra strap over my shoulder with a silky smooth graze of his hand and replaced it with his lips. He was definitely more experienced at this than I was, which was no surprise.

Hello! Gorgeous stock car racing superstar versus hermit and freak of nature.

A sound vibrated from my throat, almost like a sigh, when the tips of his hair hit my burning skin. I couldn't help it. I didn't want it to end.

Bright headlights beamed through the bay window. Colton pulled away and froze. "Shit," he groaned. Concealed by the shadow of the wall, we clung to each other, our bodies rising and falling, struggling to regain our breath. "They're home."

He lunged for our clothing, which he'd thrown toward the staircase. We hurried to get our shirts back on and threw ourselves on opposite ends of the couch. My face burned. No way would they not be able to tell what had just happened between us.

Colton turned on the TV to some random news channel just as Dean and Lorna stepped through the front door.

"Hey, guys. How was dinner?" Colton asked them, trying to appear nonchalant.

My stomach groaned at the mention of dinner. But was it hunger for food or for more of what I'd just had?

"Good," Lorna said, using more syllables than needed, and then threw some questioning glances at Colton and me. "And what about you two? How'd things go?"

"Great," Colton replied enthusiastically. I muffled a laugh and kicked him in the shin. He eyed me with a grin, then looked back at Dean and Lorna.

"Uh huh." Dean nodded. He cleared his throat and added. "You should head on out to bed. We have to get to the shop early to make sure everything's in order before we fly out tomorrow afternoon."

Colton saluted him. "Yes, boss."

"That goes for you too, Lexi."

"Aye, aye, captain." I did the same.

Lorna nudged her husband, who stood there probably waiting for us to comply. When he didn't get the hint, she cleared her throat and pushed him into the kitchen, out of sight. "Goodnight, you two."

Colton shifted forward, gave my hand a squeeze, and lowered his lips to my ear. "Will you be okay?"

I smiled. I was more than okay. I was happier than I'd ever been, but deep down I knew it couldn't last. Despite the absence of a magnetic disaster tonight—a fact that still boggled my mind—my ability would eventually drive a wedge between us. If embracing my emotions was the answer in some situations, it still wasn't a cure. And having tasted Colton's lips, tasted the freedom of giving in to what I wanted for the first time, I wasn't sure I'd be able to survive giving it all up.

But for now ... right now, I felt more than okay. I felt normal.

chapter sixteen

I hurried up the ladder to the top of the hauler the second we arrived in the infield at Bristol Motor Speedway, the track deemed the world's fastest half mile. They weren't kidding. This place looked more like a football stadium on steroids than a racetrack. I spun around, gawking at the grandstands surrounding the oval.

"Whoa."

Colton stepped off the ladder behind me.

I knew it was him. His scent had been forcing my heart to turn cartwheels ever since I'd laid eyes on him this morning.

"Impressive, huh?"

"This is insane. You're going to get yourself killed out there. It's like the size of a dirt track, only made of concrete. And the banked turns are nuts. "

"Nah, it's a lot bigger than that, and the banks ain't as bad as you think," he said, shoving his hands into his pockets and rocking from the balls of his feet to his heels. "They used to be banked even higher than this. Thirty-six degrees, I think. That was before my time, though. They dropped the angle to about thirty when they resurfaced it seven or eight years ago."

I looked up again. "I feel like a tiny raisin at the bottom of a fruit bowl."

Colton reached for my belt loop and pulled me against him. "Hey! You comparin' us drivers to dried up fruit?"

I flicked the beak of his ball cap. "You do taste like one."

"Oh, do I?" His teasing eyes gleamed as he wet his lips and moved them down on mine. This had to be what it felt like to be a normal teen. And happy. I was definitely happy.

"Come on, guys, we have work to do," Lenny shouted from below. "We need to set up the rolling garage."

I pulled back. "What's he blabbering about?"

"Well, if you haven't noticed, there's not much room in the infield for garage space."

"There's no garage?" I leaned to the side and looked around, still holding on to Colton and swept my gaze at the infield around us.

"Nope."

"So where does—"

"Out in the open, near the pits."

"Huh." I looked down the front straight. "Not much room for forty-three cars."

Colton spun me 180 degrees and wrapped his arms around me from behind. "That's why there are pits stalls on this side too."

"That's so insane."

He chuckled in my ear. "So you've mentioned."

"Guys, come on," Lenny cried.

"Keep your pants on, we're coming," Colton yelled down at him, and then turned me back around. "After I get another taste of this raisin." He nuzzled his face in my neck and kissed his way to the edge of my shoulder.

I giggled.

Again with the giggles. Girly, happy, giddy giggles. The whole concept of giggling like a ditz felt foreign to me, but I liked it.

Back on solid ground, I spotted Carl Stacy talking to Lenny five spots over from our hauler.

"Hey, Colt," I whispered. "Check it out."

Colton jumped off the last few steps of the ladder.

"What do you suppose he wants with Lenny this time?" I asked.

"Beats me. Maybe he's trying his luck again."

"Doesn't it bother you?"

Colton shrugged. "It does, but there's nothing we can do. Lenny has a wife and four kids to support. He's gotta think of them. If Carl offers him a ridiculous amount of money that Dean can't match, he'd be stupid not to go."

"Would he up and leave mid-season?"

"Nah, Lenny wouldn't do that."

I creased my forehead. Something felt off, but I couldn't figure out what. Lenny appeared to be smiling, so I guessed everything was good.

"Colton Tayler."

Colton shifted in the direction of the drawling voice. A partial smile spread across his face. "Mitch Benson. To what do I owe this honor?" He extended an open palm to the lanky older man.

"Wanted to congratulate you on your win last week. How does it feel to win your first Cup race?"

"I could get used to it."

"I told my crew chief not to let your rookie stripe fool him. You were a rising star last year. I'm not surprised to see you in the Cup this year."

"Thanks, man. Coming from you, that means a lot."

"Rookie stripe?" I asked.

Mitch placed a hand on Colton's shoulder. "Rookies, like Colton here, get to sport the dreaded yellow tape on their back bumper so that us veterans know to be a bit more cautious around them on account of their lack of experience."

"Oh." I cupped a hand over my eyes to block the sun's glare. "I just thought that was part of the car's paint scheme."

Mitch laughed.

I glanced back over at Carl and Lenny, itching to know what Carl's strategy was this time. Mitch looked up and then dropped his hand off Colton's shoulder. "Man, that tyrant never gives up." He looked back at Colton. "Sorry about that."

"No worries, man. In the end it's Lenny's decision. No hard feelings."

"Carl's gotten me this far in my career and I respect him for that, but he can be an ass. He's desperate for me to pull a championship hat trick this season. I mean, I want to win, but he makes it seem like there's no other choice. Doesn't make it much fun anymore, you know what I mean?"

"How desperate is he?"

I probably should have kept my mouth shut, but I had to ask.

Mitch seemed taken aback by my question. "Hey, yeah, I heard about the sabotage. Listen, Carl can be a dirtbag, but I don't think he has it in him to cheat."

Colton glared at me. "Don't worry, Mitch. Even with Dean and Carl's history, we're not accusing anyone without proof."

"Well, anyway, good luck this weekend." He leaned closer. "And don't get too used to winning. The big man's not the only one working toward that hat trick."

Colton grinned. "We'll see about that." Mitch patted him on the shoulder, then strolled away. I wondered if he really, truly thought Carl was innocent in all of this.

Colton tugged at my belt loop. "What's wrong?"

"I don't know. I still think his team had something to do with your sabotage in Phoenix."

"Maybe, but I doubt Mitch had anything to do with it. He wouldn't jeopardize his career like that."

"Colton, there you are. I've been looking everywhere for you." Nancy ran over, panting over her clipboard. "Are you forgetting you have an interview with the local station in—" she checked her Blackberry "—ten minutes?"

Colton glanced at his watch. "Oh, shit."

"Yeah, oh shit. Get a move on."

He took my hand and planted a firm but gentle peck on my lips. "Gotta go. I'll see you later."

"See ya."

With a slight smile, he let go of my hand and jogged off to catch up with Nancy.

"Coming through!" Dylan hollered, rolling two radial slicks past me toward the tent being set up by the rest of the crew.

I stepped back to get out of the way, colliding into someone behind me. "Oh, sorry!"

Lenny stood there, sweating profusely and looking flustered. "Oh, no, sweetheart, it's my fault. Too much on my mind." He glanced around. "Where'd Colt go?"

"PR stuff. Nancy came and got him, but I can help if you need me to."

He pulled out a handkerchief and dabbed his hairline and neck. It was hot, but nowhere near enough to cause him to sweat this much.

"You sure you're okay? You don't look like your normal self."

"I'm fine. You go. The crew's almost done setting up here, anyway." He wobbled off before I could say another word, seeming preoccupied with his own thoughts and leaving me wondering if he was actually weighing Carl's new offer.

Since the crew didn't need me, I took a stroll around the infield to pass the time, making sure to investigate the rooftop winner's circle above one of the few buildings occupying the center of the stadium.

On my way back to the hauler, a strong hand firmly gripped my upper arm. "You're Lexi, right?" The deep, raspy southern voice sent a chill down my back. Carl Stacy stood next to me, his face shadowed by the large cowboy hat he wore.

I played dumb and arched my eyebrow. "Who wants to know?"

"We haven't been formally introduced. The name's Carl Stacy. I'm—"

"Mitch Benson's team owner."

He leaned closer. "So, you have heard of me. Only good things, I hope."

"Not exactly." I wrinkled my nose at the stench of chewing tobacco. "You're the guy trying to take Lenny away from Dean, and the guy desperate enough to sabotage Colton's chances at making The Chase."

His grip tightened. "You're a lippy little thing, aren't you, darlin'? I shouldn't have expected less from a salvage yard floozy. It's sweet you think he even stands a chance at winning the cup."

I snarled and wiggled myself out of his grasp.

"Oh, I know all about you. Lexi Adams. You're Dean's little charity case."

"You know nothing." I spun away, but Carl blocked my retreat and towered over me. The man eclipsed the sun, leaving me standing in his shadow.

"I hear you're good with your hands, that you're quick at taking things apart. Tell me. How do you do it? I've never seen or heard of a trained mechanic that can yank an engine out as fast as you did a few weeks ago. How is it that you can?"

"Natural talent, I guess."

A smirk crept up one side of his face. "Oh, I don't know about that. You're hiding something."

"I am not. I'm just used to dismantling things, that's all. Now if you'll excuse me." I took a few steps back.

He tipped his hat. "Alright, then. I'll see you 'round ... Miss Magic Fingers." He strolled off, keeping a confident swagger to his step.

Magic fingers? This guy's creep factor had just risen to a new level. If I had any doubts left about this man's involvement in the sabotage, they were gone now. His fascination with my skill made me nervous. Could he be smart enough to figure me out? I didn't care what Mitch said. Carl Stacy was a little too interested in what DSG Racing was up to not to be involved.

I shook the shivers from my shoulders and hurried back

to the hauler for a chance to hitch a ride back to the motor coach lot outside the stadium. I wasn't going to let Carl ruin my good mood. Colton would be back soon, and that was all that mattered.

chapter seventeen

It'd been three days and still I couldn't shake the creepy -crawly sensations slithering inside me due to my run-in with Carl. Something about the way he called me "Magic Fingers" really got under my skin, and I kept trying to figure out what he meant by the nickname he'd given me. No one had ever seen me use my ability, so how could he suspect that my skills were anything but a natural-born talent?

I didn't tell Colton about the confrontation. I didn't want him to worry before his race. He'd qualified third on Friday and was excited with the car's overall setup. Telling him would only dampen his good mood.

Carl's hauler sat in the parking space next to ours and, as I feared, he'd perched himself up on the roof, waiting for the race to begin. The idea of having that man so close for the next 500 laps churned my stomach.

Colton tugged my arm and whirled me around. "You coming?"

I bit my lip to hide my grin. I still hadn't gotten used to how good he looked in his race suit, ball cap, and shades. Really, what was it about guys in uniforms? I could've sat there and stared at him all day. Colton pulled me close and led me to his car. The anthem played and the jets flew by. I covered my ears as their piercing sounds funneled and echoed inside the large stadium.

When it was over, Colton removed his hat and set it on my head, pulling it so low over my eyes that I had to tilt my head back to look at him. He chuckled and pulled me toward him. "I'll see you in five hundred laps."

"Play safe."

He leaned down and captured my lips in a bruising kiss. My mind fogged and I curled my toes. I clutched his neck, not wanting to let him go, as though this kiss would be our last. Every fiber in me wanted to cling to him, but I had to let him go. His hands left my waist and gripped the top of the open window of his stock car. He swung inside, handed me his shades, and strapped himself in. Something ached in my gut, sucking the happiness right out of me and I didn't know why. He smiled at me while placing his earpiece, then pulled on his helmet. Lenny fastened his window net.

It was time to go.

Why was I so worried? I was going to be in his arms again within the next few hours. I hurried to meet Dean on the roof.

"Drivers, start your engines!"

Fans cheered, cars roared to life, and my heart hammered inside my chest. This race, although five hundred laps long, was going to be fast-paced. The cars took to the track, the green flag dropped, and I sat on the edge of my seat. Colton drove great, keeping up with the best and staying out of the few crashes that happened early on.

Dean tensed when the pits opened and it came time for the first scheduled pit stop. Dean always tensed at this point. Colton wasn't the only one with a job out there; the entire pit crew had a hand in the team's success. A speedy, well-executed stop meant the difference between coming out in front or in last place.

Colton ducked onto pit road and tucked the car quick and easy in front of his marker. We were off to a good start. Within a blink of an eye, the crew had jacked the passenger side ready for the tire change, but then they stalled.

"Come on guys, let's go!" Colton yelled.

The crew scrambled. Something wasn't working.

"What the hell's going on, chief?"

I could see Lenny wiping his brow, looking stressed and panicked. Dean cued his mic. "Come on, guys, everyone else is already back out on the track."

"Guns are jammed, boss!"

"What do you mean 'Guns are jammed'? *All* of them?"

"Dammit!" Colton said.

"All but one," Lenny replied, his voice shaken.

"A four-tire change with one impact wrench? Son of a—" Dean tore past me and practically jumped down the ladder. By the time he reached the pit stall they had managed to get Colton back out on the track.

"Three laps down," Jimmy announced.

"Son of a fu—"

"Colton. The kids," Dean reminded him. Fans young and old could listen in during races. Colton needed to control his anger. My heart went out to him, but I kept my hopes high. At any other track, the delay could have cost him big, but with Bristol being such a short track, Colton still had a fighting chance at recovery.

Colton rounded the first and second turns and an eerie feeling fell over me again. I refocused, looked around and saw Carl staring at me from his hauler. He flashed me a crooked grin before leaning over his railing to spit. I scrunched my face in disgust. *That's attractive.*

He continued to stare my way with an all-knowing gleam in his eyes. Like a man with a secret he could hardly contain. Had this last pit stop issue been his fault? Had Carl found a way to sabotage the crew's tools? I blinked and forced my attention back out to Colton coming around for his next lap.

"You're gaining positions," Colton's spotter blared through my head set. "Hang in there."

Colton said nothing. I took a peek down at the pits. Dean, paced furiously while race officials tried to calm him down. I felt for him. His first Cup season had barely begun and twice his team had fallen victim to sabotage. NASCAR still wasn't even in a position to do anything about it other than add this latest incident to the ongoing investigation.

In no time, Colton made his way back up the field into the lead, still gaining positions.

"You're doing great, Colt. You're running faster than the leader. At this rate, you'll catch up to him quick," Lenny told him.

Colton remained silent. My heart ached for him to respond. I desperately wanted to hear his voice, but dead air filled my headset.

Dean remained in the pits, probably wanting to keep an

eye on the tools and equipment after they'd been replaced and inspected. The following stops moved as flawlessly as they usually did, and with thirty laps left to go, I couldn't stand still. Every nerve in my body was on fire.

Colton ran with the leaders again.

I shot a glance at Carl. He couldn't be too happy that this incident hadn't kept Colton away from Mitch.

They were now neck-and-neck for the second spot. Colton went high then tucked down close to Mitch. I noticed Carl wildly gesturing as he shouted into his mic, but I couldn't hear what he was saying.

"Twenty laps to go," cued Jimmy.

Cars rumbled around the track more loudly than at any race I'd been to so far. The bowl-shaped stadium and concrete banked track amplified the noise, intensifying the atmosphere.

Colton and Mitch moved ahead of the leader.

This was it, the chase to the checkers. I didn't know whether to be sick or to scream my lungs out with encouragement.

They slowed and banked into turn four. Mitch jerked up against Colton, forcing him up the bank and into the wall.

"What the ..." Colton yelled in my ears.

"Again." I heard Carl cheering from his rooftop. Mitch ducked low, and up he went again, crashing sideways into Colton's car.

"Someone tell that guy to lay off!" Colton screamed.

"Message is on its way," Lenny shouted, telling Colton he'd already radioed the race officials to relay the message.

"Take that car out of this race or your career is over," Carl yelled. I snapped my head toward him. Had I heard right?

Mitch dipped low into turn one and bashed up against

Colton, sending him into the SAFER barrier. My eyes grew wide. This was all Carl's doing. He was threatening Mitch's career to get him to do his dirty work.

The former leader came up quick behind Colton, boxing him in with nowhere else to go.

"Behind you," Jimmy called out, but it was too late.

The nose of the fourth place car scooped up Colton's rear end and propelled it up into the air.

The scream that escaped my throat burned on its way out.

Colton's car tumbled at speeds only an Olympic gymnast on a competition floor could achieve down the embankment, end-to-end.

My chest ached from screaming.

Carl watched the scene, smiling and enjoying every second.

"You did this!" I screamed at him.

Violent pulses hammered inside my head, trying to let my curse break free. My mind hazed with static and magnetic energy. I gripped the aluminum railing, watching Colton's car get ripped to shreds. Chunks of rubber and plastic broke off and propelled into the air each time his car made contact with the ground. Another car collided with him, sending him back up the turn only to roll back down after smashing into the wall again. The next blow came from the inside, crushing him against the SAFER barrier.

I leaned over the railing, trying to see through the thick gray smoke rising from the scene. Mitch was going after him for the final blow. Burnt rubber, leaking fuel, and hot motor oil filled my lungs. Sparks of tiny, white lights exploded in my head and an excruciating pain sliced through my temples. Every inch in me filled with hurt. My ability simmered, fueled by my rage, and I could no longer control it, I could no longer contain the beast that was ripping through my defenses. Pain seared through me as I involuntarily reached my arm out toward the track. I tensed and tried to refocus, but when Mitch's car hurtled up into the air, I knew my last attempt at containing my curse had failed. All I could do now was watch through a haze of my tears as the roof of his car hit the pavement on the high side of turn two with a sickening crash. It skidded to the bottom of the track, its body torn to pieces, roll cage exposed.

Colton. Where was Colton?

Eyes frantic, I searched the rest of the chaos until I found him, his car back on all four tires at the base of the bank nearest to the flat surface in front of pit road.

Race officials and paramedics rushed onto the track. I tumbled back, clutching my shirt where my heart felt like it was pounding out of my chest. My scorched lungs squeezed and burned with my every breath. This had to be a dream. This couldn't be real. I hadn't just lost my marbles in front of all these people. I hadn't ...

I rolled onto my stomach, gripped the bottom rail of the railing, and lifted my heavy head. Carl Stacy stared back at me, his eyes as wide as his sockets allowed, mouth agape in horror. Why was he staring at me like that? Had he seen what I'd done?

Tears streamed down my face, pooling over my lip. I wiped them away with the back of my hand.

Blood.

Bright red smears covered my fingers and sent my gut rolling. I frantically clawed at my face with the pads of my fingers and the back of my hands, seeing more red, more blood. Not only did I have a nosebleed, but I was crying blood. I looked up at

Carl, at his unchanged, fear-stricken face. He saw everything. He'd seen what I'd done. He knew it was me.

"Lexi!"

The hauler swayed with Dean's hurried steps up the ladder. "Come on, we'll meet Colt at the medical care faci—"

I faced him, still on my stomach.

Dean gasped. He threw himself at the railing and leaned over the edge. "I need a medic! Damn it, I need a medic up here, now!"

He knelt down next to me and pulled off my ball cap and headset.

"Christ, Lexi, what the hell happened?" His hand brushed back my hair. My short, gurgling breath struggled to reach my scorching lungs. One word managed to slip out my lips.

"Colton?"

"Shh … Colton's going to be fine." Dean looked down at his shaking, blood-covered hands, then wrapped them around me, rocking me back and forth.

"Lexi. Oh, Lord, Lexi. What happened to you?" His voice faded. My heavy head fell against his chest. I was numb, unable to feel anything. Haze and darkness enveloped my mind. I tried to fight it, tried to stay awake, but everything swirled … and then it all went black.

chapter eighteen

I opened my eyes just a sliver. Flourescent lights turned the inside of my eyelids a pale orange. Panic bubbled up inside me, and I sat straight up on the bed, eyes wide. *Where the hell am I?*

"Lexi, calm down," a voice sternly instructed.

I curled my fingers around the metal bed rails. Pain stabbed the back of my left hand. There was medical tape crisscrossed over the hilt of a needle jabbed into my skin, hooking me to a fluid bag hanging from a stand to my left.

This was it, wasn't it? My worst nightmare come to life. I'd been thrown into an institution, or locked up in a research facility. "Oh, God, no. Not now, please."

"Shhh, Lexi. It's me ... it's Dean."

This time the voice registered. I looked at him. "Dean?"

"It's me, kiddo."

I took another panicked look around the room. "Where am I?"

"You're in the hospital."

Hospital? I took a moment to digest the word and then

forcibly relaxed.

"Why am I in a hospital? What's happened … oh, God, did I …?"

"Shhh. It's okay. Just lay back down. You're okay." Dean put his hands on my shoulders and guided me back down until my head rested on the pillow. He leaned over me, his face etched with worry and relief.

Quick, unsequenced images of an accident sped through my mind. The bittersweet smell of fuel, the scorching scent of burning rubber, and the sound of twisting metal began to accompany the memory flashes. It was all coming back to me.

"Colton!"

"He's okay. Colton is fine," Dean tried to reassure me, but the look on his face told another story. Was he lying to me?

"Where is he? Where's Colton?"

"The doctors cleared him to leave yesterday. He wanted to stay here with you, but I made him go home. He's pretty banged up, but after a little rest, he should be good to get back in the saddle for next weekend's race." A faint smile formed on Dean's lips, but the look of concern still lingered in his features.

Bad news was coming.

"But, Lexi, something *did* happen." I knew it.

"It's … Mitch."

My insides twitched. "Is he …?"

"No, but he's in critical condition. There was this freak outcome to the accident that no one can explain." Dean rubbed his forehead between his thumb and fingers. "Whatever it was, it saved Colton, but Mitch didn't get so lucky."

Freak outcome? As in *my* outcome? I sprung forward again, but Dean anticipated my move and held his arm out across the upper part of my chest and shoulders. "Maybe I shouldn't have told you this so soon."

"Is he going to be okay?"

"Doctors don't know yet. It's touch and go. But you shouldn't worry about that right now." He slid his arm back, pausing to give my shoulder a gentle rub.

"Lexi, do you have any medical conditions I should tell the doctors about?"

"I don't think so, why? Did they find something wrong with me?" I'd avoided doctors since my curse had morphed, afraid that my ability could be physiologically detectable.

"That's just it. They couldn't find anything wrong with you, which makes it difficult to explain why you were covered in blood. Or why the roof of the hauler dented in under you."

"What day is it?"

"It's Tuesday. You've been out for a few days."

Days? I'd been here for days? Bile rose to the back of my throat. I'd been in fear of my ability for years, but now I was just plain terrified. I'd never lost control this big before. How was it even possible?

"What the hell happened up there, Lex?"

I turned away and stared out the small gap in the window curtains. Sunlight spilled in, glaring off the dust particles drifting through the air. Probably late morning or early afternoon, by the looks of it. What could I say? It was me? That I was the one who launched Mitch's car through the air? I turned my head back toward him. "I don't know."

"You should've seen Carl's face when I brought you down the ladder. He couldn't keep his eyes off you." Dean moved his hand into mine and brushed a strand of my hair off my face with his other. "There's something you're not telling me, isn't there?"

I faced the curtains again, too ashamed to look him in the eye. How could I tell him? How could I make someone normal believe that I had the ability to magnetize and control steel and iron with a simple thought? That because of me, Mitch Benson might die? He would have me committed.

"I hate to suggest this, but maybe I should give Carl a call. Maybe he could tell us what happened."

"Dean, no. Please don't do that. The doctor said I was fine, right? Why bring him into all this?"

"Don't you want to know what happened to you? Maybe something he tells us will trigger your memory—"

I tensed and shook my head. "Please don't. Promise me you won't."

"Okay, okay, I won't." He was confused. I could tell. But what else could I do?

How could I have been so stupid? How could I have let myself lose control like that? I had this thing controlled for two whole years before Colton came along. And even then, I thought I'd nipped that problem in the bud as of late. But obviously I'd been wrong. At Gwen's party, when I'd mentally flung the pitcher of water at her, I hadn't meant to, but I'd been jealous. She'd kissed Colton right in front of me. And at the track, when I saw Mitch going after Colton again, I wanted to protect him. Protect Colton. All these outbursts still revolved around Colton and my feelings for him.

The walls were closing in on me. I couldn't breathe. "I want to get out of here. Please get me out of here." My voice cracked.

"Lexi … I really think we should at least—"

"No," I cut him off. I looked him, my eyes thick, my face burning.

Dean's shoulders fell. "Let me get the doctor and see if we can have you discharged."

He left the room. A tear broke free and rolled down toward my chin. I quickly wiped it away and inspected my hand. No blood. I exhaled in relief.

My eyes had never bled before. I'd also never hurtled a car in the air from a distance before, either. Every ounce of my body wanted to protect Colton that night, and my ability had fed on that fact. But at what cost? Would I be responsible for Mitch's death if he didn't make it? Could I live with the guilt of killing someone? I glanced around the hospital room. Had I almost killed myself?

Dean reappeared at my side some minutes later. "The doctor said you can go home in the morning. They just want to keep you under observation for one more night."

I groaned.

"They would have released you right away if the MRI machine hadn't broken down while you were in it."

"They took an MRI?" Not good ... *so* not good.

"Apparently something went wonky when they tried to scan your brain. The images wouldn't show up. Without the machine and the scans, they want to keep an eye on you a bit longer."

Polarized magnets. They were lucky I hadn't subconsciously destroyed the thing. I still had nightmares about some of Roy's fridge magnets launching themselves and shattering the window when I walked into the kitchen the day after my freakout at the high school. It took me a while to learn how to control that. Of course, Roy thought I'd actually chucked them on purpose and gave me a good smack across the face for it.

"Get some rest. I'll go call home and let Lorna and Colton know you're awake."

I let my head sink fully into the pillow and exhaled a long breath. Why hadn't I just gone back home when I had the chance? Mitch wouldn't be in the intensive care unit, and I wouldn't feel so shitty for having to lie and dodge questions to keep my secrets.

Then again, Colton probably would've died.

∎∎∎

The doctors discharged me in the morning, but my blood tests revealed a slight iron deficiency. Go figure. So after prescribing me some iron supplements—which I had no plans on taking, for obvious reasons—they suggested that I follow up with Dean's family doctor in a week. Dean had the appointment set up by the time we landed in Atlanta.

When the truck rolled to a stop outside the main entrance to the shop not fifteen minutes after leaving the airport, I looked up, dazed and half-asleep.

"Why are we stopping here?"

"I need to grab a few things from the office." He stepped out. "Don't worry, everyone's gone for the day. The receptionist is the only one still here. I called ahead and asked her to stay until I got here."

I coiled into a ball against the seat and yawned.

"C'mon kiddo. I'm not leaving you out here."

Ugh, did I have to? I reached for the handle, pushed the door open with my shoulder, and let myself slide down from the truck.

Dean pulled the front door open to let me in, and both our heads darted toward the sound of Becky's heels clicking against the industrial tile flooring as she ran toward us. She reminded me of Mrs. Carter, my first grade teacher, when she'd run down the school hallways in her four-inch heels during fire drills, looking like that gold-plated robot from the Star Wars movies.

"Mr. Grant! Mr. Grant, I'm so sorry, sir, I couldn't stop him. He insisted on staying."

"Stop who?" Dean's forehead wrinkled in confusion.

"Mr. Stacy is waiting in your office."

"Carl Stacy?"

"Yes, sir."

I clenched my hands to hide the fact that they were trembling. The image of Carl staring at me from his hauler floated through my mind. He'd seen what I'd done. But I also knew what he'd done. Did Dean know about that yet?

"Here are the papers you wanted."

Becky handed him a brown, letter-sized envelope. Dean plucked it from her perfectly French manicured hand. "Did Mr. Stacy say what he wanted?"

She shook her head. "He wouldn't say. He just barged in when I was collecting the documents you asked me for in your office, and then sat down and said he wasn't moving until you arrived. I'm so sorry, Mr. Grant."

"That's okay, Becky." He gave her a reassuring tap on the shoulder. "I'll deal with him. Thanks for your help tonight." He turned to me. "Come on, Lex."

Dean opened the door to his office and let me in first. Carl sat in the pleather sofa against the wall to my right.

"Carl." Dean strolled in behind me. "Can I ask why you made yourself at home in my office after hours?"

Carl stood, eyed me, then faced Dean. "We have a serious matter to discuss."

"Oh? This should be good." Dean moved behind his desk, but remained standing. I cowered in the corner near the door, contemplating an escape.

"This new girl of yours …" He held his hat pinched between his thumb and ring finger and pointed it at me. "I know what she did. I don't know how she did it, but *she* wrecked my car."

Oh, shit.

"Excuse me, Carl, but what in Sam Hill are you talking about?"

"This young lady here, she can move things. Move things with her mind. I saw her do it, plain as day, and I'm pretty sure NASCAR would consider that cheating."

Dean laughed. "Do you have any idea how ridiculous that sounds?"

"Oh, I know, but that girl is the devil's child and I'm going to find a way to prove it. And believe me, when I do, your little operation here"—he swept his hat in front of him— "will cease to exist."

Dean scowled. "It's one thing to mouth off some wild accusations at me, but to come here and threaten my business, my employees, my livelihood? You've got some nerve, my friend."

"I'm warnin' ya, Dean. I know what I saw."

Dean bashed his palms on the surface of his desk so hard my nerves twitched. "No, I'm warning you. That stunt you pulled out on the track on Sunday did not go unnoticed. NASCAR might not have enough evidence to prove that you were behind the sabotage of my car and my equipment, but I know it was you and when I link you to that, adding to the crap you pulled over the airwaves, you won't even be allowed near a set of car keys."

Carl flinched when Dean raised his finger at him.

"Yes, Carl. NASCAR made me privy to your blackmail conversation with Mitch about putting Colton in the wall. You're already facing a fine and a possible suspension for that, but I can assure you that if they prove you're responsible for the sabotages, too, they will ban you for life."

"We'll just see about that. Meanwhile, I'd keep an eye on little Miss Magic Fingers if I were you." He pointed at me. "I may not have proof of her freaky-deaky psycho powers, but she had somethin' to do with what happened to Mitch and my car. You and I both know cars don't just catapult into the air like that, and she's costing me my championship."

"Get out, Carl, before I call security."

"I'm telling you, Dean, if you don't take her off the team, I will expose her. And then we'll see what NASCAR has to say."

"Get out!"

Carl put his hands up, pantomiming surrender. "Don't say I didn't warn you."

He winked at me with a grin sprawled across his fat, mustache wearin' face, and walked out. Dean fell into his desk chair, pinching the bridge of his nose.

I'd done this. I'd caused him all this stress, when all he tried to do was give me a better chance. I couldn't let this go on.

"Send me home."

Dean let his hand fall on his desk and narrowed his eyes.

"What?"

I moved toward him. "Send me home. You don't need me causing you any more trouble."

"Don't be ridiculous. Carl's just blowing smoke. I am not sending you back to that sadistic ..." He pursed his lips and took a deep breath through his nose. "You deserve better than that."

"You have to. There's no other choice. I can't be the cause of you losing your teams." Tears squeezed out the corners of my eyes and streamed down my face. "Because of me, Colton's racing career could be over."

"Lexi, what the hell are you talking about?"

I shook my head, fighting to find words without blurting out my secret.

Dean stood, came around his desk, and closed the gap between us.

"Please, don't ... just say you'll send me home." Sobs constricted my throat. I couldn't stop them. They just kept coming and coming. My vision blurred from all the tears pooling along the edge of my lashes.

Dean put his hands gently around my face, forcing me to look at him. "I can't help you and protect Colton if you don't tell me what you're hiding."

"I ... I can't tell you."

chapter nineteen

Dean's phone went off, interrupting his barrage of questioning. It was Lorna checking in to see what time we'd be home. Still trembling, I tried to refocus my thoughts and get a grip on my tears. I clenched my jaw, pushed my shoulders back, and braced myself for what would come next. When Dean ended his call, he took one look at me and understood that I wasn't going to say another word.

We drove home in silence, neither one of us acknowledging the other's presence. I shuddered at the thought of having to face Colton. I'd hoped to have a little more time with him, but I'd been fooling myself. Being with him had amped up my emotions, and the need to protect someone other than myself brought with it destruction and risk for all involved. The accident proved that. In the end, thanks to Carl's threats, I'd only destroy Colton's career. And if he found out it was all because of me, he'd despise me. I didn't want to let him go, but I had to. I had no other choice.

Seeing Colton sitting on the porch when we pulled into the

driveway tore a hole in my chest. Dean exited the cab of the truck without a word, patting him on the shoulder as he passed by before heading inside. Colton stood and waited for me to climb down from the truck, his thumbs hooked in his pockets, his hair blown by the wind, covering his eyes.

Thank God. I couldn't bear to face those eyes just yet. I took my time getting out, delaying the inevitable.

Colton ran his hand through his hair, pulling it back, and looked right at me. One peek at his green and blue eyes and every ounce of courage I'd managed to collect crumbled. I couldn't do this. I couldn't hurt him. The pain was too much.

He rushed toward me the second my foot touched the ground and pulled me into him, wrapping his arms tightly around me. My knees threatened to buckle as I let my lids fall. He smelled of baked apples and spices. Lorna must have made apple pie with dinner.

I can't do this. I can't do this.

I took a sharp breath and directed all my focus and energy to stop myself from crying—or lashing out with my curse.

"Thank the racing gods you're okay. You had me so worried. I begged Dean to let me stay at the hospital with you, but he wouldn't—"

I stepped out of his hold, my jaw clenching so tight it hurt.

The smile and relief on his face faded fast. "What's wrong? Do you need to sit down?" He tried to guide me toward the steps, but I pulled out of his grasp.

"No, I'm fine."

He reached for me again, his eyes creasing. "What is it, then?"

I pulled my arms back and wrapped them around myself.

"We can't do this anymore. I can't be with you."

There. I said it. Air escaped my lungs as if relieved, but I knew this conversation wasn't going to end here.

His expression melted and his face drained of all color. "What are you talking about?"

"Us. You. Me. We can't—"

"Lexi." He took a step closer. I readied myself to retreat, but he didn't attempt to touch me like I'd anticipated. "Was it the accident? Did it scare you?"

"No. It's not that." I fought the tears trying to break free and the urge to forget what I needed to say and crumple into his arms.

"Then what is it?"

"Carl made some accusations that could ruin DSG Racing and your career. I can't—I won't be the one to ruin your dream."

"Carl what?" Colton propped his hands on his hips and looked up at the cloudless night sky filled with stars. A perfect romantic setting wasted by heartache and pain. "He's one to talk, that lowlife son of a bitch." He dipped his head down to look at me again. "You shouldn't listen to his empty threats."

"His threats aren't exactly empty. Mitch almost died because of me." I turned away and buried my face in my hands. Shit. I'd said too much. The words singed my tongue—a sign that they shouldn't have been spoken.

Colton tucked his loose hair behind his ear. "Because of you? Lexi, I don't understand."

I had to tread carefully, or I would divulge everything without wanting to. I circled around and faced him again. "You don't need to understand, but we can't keep going on like this. The more distance there is between us and the less you know …

it might just be enough to save your career"—*and your life*—"in the end. I can't control myself around you."

He moved closer and took my face in his hands. I tried to pull away, but my back was against the truck. In a moment of weakness, I leaned into his touch and let the warmth of his hands spread across my face and overwhelm my body with pleasant emotions. If he didn't back away soon, I'd lose control. Not of my ability, but of my need to stay away to keep him safe.

"Please, Lexi, don't do this. We can get through this together." If only it were that simple. I sucked in a shaky breath that lodged itself in my throat when the soft brush of his lips grazed against my temple.

"You're not making this easy."

"I can't lose you. I've never cared for someone this way before; since that day you walked into our garage in Daytona. Ask anyone, I'm a better driver, a better everything because of you. I know you don't see that, but the crew does. Dean does. Please, you can't leave me."

I opened my eyes.

"That's bull. We've spent most of the past four weeks fighting."

"I was angry because I cared. Since the moment I first laid eyes on you; I couldn't stop thinking about you. I've wanted to know everything about you. And all of that ate away at me. Ah, Lex, if you had any idea how bad it bugged me that you wouldn't let me in—"

"I'll still be here. I'm not going anywhere. Dean won't let me go home. But I can't be with you, Colt … not like this. It's too dangerous."

Colton's eyes glistened in the dim light emitted by the

fixture above the garage door. They were glazed with hidden tears that I would never see fall. He swept his thumb across my cheek, leaving a trail of tingles in its path.

"Help me understand. Please." He swallowed hard and desperately searched my eyes. "I love you, Lex."

"No!" I dug up some strength and pushed past him furiously. My tears disobeyed me and rolled down my cheeks. How dare he play the love card right now? How dare he toy with me like this?

"Don't. Don't go there. You haven't known me long enough to say that."

He grabbed my arm. "I don't care. Time has nothing to do with it. It's how I feel that matters, and I know in my heart that I love you."

How could he say those words to me now? My heart ached. Hearing him say the three words I'd craved since my mother died tore my insides to shreds.

He cupped my face in his hands and pressed his lips to mine. I felt his need, his desperation. I gave in, savoring him one last time, the soft and sweet sensations that intoxicated me each time we touched, the last intimate moment we were ever going to share together—the last I was ever going to experience. Being around him for the rest of the race season was going to be torture, but at least I could go on living my solitary life knowing that I'd once been loved. That someone once cared enough to say those words to me, and that he would be living out his dream alive and safe. Colton would get over me eventually. In his profession, opportunities presented themselves every day.

He lingered, resting his hands against my cheeks. I pulled

away and pushed past him again, this time fast enough to avoid being pulled back in. I wouldn't be able to resist him if he did. I ran inside the house, slammed the door behind me, and leaned against it.

Colton's loud groan echoed in from the outside, and I cringed when I heard his fist impact with the garage door. Lorna and Dean looked over the back of the loveseat where they sat facing the television.

"Lexi." Lorna burst to life at the sight of me back in one piece, seemingly oblivious to what was going on outside. "It's good to see you." She frowned upon seeing my tear-smeared face and puffy eyes. "Sweetie, what's wrong?"

"I'll be in my room." My words came out dry and mean, not at all how I'd intended them to sound, but I couldn't pretend that my life was all puppies and rainbows right now. Lorna seemed taken aback by my abrupt response, but Dean nodded me off and murmured something to his wife.

I stormed up the stairs, into the darkness of my room, and threw myself on the bed. I cried until my eyes burned, then coiled myself into a ball, waiting for sleep to come—if it ever would again. I twirled two discarded yellow painted wheel nuts I'd picked up in Daytona at eye level next to the bed. I'd kept them as souvenirs of my first big race experience, but now they would forever remind me of the first day I laid my eyes on the only guy I'd ever come close to falling in love with. Deep down I already had—admitting it now would only worsen the excruciating pain in my heart.

Why did it have to be me? Why did I have to be the cursed one? People got struck by lightning all the time and lived to tell the tale without twisting molecules and attracting every metal object in sight. So why me? Other girls my age worried about their looks and what house party to attend on weekends, while I got to live my life worrying who I was going to hospitalize next because I got too excited, too angry, or was too in love.

I'd been given the short end of the good life stick. And it sucked.

chapter
twenty

I kept my nose buried in my work, trying to avoid running into or even thinking about Colton—one of the hardest things I ever had to do. Everywhere I looked, there he was. Not in an "oh, my God, my mind is playing tricks on me, and everyone looks like him" kind of way, but as in he literally was everywhere I went. At the dinner table, at the shop, outside working on his motorcycle wearing his khaki-colored button-down mechanic shirt left open to a white tee and a pair of faded jeans. Sigh.

Okay, okay. I knew avoiding him would be impossible, but I hadn't quite grasped just how torturous it would really be. I'd asked Dean if I could skip going to the track from now on and just work in the shop, but even he had a hard time looking me in the eye when he told me it wasn't an option. Talk about wanting to stab myself with in the head with a flat-head screwdriver.

Colton continued to stroll around looking as hot as ever in his racing suit, his formfitting shirts, or anything else he owned, really. Seeing him only made me want to scratch my eyes out more. He respected my wishes and kept his distance—no more motorcycle rides, no more hand holding during flights to and from the tracks—but his flirty smiles and twinkly-eyed glances when surrounded by fans—mostly of the female variety—didn't go unnoticed. I hated that he could make me swoon so easily. If he only knew how dangerous making me jealous could be. Not letting myself give in to the curse ferociously throbbing in my head proved exhausting, but I held it together. In all honesty, though, I wasn't all innocent either. I caught myself looking for him when he wasn't around and stealing my own secret glances at him when he was. Even the thought of running into him influenced what I wore and how I looked in the morning. How had I become such a stereotype?

I watched the races from the flat screen mounted in the hauler's small boardroom from then on. I figured if my butt stayed on the built in loveseat, in the corner, I couldn't do too much damage. At the Auto Club 400 in Fontana, California, I opted to keep wearing my headset, but hearing Colton's voice, especially when he asked Dean if I was watching, knotted my insides. I left the thing in its cupboard in Martinsville the following week. On those two weekends, Colton placed fifteenth and twenty-fifth. There was no excuse. With Mitch still in the hospital and his replacement not doing so well in the standings, Colton should have been dominating the tracks, but instead he kept complaining that his car's setup wasn't right or that his spotter wasn't on the ball enough. Deep down, everyone blamed me. I saw it in the way they acted around me.

I worked right up till Thursday at the shop. The racing season went on break for the Easter long weekend. I'd hoped that Colton had plans to head home to his parents for the holiday but, unfortunately, the responsibilities of a NASCAR driver didn't just entail being a good driver. Nancy had scheduled him for an Easter's eve mall appearance.

My room became my only refuge. Every time I headed out to the barn, Colton would coincidently be working outside, and every second my head would play the "is he looking at me" game. It grew tiring, and I gave up. I'd been falling behind on my classes, and the end of the school year was fast approaching, so it was probably best that I stayed in the attic and worked on my studies.

Someone creaked open the door at the bottom of the stairs from the second floor hallway. My heart skipped a beat, hoping it was Colton sneaking up into my room.

"You decent?" Dean called up.

Okay. So the same thought crossed my mind every time that door uttered the slightest of sounds and not once had what I had imagined come to life. Sue me.

I pushed out my lower lip to huff a breath into the hair partially hanging over my face. What did he want? He'd hardly talked to me since his showdown with Carl and my meltdown in his office, other than to bark orders or to pass the salt at the dinner table.

"Yeah, come on up."

Dean's head appeared over the half wall at the top of the stairs. "You're keeping up with your school work, I see."

"Yep. Got exams to study for."

Arrangements had been made for me to write my exams under the supervision of the local high school's principal in a few months instead of me having to go back home to my old school to complete them.

Dean moved across the room and sat on the corner of the

bed. "I have a favor to ask of you."

A favor? He wanted a favor … from me? That explained his pleasant demeanor.

"Nancy just called." He rubbed the back of his neck. "She can't make it to the mall appearance. She came down with the flu, and her assistant is on vacation overseas. She needs someone to coordinate with mall security. You think you can do that?"

I looked down at my laptop screen and clicked the mouse over the save button of my Word document. I had it set up to autosave, but you can never be too careful and well … I needed something to fiddle with. "Why can't *you* do it?"

"I have an important meeting with the Guardian Board this afternoon. I can't miss it."

"Lorna?"

"Annabelle has an appointment."

Crap. I moved the cursor around my screen, pretending to be preoccupied while he spoke. "Who else is going?"

"Only you and Colt."

My insides cringed at the thought of spending a whole day alone with Colton after hardly speaking to him for almost three weeks. The extent of our conversations were him calling shotgun every day for the front seat on our way to the shop or to the airport and the odd, uncomfortable exchanges when he helped me load my luggage when traveling.

"You know I wouldn't ask if I wasn't in a major bind."

"I know." I bit my lip. I had to expect that working with the team would sometimes put Colton and me in situations like this. "I'll do it."

Dean smiled. "Thank you so much. I'll have Lorna prepare you a sponsor bag with your official team tee, acting PR Rep nametag, and a stack of the large promotional cards for him to sign. I'll need you to make sure Colton remembers to change up his hats, t-shirts, and shades for sponsor exposure." Dean looked at his watch. "Can you be ready to leave in about an hour?"

"An hour? As in just one?" I was still in my pajamas and I hadn't bothered to shower yet.

Dean laughed. "You better get a move on. Oh, and I'll text you Nancy's number. She said to not be shy about texting her if you have any questions or if any significant problems arise." He pulled out his Blackberry and started typing away.

Even though I knew I shouldn't be, I was giddier than I'd been in days. I couldn't wait to get out of this room, and maybe while I was there, I could get some shopping done. Hey, two hundred bucks a week when you do nothing but work adds up quick and starts to burn holes in your pockets.

I jumped off the bed and started rummaging through my dresser drawers. When the sound of an incoming text coming from Dean's phone broke my concentration, I glanced over my shoulder at him. "Uh, you're going to need to leave now or there's no way I'll be ready in time."

Dean looked up, half-aware that I'd spoken to him. I widened my eyes at him and eyed the door. Took him a while to catch on, but he finally did. "Oh, sorry. I'll leave you to it."

With Dean gone and my clothes finally picked out, I hurried down to take a shower only to find that the bathroom was already occupied. I waited by the door, as it sounded like they were almost done. I leaned my back against the wall and tapped my foot on the carpet, a subtle sign of my rising impatience. Within a few minutes, the door opened. I pushed away from the wall and turned to head inside when Colton stepped out wearing nothing but his black cargo shorts sitting super low on his hips, holding a t-shirt in one hand and towel-drying his tousled hair with the other. The clean, fresh scent of his body spray mixed with the steam evaporating out the open bathroom door and from his body.

His very … shirtless …

I shut my eyes. "Oh my God, don't you have your own shower?" *Oh yum … Oh boy … Oh crap.* Why had I agreed to this again?

"Shower head's broken." Sure it was. I reopened my eyes as he stopped toweling his hair and I stared as wet clumps of it fell around his face. He grinned, revealing a hint of his hidden dimples to tease me. Not that he needed to. His wet, glistening chest and bulging biceps were doing a good enough job on their own. I swallowed hard, almost choking on my own saliva.

"So, I guess you're stuck with me for the day."

I hardly heard him speak. I'd lost myself in the memory of him, shirtless, pressed up against me the night that Dean and Lorna caught us in the act. When I realized he'd spoken, flames engulfed my cheeks.

I cleared my throat. "Yeah, um, I guess I am."

"You'd better hurry. You've got less than forty-five minutes to get ready."

My eyes narrowed. "Well, if you'd get your sexy … er, I mean, your ass out of there, I would." Seriously? Had I said the word sexy out loud? The moment called for a facepalm, but keeping my stern expression meant more to me right now.

"Sexy, huh?"

I bit my lip. His smile shifted into a quirky grin. "Your

loss, I guess." He turned his back to me and sauntered down the hallway, giving me an excellent view of his flexing back muscles as he lifted his shirt over his head. If only I'd left the cemetery with Roy that night. I rolled my eyes at my delusions and retreated into the bathroom. My life truly was cursed, in more ways than one.

■■■

On my way out, Lorna handed me the bag of sponsor gear. "I hope I got everything in there. Oh, and here's your jacket. Colton told me to remind you to grab it."

She handed me the heavy motorcycle jacket. "Wait, we're taking the bike?"

Lorna raised her shoulders in a tight shrug. "Sorry. Annabelle has a doctor's appointment. I can't spare the SUV today."

"Right. No worries. The bike it is." Oh goodie.

"Now, go on, Colton's ready and waiting." Ha ... there's a phrase that would have been hilarious a few weeks ago.

Outside, Colton waited, leaning against his bike, arms crossed against the front of his black and green jacket. "If we're late, it's your fault."

"Keep your pants on," I snarled as I dropped the bag on the veranda. I slipped the jacket on, then hoisted the backpack over my shoulders.

"Why? You'd get a better view of my sexy ass if I dropped them." I narrowed my eyes and aimed my stare, giving him the same look an archer would use to hone in on their target. I yanked the helmet from his hand and put it on. He stepped closer and sank down to my eye level to tighten the chin strap. I closed my eyes to avoid eye contact. He looped, tightened, and tugged on the strap. My head jerked forward and a warm breath caressed my neck. Tingles spread across my skin.

Ah, come on. Hurry up, hurry up, hurry up.

"You can open your eyes now." I did, only to see him still standing inches from me. I tried not to look at his eyes, but ended up staring at his lips. Ah, geez. I blinked hard, then pulled down the visor. He took the hint. I hadn't been able to forget our last moment together, our last kiss. His lips had become somewhat of an addiction of mine. One I desperately wanted give in to.

I settled in on the seat behind Colton and wrapped my arms around his waist. I was really going to need some shopping therapy after this.

The Perimeter Mall in Atlanta was jam-packed with NASCAR fans, making me want to run in the opposite direction. What the hell had I gotten myself into? Luckily, Link was also part of the appearance and autograph portion, and his PR rep, Debra, and her daughter Ryla became my new best friends. I stuck to them like glue for most of the Q & A portion, then stood behind Colton and Link with them at the signing table on the stage facing the food court. A few times, Debra filled me in on what to do, like where to stand during the signing and when to interfere with the clingy, girly fans that just didn't want to leave. I even had to gesture to the mall security standing by to escort a few cougar-looking forty-year-olds who wouldn't take being ushered along as an option.

I can't say I was overjoyed with having to watch girls flaunt their goodies at Colton when they leaned over the table to pose with him, or seeing all the phone numbers that were stacking up in a basket at his feet.

The snotty, bubble gum-chewing, girly girl next in line leaned to look at me standing behind Colton. "Hey, aren't you his girlfriend?"

A tad annoyed, I put on my fakest smile. "Uh, nope. He's a free man."

"But I saw you on TV kissing him before the race a few weeks ago."

Before I could answer, Colton glanced over his shoulder and winked. "I was too much for her to handle." He faced her again. "So she dumped me."

The girl scowled at me. "I'd be up for that challenge any day," she said to him, and voila, another phone number was slipped across the table and added to the pile. I rolled my eyes and caught Debra holding back a laugh.

When the last fan walked off, Gwen Langdon appeared out of nowhere. Since she was the daughter of the major sponsor, Debra and I had to let her through—Colton's continued sponsorship with Guardian Auto Insurance was already in jeopardy thanks to Carl's sabotage and his low performance of late.

Colton stood when she approached. I snuck off the stage to let them talk, more for my own benefit then theirs, and went in search of the man in charge of the event to thank him. He stood nearby, clearing the ropes and posts at the back of the designated area.

Colton's gaze found mine as Gwen held his forearm and looked up at him lovingly. His chest rose and fell. A long, deep breath or a sigh, from what I could tell. I looked away just long enough to thank the event coordinator and glanced back up at the stage.

Colton pulled out of Gwen's hold. "This has to stop," I overheard him telling her. "You're my sponsor's daughter and I'm okay with us being friends, but that's all we'll ever be. I don't feel the same about you."

"But Colton, I—"

He spoke his next words at a lower volume, inaudible from where I stood. He bent and kissed her cheek. She walked off the stage, her back to me, and met up with her friends waiting for her by the escalator. I wondered what he said to her. It was unusual for her to go without a fight—or a loud, annoying whine.

I walked back to the stage, thanked Debra, Ryla, and Link for their very much appreciated help, then picked up my things and headed toward the escalator.

Colton lunged off the stage and grabbed my arm. "Where do you think you're going?"

"My work here is done. I'm going shopping."

"Oh, no, you don't." The hint of a laugh escaped with his words.

"And why the hell not?"

"Are you kidding me? Fans are still crawling all over this place. I can't just go walking around."

"Who said anything about you tagging along?"

He smirked and narrowed his eyes. I turned on my heel and waved him off. "You can wait outside."

Colton wrapped his fingers around my arm again. "Come on, Lex, I'm serious."

I gave him a look and twisted out of his grip. "So am I."

He let out a deep sigh. "Okay. But can I at least take you to a different mall?"

I arched an eyebrow. "What's the catch?"

"No catch, I swear."

I looked up at a store on the second floor I'd been dying to visit since we'd got here and sighed. "Fine."

Colton smiled, revealing the hidden dimples I never thought I'd see again. "Thanks. Just let me find a bathroom so I can change and then we can go."

Colton replaced his Guardian t-shirt and ball cap with a form-fitting, plain white t-shirt that accentuated all his best features. The boy was seriously delusional if he thought this was going to deter his die-hard fans from recognizing him. Even without the ball cap.

After a few hours of shopping at a nearby strip mall, we ended the day with a late and awkward dinner at some buffet restaurant on the company card, and then headed back to the house.

I dismounted the bike, not looking forward to what I anticipated would be our most awkward moment of the day. I managed to unfasten my helmet and pull it off before Colton threw the kickstand down and got off. I held my helmet out to him.

"Well, I can't say today wasn't fun."

He pulled his helmet off, ran his fingers through his hair, and moved closer, placing his helmet on the seat of his bike. I held my helmet out further, but he ignored it.

"Colton."

He blinked slowly at me, then took the helmet from my hand, our fingers touching. I flinched as if I'd just grazed a loose spark plug wire, but removed my jacket to hide any hint of reaction that might have swept across my face.

"I had a good time, too," he finally said, taking the jacket from me and throwing it over the tank of his bike. He unzipped his own but didn't remove it. I wanted him to. It was too hard to focus on anything else with him looking so good wearing it.

"So … I guess I'll see you at dinner tomorrow, then." I turned to leave, but his hand lightly gripped my shoulder.

"Lexi, wait."

I froze for a second. "What is it?"

His hand lingered at the base of my neck. Shivers whirled down my spine, but I refused to let it show. "Colton, don't."

"Why not?"

I turned around. "We talked about this."

His eyes locked onto mine. Crap. Eye contact. I was doomed. "But you never told me why. I still love you, Lex. I can't stop thinking about you."

He still thought about me? I shook the thought away. "I can't tell you why. You'll just have to trust me that it's better this way."

"How is it better when we both want to be with each other, and trying to stay apart is almost unbearable? Every moment I'm with you, I can't seem to catch my breath."

My eyelids fluttered as he grazed my cheek with the back of his hand. "Colton, please," I begged. But what I really wanted was to sink into his arms.

He dipped his head. "Nothing you could say could stop me from wanting those lips."

"You don't know what you're saying."

He hooked the back of my neck and pulled me against him.

My breath hitched as his lips moved over mine. He kissed me hard, releasing weeks of pent-up frustration. I knew exactly how he felt. I parted my lips and returned his kiss with the same intensity. He molded himself against me, showing how much he wanted me. How much he'd missed me. Only this was wrong. I couldn't keep stringing him along. I couldn't let him think we still had a chance.

I slipped my hand inside his jacket and put it to his chest. The rush of his pulse against my fingers sent my heart racing faster. I indulged in his caresses a few more seconds before pushing him away. He raked his teeth over his bottom lip and stared at me.

"Colton, we can't do this."

"Why not? At least tell me that."

"Please, try to understand."

"Well, I don't."

He reached for me again, but I stepped back. My eyes blurred. I blinked away my urge to cry and tilted my head slightly. "I'm sorry." I brushed two fingers over my swollen bottom lip. "I'm so, so sorry." I turned and ran inside.

Lorna came out of the kitchen and greeted me with a smile as I shut the door behind me. "Glad to see you two patched things up. I didn't mean to spy on the two of you, but you were just outside the kitchen window."

She bent to hand Annabelle her evening cookie snack. Annabelle clapped her hands. "Lekki and Cotton, yay!"

I let out a groan. "We are not back together."

"But I just saw the two of you—"

I ran up the stairs and into my room before she could finish her sentence. I didn't want to explain. I didn't want to be questioned. I just wanted to be left alone.

I could still taste him. My chest hurt. Everything hurt. I grabbed my ribs and bent at the waist as I eased myself down on the bed. I didn't know what else to do to alleviate the sharp, stabbing pains of my broken heart.

Without shedding a single tear—a battle I'd finally won for once—I looked up at the dresser mirror. The last words I'd spoken to Lorna lingered on my tongue as if I needed to say them again and again. Maybe I needed to. Maybe if I, did they would finally sink in for good.

"We are not back together. We will never be together again."

chapter twenty-one

With Mitch Benson released from the hospital, the media once again focused on last month's incident. Reporters spun stories of Carl's threats to Mitch and speculated about the "why". Rumors of bankruptcy rose for Stacy Motorsports, and Carl was being put under a lot of pressure. How the man could be so close to bankruptcy with two championship wins under his belt was beyond me. And wasn't he starting up a new team? I didn't know what to think of the recent media uproar, but it was hitting a little too close to home for my comfort.

"Time to go," Dean shouted from downstairs.

I flicked the TV off and grabbed my bags. This week's schedule was screwy due to this weekend's race being on Saturday night under the one and a half miles of lights at the Texas Motor Speedway instead of the usual Sunday afternoon races we'd had up to this point in the season. And with Guardian Auto Insurance's big decision hanging over the team's financial head, Dean was on edge.

"Fort Worth, Texas, here we come," I mumbled, then

dragged my feet down the stairs and out the front door. Colton's advances last weekend shook me up, and I still hadn't quite recovered from it. Other than the totally awkward Easter dinner and the morning commute to the shop yesterday, I'd managed to stay clear of him the last few days … until just now, when I tripped off the top step of the veranda stairs and landed against his chest.

"Whoa, careful." Colton straightened me.

I stared up at him, eyes wide like an idiot. My heart flipped, and my mouth screamed for moisture. "Sorry, I—"

Colton's face hardened. "It's fine." He let go of me, picked up the backpack I'd dropped, and carried it to the truck.

God, why was Dean insisting that I attend every race? I dismantled things quickly, who cares? Since starting with the team, my skills had only been urgently needed once, and the fact that I'd almost publicly exposed my ability and put Colton's career and DSG Racing in jeopardy didn't seem to be noticed by anyone.

On the flight I sat near the window in one of the single seats away from Colton. He sat in his usual spot on the floor, with his head against the wall and his forearms resting on his knees, legs apart. Today he stared at me, jaw clenched and brows lowered. What the hell was his problem? I should be the one angry with him. Angry that he'd set back my efforts to get over him, to keep my distance. God … I was doing this for him too, for his safety.

The seatbelt light came on. Colton staggered back to his seat and buckled up, seeming more on edge without me there to help him through his fear. Moments later, we touched down and circled to a stop. From my window, I saw a mob of reporters and camera crews charging toward the plane.

"Uh, Dean?"

Dean twisted around. "What in Sam Hill is going on out there?"

Colton unbuckled his seatbelt and rushed to the window. "Something definitely has them all riled up."

"Okay." Dean packed up his briefcase. "You two—not one word to these vultures. Not until I find out what this is all about. You got that? The words 'no comment' are the only ones occupying your entire vocabulary, English or otherwise. I want you to head straight for the rental car over there." Dean pointed to a black Chevy sedan across the tarmac. I clenched the armrest tight. The last time I'd been surrounded by the media folk was when Colton won in Vegas, but I highly doubted they were all here for a celebration.

Dean exited the plane first. I followed him down the air stairs, clinging to the shoulder straps of my backpack, and Colton stayed close behind.

Large microphones and even larger news cameras were shoved in our faces the second our feet touched pavement. Dean pushed through the crowd, holding his briefcase up in front of him to shield his face.

"Do you have any comments regarding Carl Stacy's allegations that you are a cheat and a fraud?" some sassy redheaded reporter asked.

"What do you have to say for yourself, Mr. Grant?" A man forced himself in front of him.

"Colton? Colton? Is there anything you can tell us about the allegations against your employer?" I heard a woman ask.

Colton kept walking. "No comment."

Panic swelled in the pit of my stomach. I'd hoped that, after three weeks, Carl had given up on his threats.

A tall, blonde-haired woman pushed herself between Dean and me and stopped me dead in my tracks.

"Lexi, would you care to explain your involvement in this matter?"

I flinched at the microphone pointed at me. "How ... how do you know my name?"

"Lexi, it's been said that you are the key to DSG Racing's success since the start of the season. Tell me, what skill could a seventeen-year-old girl possibly contribute to help this race team cheat?"

She shoved her microphone in my face again. I opened my mouth to recite our instructed response, but my throat tightened and I froze.

Everyone knows.

Images of lab rats and men in hazmat suits flashed in my mind. Colton wrapped his arm around my shoulders and pushed the woman's mic away from me with his free hand. "No comment!" He brought his face close to mine. "Come on, Lex." He tucked me close and guided me through the crowd.

"Colton, were you privy to your boss's and your girlfriend's plans?"

Colton looked back. "What part of 'no comment' do you people not understand?"

Dean was already in the driver's seat. Colton helped me shimmy myself out of my shoulder straps and threw my pack and his gym bag into the trunk while I climbed into the back of the car. Colton came in after me and pulled the door shut. Dean stepped on the gas and got us out of there.

"Can someone tell me what the hell is going on?" Colton shouted.

My body trembled as I stared blankly at the back of the driver's seat. Carl had finally opened his big mouth, and now Dean and Colton's careers were about to end.

"I'm not sure yet, but I have a pretty good idea."

Colton wrapped his arm around me again and pulled me closer. "You plan on sharing that idea with the rest of us?"

Dean glanced at me through the rear-view mirror. "Let's get to the track first. I'll make a few calls, and we'll have a staff meeting."

I shivered. My head pounded. I could sense my ability brewing below the surface. This was my fault. All of it. I'd warned Dean to send me home. Oh, but no. He couldn't do that. Now we were all going to pay the price for my stupid curse.

A new flock of reporters waited for us at the track, near the motor coach and the hauler. There was no escaping them.

Colton had been tasked with keeping an eye on me while we waited for Dean to give us word on where and when to meet. I paced the somber confines of my room, attempting to crack my knuckles. I'd never cracked my knuckles before, but it seemed like the perfect time to start. Besides, my teeth had massacred my lip enough. Colton sat on the bed, his face buried in his hands.

"Could you please stop with the pacing? You're driving me insane," Colton snapped.

"I'm sorry, I can't help it."

He looked up and glared. "Well, park it before I do it for you."

His tone startled me. Only an hour ago, he'd draped his

arm around me and let me lay my head against his chest in the car. Now he was back to being bitter and pissed off.

I stopped in front of him. "What the hell is your problem?"

Colton straightened. "My problem?" He threw his head back. "Ha. You really want to know what my problem is? You." He pointed a stern finger in my direction. "You're my problem."

My jaw dropped. I had no words. "You say you care, but you don't want to be with me. You say you're dangerous and you act all secretive, and now we're being accused of cheating and those reporters seem to think that you're at the center of it all." He pointed at the media crews camped outside. "There's something that you're not telling me. If you truly cared the way you say you do, you'd trust me enough to tell me."

I opened my mouth to respond when my iPhone chimed. I hesitated.

Colton's eyes grew livid at the distraction. He stood and turned his back to me. "You going to check that?"

I pulled my phone from my pocket and swiped my thumb over the screen. "It's Dean. You know how to get to the meeting rooms?"

He gripped the edge of the dresser. "Which building?"

"The media center."

His head fell forward. "Shit. When?"

"Now."

He inhaled a sharp breath, pushed himself from the dresser, and moved past me. "Come on. We better get going." He snatched his ball cap off the bed, slicked his hair back, and placed it on his head, using his other hand to adjust the back in place. "And put your game face on. We'll be entering the proverbial lion's den."

Another barrage of questioning followed us out to the meeting room. A few reporters were bold enough to grab me by the arm to force me to face them, but Colton was quick to pull me out of their grasp and rush me forward again. When we arrived, the boardroom had no seats left around the glossy oak table. Colton's crew, along with Link and his crew, filled every chair. The place had standing room only. Colton eased the door shut behind him, while I stood near Nancy, Debra, and some of the race officials against the wall. Colton removed his sunglasses and stood next to me, our shoulders pressed together.

"I'm sure you all know why I've called you here." Dean leaned forward, his palms on the table. "Carl Stacy has made some highly untruthful and damaging accusations about the day-to-day operations and integrity of DSG Racing and its employees."

"What's he accusing us of?" Debra, Link's PR rep asked.

Dean glanced at me. "Mr. Stacy is accusing us of cheating. He believes one of our staff members has a special set of skills that's given us an advantage against the other teams. This mainly concerns the Cup series team, but I wanted you all here to show a united front."

"What kind of skills?" asked another crew member.

Dean hesitated, then continued. "Carl believes this person to have skills of the ... supernatural kind." Everyone around the room snickered or laughed. I sunk back against the wall and avoided Colton's piercing stare, which was burning its way through the side of my face.

"It also seems that he has not divulged this information to the media as of yet, which is what has them all riled up. He publicly accused us of cheating and has simply told them that all would be revealed at Saturday night's race."

"What's he planning?" Colton asked.

"Your guess is as good as mine."

"Well, you better figure it out, Grant." Mr. Langdon stood from his chair. "The board's already on the fence about continuing their sponsorship after all the negative publicity. If anything goes wrong this weekend, I can't guarantee we'll be in business together much longer."

"We are doing our best here, Paul."

"Right now, your best isn't good enough." Mr. Langdon made his way to the door.

"Paul—"

Mr. Langdon stopped in the doorway. "I've got to go do some damage control with the board before they hear the rest of the details on the six o'clock news."

Mr. Langdon left and all eyes turned back on Dean. Creases formed on his face and the obvious tension in his shoulders and neck seemed to be getting worse despite his rubbing them constantly. He returned his attention to the crowd in front of him.

"I want you all to be on high alert and ready for anything. Again, 'no comment' is your new best friend. I ask that you report anything that could be considered suspicious or anything you think might be relevant to the situation to me or to any race official close by. Keep an eye on your equipment and double-check everything. Triple check, even. Thank you for your time."

Everyone filed out of the room and went about their business. I remained against the wall, unmoving. I had to tell Dean. I had no choice. This was going too far.

Colton pushed himself off the wall, nudged me, and turned toward the door. "You coming?"

"I need to talk to Dean."

Dean looked up from his papers. Colton's shoulders squared and his chin lifted a fraction of an inch. He knew I was about to tell Dean what I'd been hiding since the day I arrived. He also knew I didn't plan on letting him stay to hear it. He collected himself and left the room.

As the last person exited and closed the door, I stood up from the wall. "You have to send me back, Dean. Send me back to the salvage yard. It's your only hope of saving yourself from this."

"Lex, I don't want you to worry about all this. His allegations are ridiculous. This will all blow over in a week or two."

"But what about the sponsorship? This will ruin any chance you have of keeping Guardian on board."

"Even bad publicity is good publicity. Let's just hope the board sees it that way, too."

"You can't take that chance. You heard what Mr. Langdon said—the board is already on the fence. Can you afford to finish the season without them?"

Dean said nothing, only pursed his lips. He knew I was right. DSG Racing couldn't afford two race teams without that sponsorship. I'd overheard him telling Lorna just that a few nights ago.

I had to do something.

I'd feared this moment since my first day of high school, when I'd first discovered what I could do. I had to tell someone. If I didn't, I'd be ruining multiple lives along with my own.

Lives I cared about.

I glanced down at my feet, not sure I wanted to see his reaction. "Carl's allegations aren't false. Not entirely, anyway."

"What are you … Lex?"

I stepped closer to the table, avoiding Dean's darting stare piercing through me like a laser. "I haven't figured out what I am, exactly. My father didn't stick around long enough to tell me." I looked up at him, then took a deep breath and readied myself to drop the bomb. "What Carl said is true. I can move things, move them without needing to touch them. Only things made of metal."

"Lexi, listen. I appreciate what you're—"

"No. You listen." I squeezed my eyes shut. Avoiding Colton was one of the hardest things I'd had to do, but this was a close second.

I opened my eyes again. Dean's arms were now crossed.

"You have to send me back now. If Carl succeeds, if he goes public, we all go down. Me, Colton's career, your company, all of it. Carl's not crazy. Creepy, in a perverted kind of way, yes, but not crazy. I'm the one who threw Mitch's car into the wall to keep him away from Colton in Bristol."

Dean's eyes grew wide.

"I didn't mean to do it. My ability feeds on my emotions and sometimes I lose control. It doesn't happen often anymore and it's never done anything this drastic before, but when I saw Mitch collide with Colton again, I lost it. And Mitch Benson paid the price. It's why the hauler's roof caved in. It's why I was bleeding from the eyes and nose."

Dean shook his head. "This is crazy. This is—"

"The truth." I moved closer to him. "Carl witnessed it all.

He knows."

He reached for his forehead, massaging his temples with his thumb and middle fingers, but it did nothing to ease the deep creases between his eyebrows. "I don't believe this. I can't believe this. This is too …"

My gaze fell to where the fancy pen he always carried around lay on top of a pile of papers near his briefcase. My heart raced. Showing him was the only way he'd believe me.

Here goes nothing … or maybe everything.

I released the breath I'd locked in my throat, singled out the pen from the other objects I detected in the room, and levitated it off the table in front of him.

Dean's hand fell to his side. A look of pure fear contorted his face. He slowly stepped back, keeping his eyes on the pen as if afraid it would attack him.

My posture weakened at the sight of his reaction, but I continued. I turned the pen over and unscrewed the ends. The aluminum center and plastic ink refill inside fell and rolled to the floor. I twirled the two remaining ends around each other in a sort of dance. I looked back at Dean's face. I'd known since I was old enough to understand that I was different and after Mama died that I was a freak, but seeing it confirmed in his expression made it that much more real. And I had no words left in me to say. A dull pain spread through my entire body. Now Dean knew the real me. And I was pretty sure he didn't like it one bit.

I looked away. "Please send me away or lock me up, at least. You'll lose everything if you don't. I don't want to be the reason you, your family, and Colton sees the dreams you've all worked so hard for get taken away."

I shoved back my urge to cry and continued. "I knew I should've gone home when I had the chance. This is the reason I couldn't go to school like a normal student, or tell anyone what kind of man my stepfather was. I would have never survived in foster care. I knew my place with Roy."

Dean fell back in his chair, displaying the many stages of grief all at once. I bit my lip and brought the floating pen pieces back onto the tabletop. Dean's eyes stayed glued to the objects, as if they were a new specimen, of sorts. His silence tortured me, making me wish I'd left things as they were.

"Please say something."

He got up slowly, moving his focus toward me. My breath caught. His lips thinned and his eyes narrowed. He rounded the table and reached for me. I flinched. His fingers wrapped around my upper arms with gentle force.

"Have you done anything else, other than what you did to Mitch?" His voice was stern, serious, but not enraged.

"No, I would never—"

"Colton's success is all his own? You've never helped him along?"

"Nothing besides removing that engine a little faster than normal, no. I can't project it that far. Anywhere other than Bristol, it would've been impossible for me to do anything to give Colton an advantage."

His jaw clenched. "Who else knows?"

"No one." A tear rolled down my cheek. A tear of fear, or was it of shame? "I swear, I haven't told anyone. Roy doesn't even know."

He let go and pointed his finger in my face. "You keep this to yourself. You tell no one else, you hear me?" He grabbed me again and shook me slightly. "And you stay as far away from Carl Stacy as you possibly can. Don't you fall for any of his tricks, or this is over." He let go of me, backed away, and bolted straight out the door.

I buried my face in my hands and allowed my fear to release its tears as I fought to bring my breathing back to normal.

Or this is over.

What had he meant by that? Was I welcomed back to the hauler? Was he relieving me of my duties? My contract?

I composed myself, left through the main doors, and headed for the infield, head down. A large shoulder slammed into me and whirled me around.

"Oh, I'm sorry. I—"

Carl Stacy's eyes stared daggers back at me from under his large hat, attacking me with his scowl. I swallowed hard. Already I was breaking one of Dean's rules.

"I'm onto you, Magic Fingers. I *will* expose you for the abomination you are. There's no sense in hiding anymore."

chapter twenty-two

I stared up at his hate-filled face, my feet stuck fast, breath and words caught in my throat.

"Lexi!" Colton's voice came from somewhere in the distance. I wanted to look in his direction, but I couldn't move. Carl's devious grin twitched his peppered whiskers. He leaned in closer.

"If you're smart, sweetheart, you'll run along and join the circus."

Sweetheart? Only Lenny called me that.

"Lexi!" Colton called out again, this time closer. His arm hooked around my waist and pulled me back.

"Stay away from her, you creep," Colton said with a contorted look on his face I'd never seen before.

Carl tipped his hat and sauntered the other way.

Colton grabbed me by the arms. "You mind telling me what you were doing with him?"

I wiggled out of his grasp and balled my hands at my sides. "Relax. Nothing happened. I'm fine, by the way." I turned and marched away.

Colton followed close behind. I could practically feel him breathing down my neck. "I said nothing happened. Now, can you quit following me?"

"Trust me, I got better things to do than to follow Little Miss Secrets around the infield, but I can't. Boss's orders."

I growled at him. "I don't need a babysitter."

"Oh, no, not at all. I'm instructed to keep you away from Carl, and where do I find you? With Carl."

"I can handle him."

"Yeah, you really handled him back there."

I forced my legs to go faster, but Colton matched my pace. "Go *away*, Colton, I don't—"

He sidestepped around me and blocked my path. "Lexi, talk to me. Tell me what you told Dean in there. Tell me what has him so wound up. It's not like him."

"I can't, Colt. He swore me to secrecy."

"Ugh. Again with the secrets. When are you ever going to trust me and realize that nothing you say to me can change the way I feel about you?"

"Not everything is about you!" I spat back. But wasn't it? Wasn't all of this about him? Weren't my feelings for him the reason we were in this mess?

Colton's lips thinned into a straight line while his jaw worked.

"Just drop it. Leave me alone." I aimed my eyes at the ground and walked past him. Colton gave up and followed at a distance as I made my way back to the motor coach. Debra and Nancy must have worked their PR magic after the meeting, because not a single reporter tried to trample us with cameras and large, fuzzy microphones. I welcomed the change.

I spent the next two days locked up in my room or in the hauler, escorted either by Colton, who had since stopped talking to me, or Dean, who I didn't dare talk to. At least, from what I could tell, he planned to defend me against Carl's allegations.

■ ■ ■

I'd never been so fidgety and distracted in all my life. My nerves were shot and my stomach wouldn't stop twisting into knots. No one had a clue what Carl's plans were yet, and the race was today.

Wearing my usual Guardian Auto Insurance swag, I headed down to the track early with Dean and Colton. Dean ordered me to hide out in the hauler and watch the race on the flat screen. I couldn't blame him. Whatever Carl's plans were, they definitely involved me—the more out of sight I was, the better.

Colton qualified third on Thursday, but my excitement for him and the race sank far below the nagging thoughts that plagued me. Carl had kept his distance from the media since his big announcement. He had everybody on edge, which was exactly what he wanted.

News reporters still buzzed around, waiting in anticipation for the proof of cheating Carl had promised. My nerves were frozen into ice cubes of tension. Countless scenarios played out in my head—Carl storming in here with camera crews to accuse me in front of them, or with a slew of doctors and government research scientists to haul me away kicking and screaming.

During the pre-race coverage, speculation of self-sabotage and illegal modifications haunted the team. Reporters went as far as digging into some of the crews' personal lives, airing their dirty laundry on the local news channels. Had that reporter who knew my name done the same with me? Had she sought out Roy and asked him about my life prior to having been sent here?

No. Not possible. Not yet, anyway. She would have blabbed about me all over the news already.

The anthem played, the jets roared overhead, and the famous four words were spoken. The rumble outside shook the hauler as the cars took to the track in single file on the flat screen. The sight gave me goosebumps. They rounded the corners, now grouped together two-by-two in a perfect formation of candy-shelled paint schemes, shining under the bright lights of the track. I desperately wanted to go out and watch the event live. Unlike Bristol, this track was large enough that my ability could never reach far enough to cause any damage. Still, Dean would have my hide if I disobeyed him. He'd specifically instructed me not to leave this spot, and I had no intention of pissing off the only other person who had the power to lock me away.

It's funny how you take such little things for granted. For the past few weeks, I'd willingly locked myself up in here, able to come and go as I pleased, but now that I wanted to go out, I was forced to stay put. At least Dean let me keep my headset and scanner so I could listen in on the team.

"Great job, guys," Colton said as he took to the track after the first pit stop. He had led a few laps in the beginning, but then dropped back down, holding it steady in fifth place.

"Looking good out there, Colt, keep up the good work." Lenny said.

The media kept a close watch on the whole team, and so did NASCAR. Four officials had been assigned to our pit stall instead of the usual one or two. They also weren't taking any chances.

A close-up of the crew came on the screen. Lenny didn't look so good. Sweat poured from his forehead and neck, his expression tight-lipped. He spent his time taking his cap off, putting it back on, and then readjusting his headset. Something was way off.

Colton gained two positions and ran third with one hundred laps to go. The cameras closed in on Lenny again, looking green and sick to his stomach. It was hot out, sure, even for a night race, but not any warmer than any other race weekend we'd had. The media seemed to be drawing the same conclusion. Something wasn't sitting right with him. He had the same look on his face as that time in Bristol, right after he'd spoken to Carl.

With less than seventy-five laps to go, Lenny cued his mic. "I can't do this. Boss, we need to talk. Now. Colton, I'm handing you over to Dylan."

"What? Why?" Colton said. No answer was given.

The hauler's side door slammed shut, and voices came from Dean's office. I scrambled off my chair and hurried to lean up against the adjoining wall.

"You mind telling me why in God's name you walked away from your driver in the middle of a goddamned race?"

"It's my fault, Dean." Lenny's muffled voice shook.

"What's your fault? Spit it out. We don't have time for this."

"The sabotage, conspiring with Carl, it was all me."

"What?" Dean yelled, and a bang followed, like he'd slapped his palms against his desk. I pictured his eyes bulging as they had when he'd spoken to me in the boardroom the other day.

"Tracy's pregnant again. That's baby number five. Five, Dean. How am I going to feed all those mouths on one salary, no matter how much I make? So I panicked ... I—"

"Get to the part where you screwed us over, Lenny."

"I'm so sorry, Dean. Carl offered me a substantial amount of money, enough to retire on. All I had to do was—"

"Do you have any idea what you are admitting to? NASCAR's going to have your head."

"I know, Boss, I—"

"Don't call me that. You lost that privilege the moment you sabotaged your own team."

My mouth gaped open. Lenny? Fired?

"I know, I get that, but listen to me for a second. Colton's in trouble."

"Trouble? What kind of trouble?"

"Carl's got something planned. I wasn't privy to this one. I refused to help him, but I think he plans to—"

"Did you see that?" The TV sportscaster's words blared through the flat screen's speakers. I snapped my attention to the broadcast. "It looked like a flash of flames from inside the number 129 car."

"Colton, are you alright?" Dylan urgently came through on my headset hanging around my neck. My heart skipped. I held my breath and raised one of the earpieces to my ear, waiting for him to answer.

"Colton, can you hear me?" Dylan pressed on.

Colton's car veered to the bottom of the track without any signs of slowing down.

"Colton!"

I banged on the wall. "Guys. Get in here now."

Dean and Lenny ran in. "What?" Dean snapped. I pointed at the screen with my trembling hand.

"There seems to be movement inside the car." The sportscaster continued as the cameras closed in on Colton's car. "But he doesn't seem to be stopping."

Dean threw his headset on and cued his mic. "Colton …?"

"Officials are reporting that Colton Tayler is not responding to his crew."

"Son of a bitch. Lexi, shut that damn guy up."

I lunged for the remote on the table and hit the mute button.

"Colton, damn it, answer me," Dean yelled again.

"I have no brakes, Dean … I have no brakes." Relief came in a quick exhale at the sound of Colton's voice.

"Coast her to a stop, Colt," Dylan told him.

"I can't," he said, pausing to let out a hiss of pain before continuing. "Throttle's stuck."

"What's wrong Colt? You sound in pain. Are you hurt?" Dean asked.

"My legs are burning. Something blew up at my feet and screwed everything up. The firewall's fucked."

My hands flew to my mouth.

"Damn it." Dean turned around in circles, rubbing the top of his brow as he seemingly tried to collect his thoughts to order his next move. "Hit the kill switch, Colt."

We all stared at the broadcast following Colton around the track, but he wasn't slowing down. The vise grip of fear clamped down on me. This was it. This was Carl's plan.

"It's fried, Dean—nothing's happening. I can't stop it."

chapter
twenty-three

Dean bolted out the side door and ran out to the pits. Lenny and I followed.

Dylan ran over the second he saw us. "Boss, I don't know what—what should I do?"

Dean patted him on the back. "It's okay, Dyl. This ain't your fault." He gestured to one of the officials. "You! Call a caution—something, anything. Our boy can't stop. We need to give him wide open space to run until we figure this out." The man nodded and got on his radio.

Dean turned to Lenny, one hand propped at his waist, the other rubbing the back of his neck. "Okay, talk to me. How long do we have? Fuel, tires …?"

"We just refueled on the last pit stop, but his tires aren't going to outlast that."

"What are his odds?"

"If the tires blow, there's a slim chance it could slow him down enough to kill the engine, but more than likely it'll put him in the wall. At full speed like that, with no way of slowing down ..."

We all knew the end of that sentence. Bile rose to my throat.

"SAFER barriers should reduce the impact," Dylan said.

Lenny's head leaned slightly. "Do we want to take that chance? We don't know what kind of damage that explosion did to the inside of that car. If it's as bad as Colton says, the car could buckle right into him."

"Red flag is out," Jimmy said. "Race is on hold and all teams have been instructed to line up on the inside of the back stretch."

Dean cued up. "Good. That'll give us some room."

"Guys, what do I do? Tell me what to do." Colton sounded frantic.

"Just hold it on the track. Dip low in those turns to keep your apex wide. We're working on a plan, just hang in there."

"Ten-four, boss."

Colton sped around the corners without any sign of slowing down, just like my heart was doing against my rib cage.

"What if we get him to drive through the grass?" Dylan suggested.

"The car's running flat out." Lenny shook his head. "He'll just spin the wheels on that grass. It ain't going to slow him down or be enough to blow the engine. He'll just run out of room and dart right back onto the track, possibly even head straight into the wall."

Dean threw his arms up. "Damn it. Then what other options do we have?"

"Crashing is the only option," Lenny said. "Either we let the tires blow out and hope for the best, or we create our own controlled crash environment and funnel him in. Keep the impact to both sides of the car until he slows down enough to snuff the engine. And again ... hope for the best."

Hope for the best? That wasn't good enough. Colton had no chance in hell of making it out of that car in one piece.

My body grew numb. I had to say something. "You can't be serious. This is his life you guys are talking about risking."

Dean spun around and narrowed his eyes in my direction. He was either pissed, or the track lights were too bright. I went with pissed. "You shouldn't be out here. Get back inside that hauler."

"No freakin' way. Not with Colton's life on the line."

Dean ignored me. "Get security down here, we need to clear out the pit area. Media, the other teams—get them all out of here," he instructed the officials. "Get some trucks, anything to block the end of pit road. We're also going to need fire trucks and medics here, stat."

The officials scrambled, and more joined them. The pit stall was in total chaos while I stood in disbelief, watching Colton circle the track. Intense pressure built behind my eyes and cheekbones, and I couldn't get my chin to stop quivering. "Dean, you can't do this. You're going to kill him, you're going to—"

Dean stopped what he was doing and glanced over his shoulder. "Lexi, I told you to go back to the hauler."

"Dean, you can't—"

He lunged toward me, gripped both of my arms, and shook me lightly. "Lexi, you can't stay here. You have to go back inside the damn hauler."

I leaned forward and kept my voice low. "Let me stop him, Dean. You know I can do it."

He shook his head, his eyes creasing. "Absolutely not. Out of the question."

"Tell him to drive down pit lane, and I'll stop him. The track's too big, I can't reach him that far out."

Dean gave me another stern shake. "Lexi, no. This is exactly what Carl wants."

"You think I don't know that? But what other choice do we have?" I rolled my shoulder back to make him loosen his grip. He wasn't hurting me, but the way he was holding me brought back way too many bad memories.

Dean let go, turned around, and waved me off. "Go back to the hauler, Lex. Let us take care of this."

Tears streamed down my face, blurring my vision. "It's suicide. No, worse … this is murder. You can't possibly—at best, he'd never be able to race or walk again. I can't let you guys do that to him."

He flung himself around again. "Lexi, damn it, I don't have time for your tantrums!"

I stepped back and my brows shot up. "Tantrums? You're about to kill your nineteen-year-old driver, and you're angry about my tantrum?"

His shoulders dropped. "Fine. Stay there, but don't you dare move a muscle."

I felt so useless. All this power at my fingertips and I was benched. I sat on the edge of a discarded tire leaning against one of the toolboxes, biting off what was left of my nails, and bounced my knee, using the tip of my foot against the pavement.

Dean disappeared into the crowd of screaming officials, team crews, medics, and firefighters, all planning out their timing and positioning while Colton continued to dip low in the turns and keep high on the straights. Everything was happening at lightning speed, yet somehow it all felt too slow.

"How are you holding up, Colt?" I heard Dean ask him through my headset.

"Something cut through my suit. My leg's burning like a bitch, but I'm handling her. So far, so good."

"Keep it up. We're working on getting you stopped. Keep trying the kill switch—you never know."

"Ten-four, but no luck so far on that switch."

A shadow cast over me. I knew right away who it was. The creepy crawly sensation snaking under my skin gave him away.

"You should be out there saving your boyfriend." Carl stood behind me, breathing down my neck, but I didn't dare look back at him.

"He's not my boyfriend."

"Does that matter? You can't just let him die." I could almost hear the smile forming on his lips. I never thought anyone could be this evil. Roy was an angel compared to this man.

"He's not going to die. Crashes happen all the time, you know. He'll be alright, no thanks to you."

"You don't believe that for a second, do you? You know, even if he makes it out alive, he'll never be the same again. And you know what, sweetheart? It's all going to be your fault. You want to live with that guilt?"

The slimy tone of his voice and the stench of chewing tobacco was enough to make me want to hurl. I clenched my stomach, trying to ride out the churning waves of nausea crippling me. As much as I hated to agree with him, Carl was right. If this crash didn't kill him—and that was a big *if*—odds were Colton would never race again.

An abrupt stop like that ... at nearly two hundred miles per hour ...

I could picture it, feel the impact in my bones, the flames rising, the whiplash.

"No!"

Dean turned to face me and his eyes grew wide. "You." He pointed over my head and walked quickly toward us. "What the hell are you doing here?"

"Why, I've come to offer my assistance, Mr. Grant."

"Bullshit." Dean pulled his clenched hand back. I dodged out of the way just as Dean's fist collided with Carl's jaw, sending his stupid cowboy hat flying off his head.

"You son of a bitch, you're killing my boy!"

Dylan ran toward the commotion, hooked his arms underneath Dean's from behind, and pulled him away, kicking and thrashing. Carl held his hand to his bloody lip and straightened. "You have the tools to stop this. You just don't want to show the world your secret weapon. You'd rather sacrifice your driver than admit that you're a cheat."

"The only cheat here is you," Dean spat back.

Lenny pushed through the gathered crowd. "I can vouch for that."

Carl's smile dropped.

"He paid me to sabotage my own team. He told me about the guys on his unofficial payroll dedicated to manipulating and distracting officials at the inspection booth. Tell me, Carl, do they know you're too broke to pay them this week? Do they know you've gambled all your money away?"

Carl's nostrils flared. "You ... you little snitch!"

Lenny moved closer. "You've gone too far. Sabotage is one

thing, but you're toying with a life in that car. You want to be known as a murderer? I sure as hell don't."

Carl looked down at his blood-covered hand, pulled out a handkerchief from his pocket and dabbed his lip. "You can't prove anything."

"I can, and I will. See you in court," Lenny said. Just then, two security guards appeared behind him. "Take him, boys. Take me, too, while you're at it. I'm just as guilty."

"No." Dean gripped Lenny's shoulder. "We need you here. We'll deal with your actions later."

"Uh, guys? Guys …?" Colton's terrified cries blared through our headsets.

Dean scrambled to cue his mic. "Everything all right, Colt?"

"My ass end's all over the place, tires are getting greasy. It's getting hard to hold it in the turns."

My breath hitched. His tires were on the verge of blowing out.

"Keep trying to hold her steady, we'll be ready soon."

"Ready for what? What's going on down there?"

Dean closed his eyes, knowing all too well he'd be sending him down the path of possible death soon. "We'll let you know what to do in a few."

The guards cuffed Carl and took him away. "You brought this on yourself, Dean," he yelled.

"Rot in hell, Carl!"

I pulled Dean aside. "Dean, he's right. This plan's not going to work. I can save him. Please let me save him."

"I can't let you expose yourself. Imagine what they would do to you." He began to walk away from me, but I stopped him.

"But what about Colton's life? We have to take that chance."

"Lexi, please. Step aside and let us do what's best." The corners of his lips drooped. He didn't want this outcome, either. He just wanted to protect me. Even though he hardly knew me, even after all the stress and pain I'd caused, he still wanted to protect me.

The official came up behind Dean. "We need you."

Dean tipped his head at the man. "I'll be right there."

"Dean, please. It's Colton in that car. The son you've never had."

"Just pray, Lex," he said, then patted me on the back and took off toward the scene of flashing lights.

Three large trucks, drained of fuel, were in place at the end of pit road: two side-by-side angled toward each other, and a third parked across the back as a sort of barrier. Crew members hurried to stack discarded tires in front of the third truck. Medics readied themselves off to the sides with a stretcher and other gear, while firefighters held their hoses, ready to douse any flames that might ignite.

My muscles ached. I couldn't stand here, helpless. I couldn't let Colton get hurt—or worse, die. Not when I had the power to save him. I might never be able to understand why I had this ability, but damn it, what was the point if I couldn't use it now, when it was needed the most?

It was obvious to me that my control issues stemmed from fighting the way I felt about Colton and about myself. Every time I fought against my emotions or tried to change them, my control weakened. Some emotions I had no control over, and that was something I was going to have to work on, but right now, I needed to accept what I was. I had to do something, and to hell with the consequences. They could lock me up in a loony bin for the rest of my life for all I cared, as long as Colton was safe. I needed Colton to be safe.

I ran and hid behind one of the toolboxes in the neighboring stalls and cued my mic. "Colton."

Colton answered right away. "Lexi? What are you—"

"Colton, listen to me." I wasn't as well hidden as I'd thought. Dean was coming, his face blazing red. I was in big trouble.

"Next lap, turn onto pit road," I said harshly.

"Why? Where's Dean? What's going on?"

Dean gesticulated furiously at me, telling me to stop.

"Colton, do you trust me?" Silence. "Answer me. *Do you trust me?*"

"I do."

"Then drive down pit road and head straight. No matter what you see, no matter what's in your way, just drive straight and don't flinch, you got it? Whatever you do, don't flinch."

"Ten-four."

Dean reached me. "What are you doing?"

"Saving his life."

"Lexi, you can't do this."

"I can and I will. I don't care what happens to me, as long as he's okay."

"Call him off, Lexi. We're not ready for him yet."

"You do it. You have a mic, you call him off. You're the one orchestrating his death."

Dean stared into my determined eyes, his slowly filling with understanding. He knew I was right.

"That's what I thought. Now either help me pull this off, or get out of my way."

Dean stood motionless.

"I love him, Dean. I have to do this."

Finally he motioned to the team to take their places, then cued his mic. "Colton, do what she says."

"Ten-four."

"Go," he mouthed to me. "But lay low," he added in a whisper.

I pushed past the crowd and stood behind the medics near the trucks. I placed myself close enough to the edge to have a clear view, but still hidden. I pulled my headgear and ball cap off, let my hair fall forward like curtains down both sides of my face then slapped my ball cap back on, repositioning it so it came down low over my eyes. With everything in place, I glanced around. Everyone was too distracted with what was happening to notice me. Good, 'cause I was scared shitless, and I didn't need an audience that would freak when the currents about to rush through me turned my eyes red and streaked my face with blood.

Colton roared down the backstretch, past the other drivers that lined the low side, and entered turn three.

I turned away, activated my mic, and whispered into it, "This is it, Colton. I'm—we're ready for you."

"Colton." Dean's voice followed. "Start mashing on that brake pedal. There's still a chance they might reengage on the flatter surface."

My head snapped to where Dean stood on the other side. He winked.

I couldn't believe it. He was fabricating a cover, hoping to twist the facts for the media and for NASCAR once all of this was over. Even now, he was trying to protect me.

Colton rounded turn four, ducked down, and aimed for the pit lane entrance. The car's back end wobbled.

"Keep hitting those brakes, Colt," Dean reminded him.

"What if that doesn't work?"

"Aim for the trucks straight ahead, they'll funnel you to a stop."

"Are you nuts?"

I went for my mic. Dean was scaring him. "Colton. You said that you trusted me, yeah?"

"Yeah."

"Then shut up and do what I say."

"Ten-four."

I braced my feet on the pavement and clenched my fists at my side for added channeling. Colton entered pit road; the speed and power of his car made the ground rumble under our feet.

"Brakes aren't engaging," Colton's panicked voice came over the airwaves.

"Keep trying, Colt. Pump them hard, they'll catch," Dean assured him.

The Angel Car entered my reach. My temples started to pound. My senses tightened, vibrated, and engaged. My ability knew what I wanted, what it needed to do—and this time I had control. I lowered my head, dropped the mental barriers I'd built over the years, and aimed everything I had toward it. I focused on the brake pads, clamping the calipers tight against the disks. Thick smoke rose from the wheel wells. The car protested with high-pitched screeches and groans from metal grinding on metal. The stench of burned rubber engulfed us all.

I focused on the chassis of the car next, throwing my energy at it hard. Sparks flew in my head and my limbs threatened to give out, but Colton needed me. I had to succeed. I couldn't lose him.

"The car's slowing, but not enough. This ain't going to work."

"Keep pushing them, Colt, don't stop," Dean said in my ears.

His tires squealed. The front ones locked, but the rear ones pushed against the unnatural counterforce. I stifled a scream of pain in the back of my throat. My eyes blurred, and I could taste blood.

I had to get closer. Everything inside me screamed that I needed to get closer. I glanced up to where Dean stood. While everyone was looking out at the car careening towards us, Dean was staring at me. I mouthed the words "I'm sorry," then pushed past the medics in front of me and jumped the barrier.

"Hey! You. Get back here!" one of them cried.

"Someone get that girl out of the way."

People reached out to stop me, but I managed to slip their grasp and plant myself firmly in the center of the road.

With a final jolt of energy from deep within me, I gave it all I had. I prayed to God that no one could see my face behind my hair.

"Lexi, what are you doing?" Colton shouted. "You're going to get yourself killed."

I found a sliver of strength and moved one hand to cue my mic. "I'm not leaving you, Colt. I can't and I won't."

My eyes squeezed shut as the RPMs dropped. The engine sputtered and finally choked out. Without the engine's power fighting against mine, it made the car's remaining momentum easier to handle. I reached out toward the car—not a dozen feet away now—my arms aching, my body about to give out. The front tires blew out as I lowered my hands, and the hood of the car rolled to a stop under my palms.

I opened my eyes and looked straight through the windshield at Colton's wide, terrified, unblinking eyes behind the open visor of his helmet. I'd done it. I'd stopped the car. Dean would eventually explain to him what had really happened and why I looked the way I did. I would forever be a freak in his eyes, but I saved him. That's all that mattered.

The crew and officials charged the car, unfastened his net, and yanked him out. Before anyone could see the streaks of blood on my face, Dean wrapped himself around me, forcing my face against his shirt, and whisked me away. Breathless and weaker than I'd ever been while still conscious, my head fell against his chest. A dead faint threatened to take over my body and mind, and I could barely hang on to what was left of my consciousness, but I fought against it. I couldn't pass out now. Not without knowing if Colton was okay. Not with the media frenzy that was no doubt about to follow.

Life as I knew it would soon be over, but Colton made it out alive, and I was more than okay with that.

chapter twenty-four

I sat on the built-in couch with a wad of wet paper towels in my hand. Dean had given it to me to clean myself up before he left. My orders were to stay in the hauler till the infield cleared—not like I had the energy to go anywhere, anyway.

What was going to happen to me now? Would they lock me up? Send me to a psych ward? Or worse yet, send me to be experimented on—by the government, perhaps, or some university? Would NASCAR decide Dean was cheating just by having me around? My mind raced. The newscasters weren't helping with their instant replays of the car skidding to a halt in front of the trucks and an unidentified person jumping in front of it. I let out a grunt and shut the stupid thing off, unable to listen anymore.

The paper towels dried up as time went on, and the reflection off the heavily varnished table in front of me revealed a face right out of a horror movie. I sucked in a breath, slowly eased myself up off the couch, and ventured toward the workshop aisle of the hauler. I knew the guys kept bottles of water in the bar fridge, and there had to be some clean rags lying around here somewhere. My whole body ached something terrible, but at least I hadn't fallen unconscious out on the track. Colton would've …

Stop it. Stop thinking about him. After today, he would probably never speak to me again. Torturing myself with what ifs only made it harder to accept.

I snooped around and found a few clean shop rags in one of the cupboards. Reaching around, I grabbed two bottles of water from the bar fridge and set them down on one of the empty workbenches. I found a scrap piece of sheet metal and propped it up to use as a mirror. Its embossed surface distorted my reflection, but it would have to do.

The cold water stung. With the amount of pain I felt, I almost expected to find cuts and bruises under all that caked blood, but as I washed away the dried flakes of blood, I found my skin intact and smooth. I tossed the rags in the bin with the other filthy ones due for washing, then reached behind me to grab one of Colton's clean t-shirts off the shelf. Mine was crusted with blood, and I couldn't wait to take it off.

I changed right out in the open. I didn't see the point in hiding. Seeing me in only my bra wouldn't be that big of a deal after watching me stop a thirty-four-hundred pound stock car coming at me at nearly two hundred miles per hour.

I threw my bloody shirt in the bin with the rags, then headed back toward the boardroom, holding on to whatever I could to keep from collapsing to the floor. The sound of the aluminum back door opening and closing at the far end of the hauler startled me into turning around. I gasped. Colton stood in the aisle, fire suit hanging from his waist. His right pant leg was hiked up, a large white bandage taped to his calf.

"What are you doing here?"

He said nothing, but his eyes creased. My knees threatened to give out. I leaned against the wall behind me, trying to keep myself balanced. Right now I needed to stay upright. I hadn't expected this confrontation so soon, but I'd be damned if I let myself crumple to the ground like a dry leaf.

His chest rose and fell noticeably with his every breath. He reached for his ball cap and tossed it on the workbench next to him, hair falling in curtains around his face. His eyes darted back to me. Not only did he meet my gaze, but he stared through me as if trying to see my very soul. My cheeks burned. I couldn't read him. That scared me most.

He stalked toward me, slow at first, but ending in long strides. I stepped back. "Colton, I'm so sorry I couldn't tell you, I—"

His left hand grabbed my waist. Pulling me closer, he tilted my head back and pressed his lips against mine. I froze, not knowing how to react. Should I kiss him back? He slid his hand up to the back of my neck and threaded his fingers through my hair. I couldn't deny him—I wanted him too much. I ran my hands up his arms and returned the kiss.

My toes curled, and tingles fluttered from the pit of my stomach into my chest. The sensation spread to every point of contact as Colton tugged at my hips and brought me closer. Shivers rolled down my spine. The soft sweep of his lips made me dizzy and crazy all at once, and the pressure from the constant pulsing senses of my ability danced in the back of my head, calm and controlled.

Colton slowed his pace, and then broke the kiss. Trembling lightly with his eyes still closed, he leaned his forehead against mine. I didn't want the moment to end.

"You saved my life."

My eyes stung, but no tears fell. I'd cried them all earlier, and my body was too weak to shed more.

"I'm so sorry. I never—"

He pressed his finger against my lips.

"Dean told me everything. You risked everything to save my life."

He tilted his head back and opened his eyes—his mismatched eyes, which radiated heat and respect. "I'm not letting you go."

His words washed over me like a cold ocean wave, and my legs couldn't hold me anymore. Finally, they let go, and I collapsed.

Colton caught me. "Lexi, are you—"

"I'm fine, just—weak. It took a lot out of me."

Colton nodded and carried me to the couch in the next room. "I'll get you some water."

I wiped my brow with the tips of my fingers and tried to take deep, soothing breaths. From the corner of my eye, I could see Colton in the doorway staring at me. "Are you finally seeing the monster in me?"

He handed me a water bottle and knelt down in front of me. "You're not a monster, Lexi. You're gifted."

I choked on my first gulp and almost spat it out. "Gifted? Yeah, right. More like cursed."

"Hey ... any curse that can save my ass is a gift."

The corner of my lips twitched up.

"I'll admit the blood thing is kind of creepy, but Dean told me what you did and how you disobeyed him to do it. He also told me it wasn't the first time."

"So you know how dangerous I am. You know what I did to

Mitch and—"

"Mitch had it coming. If it hadn't been you, he would have spun out on his own somehow. He's alive, Lex. He'll be back to racing in no time—that is, if he finds a team to drive for. I'm pretty sure NASCAR's going to boot Carl out for good."

I bit my lip. Colton moved closer between my knees and wrapped his arm around my waist.

I rested my forehead against his and closed my eyes. "I'm still too dangerous. I can't control my ability completely. I could have killed him."

"But you didn't."

"As much as I want to, I can't be with you. You amplify my emotions. Who knows what I could do?"

He placed a finger under my chin and raised my face to meet his. "We can work on it together. I'm not leaving you."

There were those dimples again, the ones that emerged when he smiled. How could I say no to him?

"What's going to happen now?"

"Don't worry about a thing. Dean's working the media as we speak, and Nancy has already scheduled a press conference for early this week."

My eyes grew wide. "A press conference?"

"Don't worry," said a voice in the doorway. Dean walked in. "You're going to take a little trip until all this blows over. You need to get your emotions in check after this weekend and decide what you want to do next."

Colton looked up at him. "You spoke to Pops?"

Dean nodded.

I bounced my eyes between the two of them. "Where am I going?"

Colton stood. "You're going to stay with my parents."

I swallowed hard. "Your parents? Do they—"

"No. They know what happened to Colton, and about the accusations revolving around you, but that's it." Dean sat down next to me. "Think of it as a mini vacation. Concentrate on your studies. Unfortunately, we'll have to cut all ties with you until it's safe for you to return."

I felt a jolt of panic, and I darted my attention toward Colton. "No. I don't want—I can't leave—"

Colton dropped down to one knee and cupped my face with his hands. "I'm not going anywhere. I'll be right here when you get back. I promise." He pulled me into an embrace.

"We need to get going. The track's almost emptied out, and the crew needs to pack up."

Colton kept me close on our way to the motor coach. We packed up our stuff and headed back to Atlanta.

■■■

The following morning I packed my bags, looked back at my room, and said my goodbyes. Was I ever going to see this place again? My tears returned in that moment. Dean and Colton were quiet on the ride back to the airstrip. My goodbyes to Lorna and Annabelle had taken a toll on me, and I wasn't very talkative myself.

Before boarding, Dean took me in his arms and kissed the top of my head. "This is only temporary. No need to be sad." His words were comforting, but I was skeptical that this would ever blow over and that I'd ever be coming back. "See you soon, kiddo," he added and returned to his truck, giving Colton and me some semi-private time.

Colton came closer and pulled me tight against him. My eyes fluttered closed and I breathed him in, trying to commit his scent to memory. "Will they like me?"

"They'll love you, Lex. Trust me."

I nuzzled my face in his neck. "What if I lose control while I'm there?"

His lips grazed my ear. "Just think of me."

I grimaced. "That's usually how I lose control in the first place."

He laughed. "I believe you have it in you."

"I'm scared." I squeezed him tighter, not wanting to let him go.

"I know, but know that I'll be here waiting for you. I love you, Lex."

I wanted to say it back. I'd regret not saying it if I never saw him again, but I couldn't. The words were there, the sentiment was there, but I couldn't let them out. He pulled back, gazed at me again, and then kissed me. A long kiss. One to add to the chest of memories I planned to lock away to reminisce on later in life. "Take care, Lexi. I'll see you soon."

I climbed the air stairs, struggling not to look back, fearing that if I did I'd run into his arms.

I sat in one of the window seats and looked out at him, remembering his face the first time I saw it, our first almost kiss in the barn, the way my gift had reacted to his close presence. I missed it all already, and I wasn't even in the air yet.

"I love you," I said out loud to him, even though I knew he couldn't hear me. The plane took off down the runway. Colton dipped his head and slipped his hands in his pockets as I watched him get smaller. "I love you," I repeated, this time in a whisper as the plane lifted and I could no longer see him.

■■■

The plane landed a few hours later. I stepped off the stairs and approached the group of people standing there, waiting.

"You must be Lexi," a blonde, slender woman with deep blue eyes said to me. I looked down at her sitting in her wheelchair. Colton had told me about his mother's complications with the birth of his brother, but I'd almost forgotten. Colton looked so much like her, I couldn't mistake her for anyone other than his mother. She wheeled herself forward and tugged me down into a hug.

The tall man standing next to her extended his hand. "Welcome. Colt's told us so much about you." His green eyes shined down on me.

I worried that I was coming across as rude, just standing there not saying a word, but then out from between the two of them, Colton's dimpled face looked up at me—only this face was much younger.

"Exie," the boy screamed.

His mother leaned over the side of her chair and grabbed the boy by his waist. "Shush, Robbi, she's right here … she can hear you. You don't have to scream." I stifled a laugh unsuccessfully. "I'm sorry," she said, looking back up at me. "He grows on you. I promise." She smiled warmly, just like my mother used to. My tension drifted away.

"Come on." Mr. Tayler stepped forward and picked up my suitcase. "Let's get you home."

chapter twenty-five

Weeks dragged by without a word from Colton or Dean, and my hopes were dwindling fast. The Taylers were sweet. They cared for me as if I were one of their own. They even let me stay in Colton's room, and being surrounded by his things provided a comfort that helped me sleep at night. But with every week that crept by and every race weekend that came to a close, the walls closed in bit by bit. I didn't know how much longer I could stay here without suffocating. I needed out. I missed Colton. I missed going to the track. I'd become accustomed to NASCAR's way of life—the adrenaline, the excitement. For the first time since Mama died, I had a home, a purpose. People actually cared about me and wanted to help me achieve something better than the solitary life I'd envisioned for myself.

Funny how I needed to leave to realize and appreciate all that. And now who knew when I'd get it all back. If I'd ever get it back.

Dean's press conference went well. The Taylers and I watched in the family room as Dean convincingly announced that Carl's accusations were false, that Carl had been the one behind all the sabotages, and that my presence during the chaos in the pits was nothing more than a devastated girlfriend wanting to protect her boyfriend. And when Lenny took the mic and explained what he'd done, no one even bothered to ask any more questions about me.

"Some of the hoses hadn't been entirely severed by the blast and the brakes reengaged. We were lucky to have avoided what could've been a great tragedy," was all that was said and quoted.

In light of what happened and how well Dean had dealt with it, the board at Guardian Auto Insurance extended their offer for another fifteen races. If Colton made the top twelve, and if he did it bad-publicity free, Guardian promised them a five-year contract.

As for Carl, he pleaded temporary insanity to all his charges—fraud, attempted murder, a few misdemeanors—and that in itself had cleared my name. I couldn't be sure if he actually believed himself insane or if he'd just seized the opportunity to use it as a defense, but as long as he stayed away from us and from the sport entirely, I didn't care. He had no proof.

It'd been four weeks, and still I'd heard from no one. I was tempted so many times to text Colton or Dean to ask when I could come back, but I held back and did what they'd asked of me.

Over the weeks, Colton had gotten himself two top five finishes, one in Kansas and one in Richmond. Last week, he'd crossed the finish line first in Talladega.

The Taylers celebrated with neighbors and friends; they included me in the backyard festivities. They were so proud of their son, but what I wanted more than anything was to congratulate him in person, wrap my arms around him, and show him firsthand how proud I was of him. Now I wondered if I'd ever get the chance.

Sun beamed through the open curtains of the bedroom as I finally gave up trying to sleep in and sat up in bed. A dozen or so birds perched on the telephone wires outside, squawking and chirping loudly. Even with the window closed, they sounded as though they were perched right above my head. Who could sleep through that?

I mindlessly went through the motions and shuffled off to the bathroom while Diesel, the Tayler family's chocolate lab, circled around me, wanting to play. I showered, got dressed, and checked my phone for missed voicemails or texts. Thanks to the race schedule now permanently engraved in my memory, I knew today was Friday and that Colton's qualifying runs in Darlington were this afternoon. Something squeezed in my chest. *God, I wish I could be there to cheer him on.*

"Lexi, dear. Breakfast is ready."

I opened the bedroom door and aimed my voice down the hall. "I'll be right down."

I finished brushing my hair, straightened my shirt, and headed for the stairs. Midway down, Mr. Tayler's voice coming from the kitchen caught me off guard. *Shouldn't he be at work already?*

Another voice responded to him. A familiar voice, one I'd been waiting weeks to hear. I rushed down the remaining steps, almost tripping off the bottom one as I charged into the kitchen. "Dean!" I launched myself into his arms. Diesel jumped at us and barked.

I caught him by surprise and he laughed. "I take it you missed me?"

I pulled back, pushing Diesel out of the way. "Is Colton here? Did he come with you?"

"No, Colton had practice early this morning. He couldn't be here."

Right. I knew that. My gaze fell to the floor.

"Don't give me that face."

I wrinkled my nose. "What face?"

"The same one Colton gave me when I told him I was coming here, and he couldn't tag along."

My heart skipped at the thought.

"Besides, you're going to see him in a few hours, anyway."

I flashed Dean a toothy grin. "Are you serious? I get to come home?"

Dean raised his eyebrow. "Home? I thought the salvage yard was your home?"

"Are you kidding? After everything you and Lorna have done for me? You guys are the only real home I've had in years."

Dean placed his hand on my shoulder. "That's good to know. Now pack up. We have a race weekend to get back to."

I turned to run back up the stairs when Mrs. Tayler cleared her throat. "Your breakfast is getting cold."

I glanced at Dean. He looked as annoyed as I felt.

Mrs. Tayler turned her chair around and faced him. "The girl has to eat."

Dean nodded toward the kitchen table. "Eat your breakfast. Then we'll go."

I pursed my lips to avoid laughing and sat down.

It didn't take me long to scarf down my food and run back

up to Colton's room to pack up my things. I thanked the Taylers, gave Diesel a scratch behind the ears—I was going to miss him the most—said my goodbyes, and waved as we pulled out of the driveway.

I was finally going home.

Once on the jet and up in the air, Dean's expression turned serious.

"What's wrong?"

Dean leaned forward and threaded his fingers together in front of him. "I'm not quite sure how to break this to you. You trusted me, but I'm afraid I didn't have much of a choice."

"What is it?" My voice cracked.

"To make your story go away at the press conference and in all the media interviews, I had to inform Dylan, Jimmy, and Nancy of your—" he tilted his head and squinted slightly "—your unique skills. I needed them to back me up and help me turn the story around."

My stomach cramped. I suddenly wasn't too eager to see the crew again.

"It took some convincing. They all thought I'd gone nuts like Carl, but they came around. They've accepted it."

I gripped the hem of my shorts, digging my nails into the denim. "I don't know, Dean, what if—"

Dean reached out and tapped me on the knee. "Lexi, you have nothing to worry about. I promise you. You can trust them. Hell, Dylan can't wait to see you in action. Besides, I had them sign a confidentiality agreement as part of their employment. I kindly reminded them that what I told them fits the terms of that contract." Dean sank back into his seat.

I eased my grip and urged myself to relax. These people had

no reason to lock me up, especially if their jobs were on the line.

"What about Lenny? What happened to him?"

"I didn't have the heart to fire him after everything he did to help expose Carl, but I couldn't keep him on as crew chief. I have him driving some of the trucks and working odd jobs in the shop for the time being. It's sad, really."

"So Dylan's—"

"Dylan's officially our new crew chief, yes. I moved Alan up to car chief." Dean shifted and crossed his leg so that his ankle rested on his knee. "Now, when we get to the track, expect the other teams to gawk and stare. A lot of people noticed you were gone, and once you reappear, it might stir some talk. Just rest assured that any rumor of you possessing any kind of supernatural powers has been nipped in the bud."

I grimaced. "Supernatural? Ugh, don't call it that. You make me sound like a superhero or a demon or something."

Dean smiled. "It's good to have you back."

"It's good to be back. You know ... I did a lot of thinking while at the Taylers' and ... well, I think I want to go to college next year."

Dean perked up one eyebrow. "Is that right?"

"Yeah. I think I might want to attend the NASCAR Technical Institute. Do you think I could have a future with NASCAR? I'd do it legitimately, of course, and I'll have to work on controlling my ... sixth sense, if you will, but I think I can do it."

"Well, well ... I may just have to open up a spot for a new technician in a few years. Can't have you working for anyone else, now can I?"

I sat up straight, happy at his approval. "Really? You don't think it's a stupid idea? I mean, I'll be eighteen by then, so I don't have to worry about Roy stopping me, and I'll have to rent out the cottage Mama left me in her will to help pay room and board …"

"You really thought this through."

I shrugged. "Didn't have much else to do with my time at the Taylers'."

"Well, I think it's a fantastic idea, Lexi. You are the bravest girl I've ever met. You can do just about anything you set your mind to—in your case, literally." He smiled at his indirect mention of my ability and leaned in my direction. "Not only was your home life a mess, something we have in common, but you survived it all while dealing with this secret. How are *you* still so … so ?"

I giggled, something I still couldn't get used to hearing coming from my own lips. "I am who I am because of the cards I've been dealt. I know that now. My life wasn't all bad. I had a great mama and Colton calls my ability a gift. I guess he's right, I mean … I couldn't have saved him without it. I wouldn't go as far as calling it a gift, but I don't want to hide anymore because of it. I'll always be different. That doesn't mean I can't still have a normal life. College, friends—"

"Colton," Dean inserted.

I bit my lip and smiled. "Yeah … definitely Colton. If he'll still have me."

"Oh, I'm pretty sure that's a non-issue. As for the rest, I'll help you in whatever way I can."

"Thanks, Dean. I really appreciate it."

The seatbelt light turned on. We buckled up and waited to land.

I was that much closer to seeing Colton again.

...

When we arrived at the track, I dropped my luggage off in my room in the motor coach and bounced toward the door. "You coming?"

Dean stood at the kitchen counter. "I have to wait for Nancy. You go on without me. The guys are expecting you in the garage. Oh and"—he handed me a track and clearance credential with a smile—"don't forget this."

I slipped the lanyard over my head. It was funny how I'd missed having it around my neck these past few weeks.

I made my way through the gates and down toward the Cup series garages. As Dean had warned, people stared at me from every corner—some even stopped working to eye me as I walked by. The smell of rubber and racing fuel floated through the air. I'd only been gone a month, but man, I had missed being a part of it all.

I found the familiar equipment of the 129 Guardian Auto Insurance team outside one of the stalls up ahead. I rounded the corner and looked over every inch of the stall. A few of the crew members were huddled under the hood while another's feet stuck out from underneath. I stood in the open doorway and stared at them, waiting for them to notice I was there—everyone else had.

Eventually, I gave up and cleared my throat. "What's a girl gotta do to get some attention around here?"

Dylan slid out from under the chassis, eyes wide. "Well, look at you." He jumped to his feet and scooped me into a hug. "Welcome home."

"Hey, Lex, welcome back." Jimmy waved from behind the open hood.

"Hey." I walked around and gave him a hug. "Any of you seen Colton around?"

Jimmy jutted his chin and glanced over my shoulder. My heart thudded painfully as I slowly turned around.

There he stood, his arms crossed, leaning against the doorway. His ball cap was dipped low over his shades as the sun beamed down behind him, giving the illusion of a golden aura around him. Corny, I know, but he was beautiful. Hopefully he was still mine. I took a few steps toward him. He removed his shades and hooked them to the front of his shirt.

"Are ya lost, little girl?" He smirked.

"Who are you calling a little girl? Little man." I heard Jimmy stifle a laugh behind me.

Colton shrugged, stepping closer.

"You shouldn't speak of what you don't know."

I ran my tongue over my bottom lip. "Maybe I'm lookin' to find out."

He hooked a finger in my belt loop and tugged me closer. "Come here." The smile fell from his lips. "I missed you," he whispered so only I could hear him.

I swallowed and met his stare. "I'm never going to be normal, Colton. You know that, right?"

"Lexi, you wouldn't be you if you were."

I could see his parents in his mismatched eyes, his mother's kindness and his father's determination to succeed. Having lived with the Taylers, having gotten to know them and little Robbi, it felt like I'd known him forever. "I love you, Colton," I whispered. "I wish I would've had the guts to tell you sooner."

He smiled again, a soft, content smile. "I love you back, Lexi Adams." He pressed his lips against mine. I wrapped my arms around his waist and kissed him back with my whole heart and soul.

He knew who and what I was, and he still loved me. I could've only dreamed of such a thing a few months ago. The crew clapped, cheered, and whistled behind us, making my cheeks flare with heat. Colton reached down around my waist, lifted me high up off the ground, and lowered me back down slowly as I nuzzled my face in his neck. He smelled like Axe and Lorna's baking.

I couldn't wait to see her and Annabelle again.

Dean came in behind us and tapped Colton on the shoulder. "Sorry to interrupt the reunion, but you think you're up for another practice run?"

Colton leaned his forehead against mine.

"Let's go do this thing."

acknowledgements

Kristi Cook. What can I say? Without your kind words when I first started this crazy and amazing journey, I would not be where I am today. You were my first critique, my first author friend, and now my work's biggest fan. This story could not have found a better editor. You and the Spencer Hill/Midpoint family have given *Magnetic Shift* a home and the love it needed and for that I will forever be grateful.

To Jenny Adams Perinovic for the amazing cover art. Wow! Just wow.

Brittany Booker. I would not have made it this far without you. From the bottom of my heart I thank you.

To the many speedway staff members and industry professionals who took the time to accommodate my visits or entertain my barrage of questions. Without your combined knowledge and expertise of how things work behind the scenes, I could not have given my story the dose of authenticity it needed. Much respect to you all and thank you so much.

To the great author/writer friends who have mentored me

over the years and to my friends and family who have motivated, inspired, and supported me, I will never be able to thank you enough.

And last but not least, to the most amazing person in my life, my husband Daniel Briand. You have been my rock, my anti-anxiety coach, and the biggest reason why I'm writing these acknowledgments right now. You rode this crazy roller coaster ride of publishing with me, the ups and downs, the panic attacks, the reading and re-reading chapters to appease the doubt that constantly nagged my brain. It wasn't easy, but you managed to make me believe I could do this and for that I am truly grateful. I love you most.

about the author

Lucy D. Briand lives in Ottawa, Canada with her comic book fanatic husband and her nonchalant Siamese cat. By day she works full time as a public servant for the Government of Canada, but by night her creative mind takes over and conjures up young adult gear-head romance stories with supernatural twists.

When not working, reading, writing, or watching way too much TV, Lucy likes to cosplay, attend ComicCons, go on road trips to Walt Disney World, and play ridiculous amounts of board games. She's a geek to the core but is also a huge NASCAR Cup fan.